LEMONLIPS
The Nam Viet Duet
(Part II)

John Klawitter

LEMONLIPS
The Nam Viet Duet
(Part II)

FICTION4ALL

CHAPTER ONE

1964   U.S. Army, 3rd Radio Research Unit, Davis Station, Tan Son Nhut Air Base, Saigon, Republic of South Vietnam.   Specialist E-4 Jack Beale, linguist and cryptographer by army designation, has been granted his wish and transferred from the top secret Puzzle Palace at Fort. Meade, Maryland, to South Vietnam where the war is beginning to heat up.   At the time there are only 17,000 G.I. "military advisors" in country (in a year or so there will be hundreds of thousands).   Unfortunately for Jack's buddies, the three other members of the so-called Dimbo Patrol, they have been reluctantly assigned to the same unit.   Charley Magnolia, Larky Larkspun and Mad Denny Haller blame Beale, in short, for everything.

"Get up, get up, and get *up, get-up-get-up-get-up -- GET UP!!*" Toady chants over and over like a peeved parrot.

"Who is it?" Beale groans from under his pillow. "Check that. Never mind who it is. Go away. I'm not on duty today...." Jack Beale knows it's the company orderly, and he couldn't care less.

Beale has managed to sleep through the Huey's pre-dawn racket as they flupped away toward the bush, and through dozens of thundering flights of jet take-offs on the runway that is less than 300 yards away from his barracks, and then through the general hubris as guys on the first shift struggled into their fatigues and banged their way out the barracks screen door a dozen feet from his bunk Now it is getting on toward nine and so hot that even the overhead fans aren't much help, and he knows if he wakes one more time, he won't get back to sleep.

Toady gives Beale's pillow a tug, "Captain Nordoff wants to give you a medal!"

That works. Beale lets go the pillow, causing Toady to fly back and hit his head against the wall. Beale sits up and blinks in the light, "A medal?"

Toady angrily rubs his head. "Yes, you *stupido*! For your supposed heroism on the Pan Am flight." When Beale had first arrived in-country, his plane was racked with machine gun fire from the ground. There had been casualties. There would have been more, but for Beale, in shock but acting on instinct, had saved several lives. Toady wasn't there, and he doesn't believe it.

"First Nordoff is going to congratulate you.... and then he's going to ream your ass!"

"What for?"

"It's a rule: *Linguists doth not go up in Otters.* Captain Nordoff, Chapter 1, Verse 6. You *know* that. You heard it at the briefing!" The sweaty, fat little corporal looks grimy, like he could use a bath, but he also looks happy to be bringing Beale some bad news.. Beale is pretty sure there is something wrong with Toady, there is just the dim edge of something he can't place that makes him uncomfortable, and he is relieved when the corporal gets up from the edge of his bunk. Toady eyes his own pimply face in the full length mirror hung from the end of the wall lockers and starts to squeeze the biggest of his zits, "Dost thou not know the law, Specialist?"

"B-but I was *ordered* -!" Beale says.

"Doesn't count", Toady says, studying the white ooze on his fingers and then smearing it on the back of his pants leg, "Boo-Boo is only a lieutenant. Captain Nordoff is a captain - *and* your Commanding Officer."

Beale groans, rubbing his hands through his hair and becoming more aware of his hangover, "Can I at least take a shower?"

"Why? You're already dressed."

Beale looks down at his rumpled fatigues, "So I am." He vaguely remembers Ranley and somebody else helping him back from the EMC. "But I'm a mess...."

Toady hooks a thumb toward the door, "Captain said *right now*!"

"Bullshit, Toady", a bored and tired voice from the bunk on the other side of the wall lockers speaks up, "Give the nug a chance to clean up, or Nordoff will get him for that too!"

The corporal's voice goes thin and reedy, "The Captain *said* -"

"Toady...." The voice from under the blankets thickens until it becomes a growl, "Get the fuck out of here, you little faggot!"

The corporal backs toward the screen door, pointing a warning finger at Beale, "All right - ten minutes then, and you take the consequences!"

"There won't be any....", the rough voice mutters with a sigh, drifting back to sleep.

Beale jams his dirty khakis into the clothes sack for the native cleaning girl, grabs his towel and personals kit, and makes a naked dash for the showers. Toady watches from the shadowy under-

7

hang of a nearby bungalow, watching the easy grace of the new Spec. 4's muscles as he runs. "There are always consequences," he mutters to nobody in particular.

By the time Beale gets to the C.O.'s office, Ranley is already there with Larky. Ranley is the guy Beale reports to, a sergeant who knows how the system works. He is idly fidgeting with a brass ashtray that features a twin-boom World War II fighter plane. He has detached the plane from the round base and is making little engine noises as he loops and dives the little brass toy in neat figures. Nordoff makes a show of ignoring Ranley and Larky, turning instead to Beale as he comes in through the screen door, "Specialist, you have a Top Secret security clearance. My strict and specific orders are that you may *never, NEVER* under any circumstances leave the secure areas of this base or the Saigon city limits."

"Counter-manded, Sir", Ranley says mildly, putting his little plane through a fancy Immelmann turn.

"Not accepted!", the Captain explodes, pounding both fists on his table-desk and glaring at the sergeant.

"Then where's Boo Boo Boudreaux? Ask him!" Ranley has the plane execute a neat four-point roll, then brings it in for a touch-and-go on the edge of Nordoff's desk.

"See these, Mister?" Nordoff angrily points to the two metal bars on his shoulder.

"Yes, you outrank Boo Boo, but, if you'll pardon my saying so, you should have been there to counter-mand his counter-mand, sir. I need not remind you, sir, that the lieutenant's one bar beats

8

my four of a kind every time." Ranley buzzes the four hard-stripes on his own sleeve patch with the little brass plane to illustrate his point. "And, of course, Boo-Boo and I *both* get our orders from a two-star half way around the world."

Ranley knows that is the final word. Orders from the White Shack come from God himself, or at least from his anointed men at the Puzzle Palace back at Meade.

"Do you know", the captain shouts angrily, "that little toy you are fooling around with is entirely hand-made from old artillery casings - and *took one of the finest skilled Korean craftsmen over a year to create!"*

"Really a beauty, sir. It's a P-38, isn't it?"

"WOULD YOU PUT MY AIRPLANE DOWN AND GET OUT OF HERE!!" The C.O. yells so loud that the room seems to shake. Beale and Larky get up to leave with Ranley; but they take only two steps before Nordoff roars, "*NOT YOU TWO DIMBOS - HIM!"*

The two of them sit down again, Beale sitting as inconspicuously as possible on his hands. They have started to shake. The C.O. doesn't notice Beale's hands, or maybe he doesn't care. He shouts for five minutes, but he has to let them go.

Beale and Larky walk to the mess hall, reeling from the noise. Beale splatters a half a cup before he gets enough coffee into his mug to put it on a tray. Larky loads up on a plate-full of combined breakfast and lunch, and takes a seat across from Beale in the nearly deserted cafeteria, "If that don't beat all! All that yelling, and in the end we don't get nothing!"

Beale shakes his head, "I still can't believe it.

9

You notice the way the C.O. changed the subject? One moment he was railing about our major infraction of his rules, and then he started yelling at Ranley for playing with his little brass airplane!"

Larky gives him an amused glance, "You mean, the same way like you done, talking about the wiggly weeds when Charley blamed you for getting us into this mess?"

"That wasn't my fault."

Larky's smile broadens, "An' then he started in on how he smacked up your car?"

"Well, that was *different* . . ."

"No it weren't. If you're going to be a great writer, Ong Be, you got to stop denying what is real and what ain't!" Larky gives him a look so wide-eyed and full of righteous enthusiasm that Beale can't find any way to be angry. He takes an extra fork from Larky's tray, waves it in the air, and spears a french-fried scallop from his friend's plate, "So what should I do, oh great guru from the sagebrush plains?"

"I'll tell you one thing. We all got to stay away from that Toady. You see the way he was staring at you?"

"No, I didn't notice."

"Good thing. He lusts to jump your bones."

"That's crazy talk."

"He gave me this brochure while we was waiting for you. I got him figured out, Ong Be. He's the worst kind of pre-vert in the universe - a devout an' dedicated queer!"

"A *what*?"

"Guy like that brings a whole new meaning to the song, *I'm going to sleep with Jesus*."

They both laugh, but later, thinking about it,

Beale had to admit Larky had put his finger on something. It wasn't that Toady was gay. Toady reminded Beale of something he'd heard about the true believers being the most dangerous class of people in the world. *Nothing they do counts for nothing, so they got nothing to lose.*

CHAPTER TWO

Four olive colored jeeps with big white stars on their sides sit in the middle of the 3rd's motor pool, waiting to take their riders one hundred miles northwest to Tay Ninh, a middle sized town located up against the Cambodian border. Beale arrives first, making his careful way around the puddles and across the muddy gravel. He finds a convenient spot for his M-14, sliding it half way under his seat. He throws his heavy duffle bag in back and climbs into the driver's seat. Two clips of ammo ride heavily in his jacket pockets. He wants to load one in his rifle, but Nordoff had warned they were *"advisors* in the host country of Vietnam" and were to fire only if fired on. Ranley hadn't said anything, but Beale saw him roll his eyes and look at the ceiling in a funny way.

Larky shows up a few minutes later, sloshing his way happily through the mud puddles. He'd just been to the arms room, picked up his pappy's old .45 and had it strapped to his waist. He carries his M-14 upside down as if he knows what he is doing, and easily swings his duffle in back with Beale's. He pulls his poncho top back from his head, pops a big piece of Double Bubble in his mouth and squints bare-headed up into the rain. "Howdy, Ong Be!" he says as if they don't have a care in the world. "What a day for a picnic, huh?"

"That bag looks awful light, Larky...."

"One pair of civvies, one pair of underwear, and a bag of possibles...." Larky's grin is ear to ear, "I ain't planning on a month's journey."

"You never know....", Beale gives him a doubtful look..

"Oh bullcrappers, Mister Be!" Mad Denny says. He has snuck up behind and startles Beale by shouting in his ear. He tosses his bag, which looks lighter than Larky's, in a second jeep, and climbs in. "Ya gots to leave room for booze and silk panties and other trophies of war!"

"Where's Charley?"

"Probably hiding under his bed. He don't take to kindly to all this, particularly when I told him it was your idea."

"Oh, great; just what I needed."

"Just kidding, Ong Be, just kidding."

The rest of the party arrives in a clump, walking slowly through the warm afternoon rain. Toady is carrying his own and the Captain's bags. Charley comes last, talking earnestly with Ranley about the down-side possibilities of their trip into the bush.

Seeing Charley's nervousness, Beale tries to push the guilty feeling from his mind; he'd had more to do with instigating their trip than any of the Dimbos know. By working long hours since the other three had arrived, he had almost single-handedly caught up with all the decodes at the White Shack. And then he'd started to bug Ranley for something to do.

Saigon is still off-limits, due to new rumors of a government shake-up and another bloody Buddhist riot. Ranley and the other NCO's who live downtown seem unconcerned, but for the lower ranks there is nothing to do but work and wait for things to change. Charley spent hours scraping webs of fungus in his damp boots. Larky

13

got rot in his damp clothes. Mad Denny suffered athletes foot and jock itch and jungle dandruff, all at the same time. They all got mad and swore at Beale, who didn't seem to get infected with anything.

Beale brought it up for at least the tenth time at the NCO's table at the EMC.

"Well....", Ranley thinks it over while sipping his scotch-and-water, "about this time of year we sometimes take a run out to Nui Ba Den."

"Black - Lady - Mountain?"

Greggs, the E-7 who usually tracked freqs in Maisy-the-flying-beaver, nods, "Black Lady Peak. A little pimple of a mountain about ten klicks north of the Tay Ninh city proper. The 114th RRU out of Tay Ninh takes a mobile unit up there in the dry season. They monitor the whole delta, and it's a great view."

"Why do we go out there?"

"Nelson an' Ranley set up the station in the old days when Nelson was still a lingie. This was before he went civvie and became the little big shit he is at the Puzzle Palace."

Ranley nods, "Yeah. It being Little Brush-head's claim to fame, he wants to make sure it's 100% operational. Since he doesn't trust the C.O. of the 114th, he gets us to go out there."

Beale is ready to pack his bags, "Great! When do we leave?"

Ranley shakes his head, "Well.... that's what Nelson keeps asking. But I don't think Nordoff is in the right frame of mind for it after our recent heroics."

Beale shows his disgust, "Sure. The same thing is going to happen to us that happened to the

14

French. I see it coming." He takes a drag at his Marlboro and tries to puff some smoke rings. He's seen Lieutenant Boo-Boo do four or five in a row, and he thinks it looks sophisticated, like in the movies. He gets one decent ring out, and then his throat backs up and he has a coughing fit.

"See what coming, nug?" One of the short-timers raises a shot-glass full of brandy and gives him a friendly pat on the back, winking at the other lifers.

"We're gonna be tied down," Beale says, swallowing a big gulp of beer from a bottle somebody hands him.. "We get the cities, they get the rest. We lose the war."

The short-timer chugs his brandy, and washes it down with a healthy swig of Schlitz, drinking from the brown bottle. "Hell, they can *have* the rest, sonny-boy! There's heat out there that'll fry your brains. Bugs and rot and leeches and snakes - "

The comments run around the table like an amiable litany.

"Head high elephant grass, sticky mud up to your ass."

"Punji stakes dipped in shit."

"Bamboo Bouncing Bettys to blow off your balls."

"Don't go alone, nug. Take along some ARVNs, a bunch of simple-minded peacenik Buddhist monkey-fuckers who'll dedicate all their rounds to Mother Sky before they'll kill anybody."

Another lifer holds out his thumb, "Imagine a leech as big as your dick, *on* your dick!"

"That happened to me", Ranley muses, eyeing the massive red-gold dragon-ring on one of his fingers, "floating down the Mekong, on a Sunday afternoon...." He turns it into a melody, "The sky above was made for love, the flowers was in bloom...." He pushes his drink away, "Seriously though, brothers of the olive cloth, in this case I happen to agree with the nug. I don't want to sit around waiting for the Russian rockets to drop in on us."

"You're going to stop that with *a fling in Tay Ninh?*"

Ranley gives them his lopsided grin, "Hey, it's a start."

"You be the one to tell Nordoff."

"I'll do better than that - I'll get Nelson to tell him."

"Oh, he's going to *love* that . . ..!"

And so, a few days after their conversation in the EMC, the convoy of four jeeps pull out at two in the afternoon, the canvas jeep tops drumming in the heavy rain; they head into the unknown, into that wide area outside the city known to the Dimbos simply as 'the bush'. Ranley's jeep leads, followed by the Dimbos in the two middle jeeps, with a jittery Toady bringing up the rear with a very angry Captain Nordoff.

They leave the ramshackle outskirts of Saigon and make their way west on Route 1, a two-lane asphalt highway that cuts through the drenched flat squares of fields and paddies. They drive at a fairly constant 45 miles per hour from checkpoint to checkpoint. Route 1 continues west through Cambodia to Phnom Penh, but they leave it a few miles before the border, turning right on Route 22, a much narrower road that heads in a northwesterly direction to Tay Ninh with the tree-lined, muddy

Van Co Dong river visible on their right for much of the way.

Beale drives along happy as a clam, unmindful of the continuing downpour except for the fogging that he has to wipe from his glasses. That irritates him a little bit. Rain drums on the jeep's canvas top, working its way in any opening it can find. Beale and Larky are closed in by plastic side flaps, and their breathing fogs up all but a small patch of windshield. So in addition to his glasses, Beale has to rub the window area he can reach in front of him, wiping it clear as he can every thirty seconds or so. After a while, he gives up on that; he opens the side flaps; figuring he and Larky are wet anyway, and the stream of moist, heavy air will at least keep the center of his windshield clear. There isn't much to see but paddies, which gradually give way to brush covered hills. The elusive Viet Cong guerillas seem to have taken the day off.

Late in the afternoon, Ranley, still forging ahead in the lead jeep, blinks his lights and pulls over to the side of the road. He walks back toward the tail jeep with a map under his arm, and Beale hops out and follows him. One by one, the three other Dimbos trickle back to gather around Ranley and the Captain.

Nordoff stares at the group, his hotly accusing eyes shifting from Ranley and resting for a moment on Beale. He'd heard about Beale's zealous ways, and had little doubt about who and what had inspired their mission. The captain opens his fatigue jacket, and wipes his glasses on his damp t-shirt. Beale sees the soft, little paunch under his shirt, shakes his head. Nordoff is out of shape, a soft little man who doesn't belong in

17

Vietnam, much less in the bush. He alone has put on his helmet, and he looks odd peeping out from under the rim of his dull olive tin pot.... odd, and a little scared.

Mad Denny pokes Larky and whispers, "*Cappy-baby* looks like a *civvy* lawyer or banker playing weekend warrior." Intent on stirring up as much mischief as possible, Denny grins at Toady, "Hey, ya little creep, got a proverb for us?"

Toady is in no mood for joking, "Leave me alone, Specialist Haller!"

"How about, *I will fear no evil, cause I'm the meanest ass-grabber in the valley!*"

Charley sets aside his own concerns for a moment and adds, "*The Chicken-shits shall inherit the earth.*"

"You smart-ass people are going to end up in hell!"

"*Will* you men shut up for at least one moment!" Nordoff gives them a warning look, and Toady, who'd had the misfortune to be the last person speaking, could do nothing but glower at his tormentors. The captain turns his attention to Ranley, "Now just what is it, sergeant? Why are we stopping here?"

"We're coming up on the last checkpoint before Tay Ninh, sir."

"Yes, I know that. But I don't feel *good* stopping here! It's not a proper procedure, standing here on a raised road in the middle of nowhere. I can see at least 15 places where snipers could be aiming at us right now! We should get back in our jeeps and move out smartly; we can have this discussion in Tay Ninh."

Ranley opens the map and holds it out of the

rain under the Jeep's canvas roof. "That's what I wanted to talk to you about, sir. Rather than stay in some gringy and unsecured hotel in Tay Ninh, why don't we spend the night in Long Chu? We can show the nugs the other side of Vietnam."

Nordoff frowns. "Personally, I've never been to Long Chu. I don't know about your men, but I've seen enough of your *other side* of Vietnam around Tan Son Nhut!"

Ranley points out a small dot on the map, a spot located about ten miles north of Tay Ninh city, "It's right here, sir. A fortified hamlet."

"God, it's out in the middle of nowhere! Count us out! You can't expect me to take men with security clearances out there!"

"Our own ambassador was quoted in Newsweek just last week, the great man assured all of America that the situation throughout Nam is *completely* under control."

"Don't get smart with *me*, Sergeant!"

Toady, who had been listening to the conversation with lidded eyes, puts his hand up like a schoolboy, "Permission to speak, sir. I suggest that if Sergeant Ranley is so confident of the success of the Hamlet Pacification Program, he take his own men out there - and may the grace of God go with him."

Ranley nods, happy to get this unexpected support from Toady, "That makes sense, sir! My orders are to check the station at Nui Ba Den - and the surrounding area. You can monitor our progress from the Tay Ninh RRU. You'll be our safety valve, and we'll join back up with you in three days, on our way back."

Given his way out, the C.O. grinds his teeth,

makes up his mind and waves them away. "I don't like it, but - very well. Now let's get moving - I *won't* just sit here all day talking about it!"

At first glance, Tay Ninh seems like a nice enough place, with a sprinkle of temples, bars and hotels. But Ranley and the Dimbos soon are leaving it, and as they head out of town the soggy afternoon light begins to fail. The rain continues and their tires whine on the long stretches of deserted two-lane road. Beale drums his fingers on the steering wheel, eager to get to Long Chu. He fumbles in his pocket for a Marlboro.

"Hey, man," Larky drawls from the seat next to him, "I didn't know you smoked *all* the time."

"Yeah. It keeps the twitches down."

Larky yawns and stretches, "I don't get the twitches, pard. An' I still got 98 women to go."

"Ninety *Eight?!"*

"Yeah. You know that little Zip chick picks up the laundry? Look out, great gran'pappy, here I come!"

Beale laughs and settles back with his smoke in his lips, his hands firmly wrapped around the wheel. Larky tells him how he'd been visited by the girl, who only cost a dollar and a half *my-kim*, while he was taking a shower one morning, and then he cheerily fills Beale in on his adventures with the French Ambassador's daughter back in D.C. His conversation happily bubbles on as Beale puts the miles behind them, and Beale finds himself thinking Vietnam isn't always such a bad place after all. He is hopeful that if he is very, very careful they might all get through their tour okay.

CHAPTER THREE

The Americans pull into Long Chu, sliding their three jeeps to a halt in a muddy area at the center of the compound where they are surrounded by a gang of screaming, half naked kids who don't seem to notice they are being soaked by the warm rain.

As he unclamps his stiff fingers from the steering wheel, Beale looks around the fortified village. He is not happy with what he sees. People are jammed close together in little bamboo huts with thatched palm-leaf roofs. The settlement is plain and mud seems everywhere. Raindrops disturb the long pools of water caught in the deep tire ruts that serve as roads. He can't help voicing his disappointment, "I hope this isn't the real Vietnam, Larky."

The Texan seems to take it in stride, "Yeah. Well, Ong Be, let's make the best of it....at least it looks safe."

"Safety isn't everything."

Ranley bangs the front fender of Beale's jeep with the palm of his hand as he walks by, "Get your gear, boys, and meet me at the front gate."

Larky squints out into the gathering twilight gloom. "Oh, no - we goin' back *out there*, man?"

Beale, who has already hopped out of the jeep, slings his duffle over his shoulder with a grunt, "Good Old Red Dog - I knew he had something better than this!"

But the Self-Defense Commander of Long Chu holds them up by insisting they tour the hamlet. After walking around in the mud and taking in the cramped living quarters for a half-hour, Ranley gives the dapper Vietnamese man an elegant half-bow, bending slightly from the waist. He says politely in English, "Buddha is good, and your fortified hamlet is an abomination on the face of the earth, and I thank you for showing it to us."

The Commander bows in return, with a quiet, self-satisfied smile, "Sssank you, sir. We have much help from A-melicans."

"Yes, I'm sure you did."

Ranley and the Dimbos stand with the serious little man, who, though soaked, is dressed in spotless dress khakis, knee length pants, a bright yellow beret, and yellow and red braid on the left shoulder of his short sleeve shirt. He carries a leather-handled, chrome plated crop, a rigid whip made from a shortened golf club with markings indicating it had once been a Spaulding 9-iron, and he decapitates nearby weeds and touches the shoulders of his listeners with it to illustrate his points.

It was true that everything about the fort was new. Even the barbed wire hadn't lost its dark shine. The nearby walls were 12 feet high, and made of spiked bamboo. These walls had interior standing platforms for firing out over the top, much like forts in the frontier days of the American West. There were staked pits around the outside of the walls, and thick rolls of barbed wire beyond the pits. But inside, it was more like a crowded pigpen than a place where people lived.

The Commander points out a small hut, "We like invite you stay for night."

"What an abominable little hut for us all to

sleep in!", Mad Denny replies agreeably, picking up on Ranley's earlier conversation.

"Sssank you so much, Sir....", the little man purrs.

"Why, we'd be packed like sardines in there!"

"I ssink so, yes!", the little man nods cheerfully.

"We regret," Ranley speaks with a show of sadness, "but we must go now. Our important mission takes us out there." He waves a vague hand down the way they had come. "In honor of the Republic of South Vietnam." He salutes the twin flags, the yellow of the republic slashed with three parallel red bars, and the stars and stripes.

"Yesss. The lepublic....", the Commandant repeats sadly. ".... We use very-much tonight your extra shooting-fingers here."

"There never are enough shooting-fingers, are there?", Ranley replies sympathetically. "Still, our mission is clear. Come on, nugs - we've got to hike."

Charley throws down his heavy duffle bag. "This is *crazy*! I don't *want* to go out there!"

Ranley nods, and gives him a little smile, speaking low so he won't be overheard, "The truth is, you don't want to stay here, either. They're going to be attacked tonight."

"You don't *know* that!"

"Sure I do. They get attacked every night. Sometimes it's just a carefully aimed rifle shot or two. Or a sapper will try to crawl in over the punji stakes and set an explosives charge against the wall. But tonight there's something even better to look forward to. You can bet the VC agents are already spreading the word we're camping here for

23

the night; do you want to be in that little hut a few hours from now when the mortars start coming in?"

The Vietnamese commander has shuffled over to where he can hear the conversation. Ranley, seeing he hwas overheard, speaks to him directly, "Is that right, Commander?"

The little man nods unhappily, "VC come al-lite. But we have good fighting mans. VC no take Long Chu. We die to last woman and child."

Ranley pats his shoulder, "I know you'll do alright."

"Sssank you, sir."

Ranley turns his skeptical gaze on Charley, "You can stay if you want, Specialist; I recommend you put your M-14 on single-shot - that way your ammo might last until midnight." He starts toward the gate, heading back the way they had come.

After a fast look at the other Dimbos and the wretched little fort, Charley picks up his bag and starts after him. He looks back over his shoulder at the Dimbos.

"Just you wait - I'll get you for this, Beale!"

"Damn it, Magnolia - "

Beale would like to reason with him, but Charley is already past him, head down and making his way to the front gate.

Larky picks up his own bag, "Wait, Charley. I'll walk with you."

Mad Denny nods, "Go ahead next, Ong Be. I'll bring up the rear."

They had no sooner retreated over the drawbridge when the people inside began to pull it up, isolating Long Chu from the surrounding

24

countryside for the night. Ranley led them single-file, walking through the light rain and the failing light for a quarter of a mile back along the gravel road the way they had come. This area had been bulldozed flat, to provide a field of fire for the sharpshooters behind the bamboo walls.

Ranley paused on the road, waiting for his straggling Dimbos to catch up. When they gathered in a semi-circle around him, he saw that Charley and Beale were panting heavily. "Here, give me that." Ranley swung Charley's bag on his own shoulder. He grinned, "You're all going to like it a lot better from now on." He took a right angle off the road onto a dim footpath that none of them had noticed. The Dimbos followed, one by one, and as they did so they left the Western World and civilization, as they knew it, behind.

In less than thirty seconds they are surrounded by dense forest. Dim light still filters through the high canopy overhead. Here the rain drips from the branches, and they smell the rich, earthy odor of the jungle. Beale sees a patch of huge, white flowers - or is it fungus, clinging to the side of a tree? Some little animal scurries across the ground in front of them. The footpath is firm under their feet, and they hike along in silence, overwhelmed by the gloomy majesty of the rain forest.

Charley drops back alongside Beale, "I'm sorry I yelled, Ong Be. I know *intellectually* it's not your fault."

Beale shifts his bag to his other shoulder, and his M-14 to his other hand. "Ong Nha - I've been thinking a lot about this. I think you really are going to be okay. We all are."

"Maybe. But one thing's sure; I'm no good at
25

this shit, Ong Be."

Beale doesn't want to get into how it had come about, "What *are* you guys doing in Vietnam, anyway? You never told me exactly what happened back at Meade."

Charley gives him a long look, "Who knows the real reason? We *did* piss off Captain James. But maybe they wanted to get everybody out of town who'd been on burn bags the night Drunk Sarge hit the blender. It's *the army way.*" They march along in silence, continuing on the path for another ten minutes until they come to the bank of a shallow brook.

On the other side, the Dimbos gather around Ranley, who talks to them with quiet confidence, "We're coming to the hamlet village of Thong Nhet. The government hasn't gotten around to relocating it into one of those spiked pig-sty horrors you saw back there. These people are why we're *really* over here. Try to remember if you have any manners." His critical eye lingers on each of them.

As they move forward the jungle foliage gives way to a clearing. There is a group of houses built of logs and bamboo. They hear children laughing and playing. A gong rings once, a heavy *bong* and again a sweet, high *ping*, the trembling notes hanging in the moist, heavy air. There is a pleasant smell of food. Through the trees, they see cooking fires going in the center of a village square. They hadn't realized how hungry they were.

Beale is overcome with an unexpected awe. The hamlet is natural to the area, \ it *belongs* here. It is warm and familiar, like a well-worn farm in

26

the Mid-western United States, and it seems this is its natural place, here in the middle of the rain forest.

"Anh, oiiiiii!", someone calls in a friendly hail. Ranley motions for them to wait while he goes on ahead.

Beale's heart is singing with a strange madness, he can hardly contain his amazement and joy. After the grinding year at language school, after the months at the Puzzle Palace, after the bustle, flap and roar of Tan Son Nhut, he has finally arrived at what back at language school he always visualized as *the real Vietnam*! No muddy, rut filled streets. No people jammed behind high walls for protection. No soldiers with rifles and lives interrupted by fear and terror.

He gazes with pleasure at the tightly-woven bamboo and thatch roofs and the men robed in simple peasant's pajamas and the women and young girls in plain *ao dai*, flowing dresses slit to the waist, with cotton pantaloons underneath. The gong rings again, and he makes out a small open-air temple at one end of the hamlet, the only structure with a tile roof.

The Dimbos link arms, each unconsciously throwing a hand over the other's shoulder, and they all stare. Larky whispers, "So it ain't just made up lessons, or a movie thing...."

"Or pictures in National Geographic...." Mad Denny adds.

Beale says it all for them, "There really *is* a Vietnam..."

CHAPTER FOUR

The village elders are dressed in frayed old robes of flowing beige silk. They are flanked by Buddhist monks in orange robes and young novitiates wrapped in rough textured cloth of a deep brown color. They all stand motionless in the center of the hamlet square under the roofed open-air gathering place next to the temple. Behind them community cooking fires blaze, crowded with older *bas* preparing the evening meal. A few older men move about tending the fires, carrying bundles of charcoal. Younger men, marriage-age women, and the laughing children are now nowhere to be seen.

Ranley takes Beale's M-14 and his own gray-stocked Armalite and hands them to Charley, "Wait here. Be friendly."

"Friendly?"

"Right. Pretend you're back in Bayonne and you're on vacation in the other guy's turf. You wouldn't start a rumble on vacation, would you?"

"Nooo. . . "

"Come on, Beale." Ranley drops the small knapsack he'd brought along, and they walk together to the village elders.

"How did you know Charley belonged to a gang?"

"Teen-age stuff. A bunch of toughs called *The Spirits*. It was in his file." He grins at Beale, "Mother ASA knows all."

The elders wait on a platform of wooden planks two steps off the ground. They seem otherworldly, almost alien in their dignity. Ranley bows deeply from his waist. Beale does the same. After what seems like a long time, the sergeant begins speaking with great ceremony in Vietnamese, "Greetings, *Thua Ong*, honorable ancient ones. We come to share our lives and the night, hoping for friendship, food and a place to rest."

The old men whisper among themselves. The eldest, a tiny man with long wisps of white hair on his chin, speaks in a high, wavering voice, "You have been here before as our friend, alone and without guns. Now you bring four armed warriors of the American colonialists."

"We are on a mission to a distant place, *Thua Ong*. We will stack our guns for the night."

The old men whisper among themselves for an even longer time. At last the old one bows, followed by the others. The monks remain aloof, the calm smiles on their faces saying they would endure, no matter the decision. A second, sweeter, more high-pitched gong now chimes, followed by the deep vibration of the first, and the village of Thong Nhet comes alive again.

It is like diving through water, Beale reflects, and coming up on another side of the same world. The hamlet is now filled with activity. Little kids dart about, with dogs barking and nipping at their heels. A young girl dressed in maiden's white gives him a long side-ways glance from a doorway. He sees her luxurious hair flows down past her waist. Middle-age *bas* smile and greet him, their teeth black as pitch from chewing beetle-nut. A small kid with an impish smile comes darting forward to pinch the golden-blond

29

hairs on his arm, then scuttles away.

By the time Ranley and Beale return, a laughing, chattering group has gathered around the other Dimbos. Larky, who had guessed they might be giving up their weapons, managed to slip off his pistol-belt, stowing it in his duffle-bag before the bald-headed apprentice monks came for their weapons. Charley stubbornly hangs on to his rifle.

Ranley takes it from him and hands it to the nearest monk, "It's the only way.... they ask the same of ARVNs and the VC. Their grandfathers asked the same of the French. And before that, the Chinese probably had to stack their spears by the fire."

"I'm going to get shot in the head with my own gun!"

"That's why you keep the ammunition," Ranley reminds him. "I said *be friendly*. You don't have to be a fool."

Ranley looks across at Larky, "There's nothing wrong with a hold-out."

"Wh-whut do you mean?", Larky blurts, his face blushing red in the flaring bonfires.

"I have one or two myself." Ranley draws the blouse of his pants leg tight over his calf to briefly outline a Beretta.

A thin, wiry boy heaves Beale's bag over his shoulder, only to fall flat on his back. He quickly scrambles to his feet, insisting on another chance. "We take you to the long room," he says, speaking in the soft-voweled southern dialect. He struggles with the bag that weighs as much as he does. "That's where all single men of marriage age sleep."

Ranley nods, "There's plenty room now, and

plenty of single girls too, since the government enlisted many of his brothers and cousins."

The long room is clean and neat and dry, with rows of double bunks built in along one wall. A candle in an oilpaper case is lit by the door at each end of the room. Little girls bring gourd pots of water, and stand by, laughing and chattering, while the Americans wash their faces and hands.

Larky slips his pappy's old .45 into one of the baggy pockets of his fatigues and stuffs an olive-colored handkerchief in over it. Charley barely slaps a few drops of water on his palms. He sits back in the shadows on his bunk. One little girl, seeing him alone, steps forward and offers him a flower. The girl stares silently at him, her great, round eyes fixed on his own, holding the limp water lily out to him. He reaches for the lily and kisses her on the top of her head. She smiles, a beautiful, shy smile, and the black-haired moppets run giggling from the room.

Charley grumbles, "I don't know what's become of my instinct for survival."

"You never had any, or you wouldn't be hanging around with us," Mad Denny says. "Come on. Let's go eat."

They walk back through the warm rain to the center of the hamlet. It is now full dark, with the only light coming from the blazing bonfires. The hamlet itself is rectangular, the houses directly connected or joined by waist-high fences to keep out animals. The open-air meeting place in the center is high enough so that its conical thatch roof, supported by four huge posts, is in no danger from the fires underneath.

Ranley and the Dimbos cross their legs and sit

31

on reed mats in a rough semi-circle with the elders and a few honored villagers. The *bas* pass around wooden bowls and chopsticks, grinning their black-tooth betel nut grins and chattering with one another. They bring copper bowls filled with steaming soup, and rice with the salty *nuoc mam* aged fish sauce on the side. Other women bring gourd bottles filled with rice wine, and fill small wooden cups for their guests.

The meal is presented in honor of the American guests: There is delicately seasoned fish, and chicken, and a meat fried in banana leaves.

Larky nudges Beale, "Hey, ol' buddy - you think we could ask for some more of that pork? Closest thing I've had to good ol' Texas barbecue since I joined the army."

Beale nudges Ranley, "Larky wants more pork"

Ranley raises his wooden cup in a little salute, "Fried rodent."

"Maybe I better tell him they ran out."

"Just tell him it's pork."

The memory will last a lifetime, not only for the food as the fact that *they were actually there* in the place they had begun to question existed when they were back at Monterey and in D.C. As the meal went on, they toasted each other and Ranley, calling him their fearless leader. Then they toasted their hosts, and the beauty of the village.

The chirping language is all around them. They eye the nymph-like coppery-skinned girls who fill their wine cups. In the golden glow of the fire and the wine, the nettling army regulations and the war itself seems to dissolve, and finally fade away. There are no bat-shit rules, no snipers, no V.C. terrorists. Just a timeless village far away from anywhere.

While the *bas* take the food trays away, Ranley fishes a box of rum-soaked Crooks from a knapsack he has brought with him from the long house. He presents the box to the chief elder with a small bow. The old man insists on opening the box himself, cutting the cellophane wrapping with a small knife he draws from the back of his waist. He passes the cigars out to the others at his side and then to each of the Americans. He claps his hands, and women bring small, flaming splinters from the fire. While they puff away, Ranley dug again in his sack, this time retrieving a bottle of French brandy, which he presents with great formality.

The old man nods, responding with a little giggle and clapping his hands for one of the women. The chief elder stands, weaving slightly as he raises his copper drinking mug, "To our eternal ancestors, and yours!" He pours a small stream on the wooden planks, and then drinks the rest.

Ranley motions the Dimbos are to rise. "To the ancestors!" he says, repeating the ceremony.

When they are seated again, the old man leans toward Ranley, "I have seen many suns and moons. The sun has risen and set on my children's children's children. And I will not see many more. Yet, before I die, I wish one more thing. You my *nguoi My* friend, can obtain this for me."

Ranley nods, "Yes, of course...."

"I have the old man's foolish wish to taste one time again before I die, the great *beer My*, Bud-

33

wy-siir...." His face is blank and expressionless in the waning light, "....in the carton of six...."

What's his request?", Charley asks.

"Bud in the six-pack!"

"Good choice! Bud, the king of beers!"

Ranley waves them quiet, trying to keep a solemn face, "We shall obtain some at the *Club N.C.O. My* within three days."

The old man thanks them and then claps his hands. "I have one piece of business, if you will allow." He stands as two *bas* drape a black vest over his thin shoulders. They settle a ceremonial cone-hat of black silk on his head. He lightly claps his thin, shriveled hands again, and a peasant man comes forward from the darkness. Another of the old men rises, bows to the elder, and joins this newcomer in front of the raised platform. Their conversation begins politely enough, but soon heats up until the two men are shouting at each other. Unexpectedly, the peasant agrees, bowing at the waist and disappears into the darkness. He returns in a few moments with a huge copper kettle, which he places at the feet of the second man. Again they argue, and the man leaves again, and a short time later returns with a set of copper spoons. This continues, and the pile of goods in front of the platform grows to include bolts of silk, a butcher knife, a wooden mortar and pestle, and smaller things wrapped in white cloth. Through it all, the chief elder and the other old men sit and watch, only pausing to sip from their wine bowls, which the *bas* were now lacing with brandy.

"What's going on?", Mad Denny asks.

Ranley put his finger to his lips. "Shhh - Negotiating for a bride!"

"You're kidding!"

"Where's the bride?"

"Watching from one of the huts."

Charley finds himself remembering the Total Zip Game and Vung's loss of face to the chocolate Ex-lax.

The bartering continues. After one last, furious round when one of the bargainers looks like he is going to come to blows or leave the hamlet, the peasant retrieves a huge water buffalo, which he leads to the edge of the firelight. The old men all come to look at its teeth and prod it in the ribs and genitals. Satisfied, they return to their seats and nod to their negotiator. It's a deal.

CHAPTER FIVE

Larky can't remember the last time he'd had so much wine. He finds himself thinking about the people of Thong Nhet; they remind him of ranchers and farmers, more like Texans or folks from Oklahoma, only maybe with odd accents. He chuckled at the strange combination of sense and nonsense that idea made. *This was like a batch of good old boys - who were also sort-of outer space aliens - at an engagement barbecue!* Texas was about the same as Vietnam, he figured, with two seasons, the wet and the dry - though back home there it was generally more dry than wet while here it was reversed. These folks had their spring planting and fall harvest feasts, and their drunken howling at the moon in the New Years Tet Celebration. They were as animistic - as close to the land - as the Indians, and surely as devout and superstitious in their Buddhism ways as the Baptists were back home.

Larky doesn't know it, but for some time now a beautiful woman has been watching him, looking out through the slats across her open window while she sits naked on a small stool in front of the rusty old mirror in her bedroom. The night breeze billows through Than-An's long, black hair as she runs an old ivory handled brush through it. There is too little light in the room and only the glow of the distant, dying fires faintly outlines her delicately curved body, smooth except for the lush patch of black hair between her legs.

Her husband is away, and she is restless again,

impatient with hunger to be touched and held. She stares at the stocky American. He is shorter than the other *nguoi my*, only a few inches taller than she is, and she likes that. He has a nice, boisterous way, she could see it even at a distance, and she likes that too.

She knows that if they ever held a contest (which they wouldn't), she would be the village beauty. That bores her, for the entire village bores her. The problem is, Than-An doesn't know how beautiful she is in the real world *outside* Thong Nhet. And the punishments would be swift and cruel if she was caught making love to anyone but her husband. But on the other hand there will be no punishment, for she is always very quiet and very careful.

As a little girl, she'd dreamed of going to Tay Ninh. It was a big dream, for to go even 10 kilometers was often the trip of a lifetime. But her mother had said no, and had browbeaten her father - after she had him already half-convinced with smiles and little-girl sweet talk. She had never forgiven her mother for that. It wasn't as if she was asking to go to wicked Saigon, where the legendary potbellies took down little countryside girls, plying them with liquor and drugs until they spread their legs for piasters. But it wasn't to be, and she had never been to Tay Ninh, or anywhere.

The other women in the village whispered behind her back that she must be a clay doll, perfect but cold in bed. Than-An took bitter amusement from that -- having had fiery affairs with four of their husbands since she was married, burning passionate relationships that had left the men exhausted, jealous and wary.

37

Now she strokes her brush through her long, black hair, eyeing the smooth curves of her own nakedness and the flatness of her childless belly. The villagers are drinking rice wine and soon will be drifting away to their beds. She watches from her window until she can barely stand to wait any longer. And, as if in answer to her call, Larky rises and staggers away from the circle of men around the fire. Than-An gathers the upper part of her thin silk *ao dai* around her like a shawl, and tiptoes from the house.

Larky wanders away from the fire, looking for a dark and deserted corner of the hamlet to take a leak. It isn't that easy with kids and dogs everywhere, and after looking around hopelessly for a while, he strolls out the still-open gate and down the path the Dimbos had walked along earlier that evening.

Than-An waits, and then drifts soundless up behind the unsuspecting American soldier. This is her hamlet village. She might not have known the streets of Saigon or Tay Ninh, but here she knows every rock and blade of grass. She waits for the *Nguoi My* to finish urinating and then moves swiftly behind him and slips her arms around his waist.

Larky violently breaks her grip, fumbling for his gun. The t-shirt he'd put over it wasn't helping, and when he sees who his attacker is, he doesn't know what to do. He rubs his eyes, weaving slightly in the night while the warm rain patters down through the trees, wetting his head and shoulders. He can't believe it. Directly in front of him the rain is falling on the bare shoulders of a half-dressed woman, a beautiful dream-woman. The raindrops are running between her pert, uplifted breasts, and he swears to himself she is surely the most beautiful women he has ever seen. The wine and the moment are too much for him, and he blubbers foolishly in English, "What - what's going *on*, lady...?"

"Zut!" she whispers, smiling and raising a finger to her full lips. She comes slowly closer, and closer still, until only her finger is between their lips. And then she takes her finger away, and their lips meet in a full kiss.

Her hands fumble with his clothing, and in a moment his pants drop around his knees.

"You - you're a goddess!" Larky whispers.

Than-An caresses him, holding him in one hand, knowing he is completely in her power. She pulls him down with her to lie on the wet sand next to the pathway, easily guiding him to fill the screaming cry of desire that her body has become. The rain is in her eyes, and he is inside her, big and right and good.

Larky is one of those guys who can make love a long time after he's been drinking wine, and this stranger of his desires spasms again and again until he finally gives up with a tremendous gasp of elation and collapses on her, feeling weak as a new-born kitten.

This is the part Than-An hates, and she endures it for as long as she can. Then she pulls away from him, rises and wraps her thin silk around herself. She points out the bamboo hut where she lives. "Come to me there. Later."

She is surprised when he answers in halting Vietnamese, "You are beautiful as a princess."

39

Her lips meet his, and she repeats, "Later, my sweet *nguoi My*."

He feels the brush of her bare hip against his own, hears one faint whisper in the brush, and she is gone like a ghost-lover. He gets himself together as best he can and returns to the fire, feeling foolish and befuddled and content at the same time as he hums under his breath, "Ninety-eight bottles of beer on the wall, Ninety-eight bottles of beer - if one of those bottles should happen to fall. . ."

Beale smiles at him, handing him a full cup of wine, "Hi, happy warrior - I was just going to look for you. Any trouble?"

"Uhh, no, Ong Be. I was jest - jest experiencing that true Nam Viet you're always telling me about...."

Ranley raises his glass, "To Nam Viet! And to lingies, the only hope of the war!"

"Hear, hear!", they all cheer.

The chief elder claps his hands, and a line of young girls gathers on one side of the dying fires. They wear white *ao dai*, and look like a little flock of doves. One of the old men plinks a lute, and another plays haunting notes on a flute. The girl's voices sound sweet in the night, singing a classic lullaby

Bay la, la, bay la
Bay la, la, bay la

Their song finished, they are about to leave when Mad Denny staggers to his feet and walks over to them. Ranley lurches up to intercept him, but Beale stops him, "No. Wait and see what happens."

Mad Denny Haller stands in the center of the little girls like a tall frog surrounded by waist-high daisies. He takes the flute and hoots it for a moment. Then he sets it down and picks up the stringed instrument. This he studies carefully, his eyes blinking in the firelight. He begins to re-tune it, turning the wooden pegs until he is satisfied.

Charley groans, "Uhhh, Ong Be -- maybe you better stop him."

"No, you guys!" Beale gives Mad Denny a little salute of encouragement, "Dimbos forever!"

Denny strums the instrument like a ukulele, and begins singing in a clear, tenor voice.

Bay la la bay la bay la la
Bay la la bay la bay la la

The villagers link arms with the *nguoi My*, and their voices rise as sweet threads of sound in the night.

Looking back, Beale would remember the way their tough-guy sergeant smiled, as if seeing them for the first time. It was important to him because he saw Ranley as their link with the past, with American intentions that he believed in his heart had once been noble and good.

CHAPTER SIX

Larky wakes to find he is butt naked from his fatigue jacket down to his boots. His underpants and trousers are on the floor, unbelievably soaked and muddy. He grabs them, feeling for the firm contact of his pistol and then breathing a sigh of relief, "Oh, Daddy," he mutters softly, "if I'd lost our .45!"

He sits back on the bed, holding his head between his hands. Bits of his amorous adventures start to come back to him then; what a night he'd had! After the others had drifted off to sleep, he'd gone back out through the rain to the house his mysterious lover had pointed out to him. By this time, the village fires were just low beds of coals, and he'd made his way uncertainly through the darkness, at the last moment seeing a soft, indirect glow of a candle. He thought it was hers, but still he couldn't be sure. She moved slightly as he approached the dark doorway, revealing the outline of her body. *Hot Damn!* he thought to himself, *doesn't she ever wear any clothes?*

"Zut!", she said again, signaling he should come closer. When she stood one step above him in the doorway, she had to bend her head down to kiss him. He cupped her breasts gently in his hands, softly kissing the nipples of first one and then the other.

She whispers something to him he doesn't understand and takes his hand. He thinks she'll take him inside, but instead, she leads him halfway across the hamlet to the central meeting place.

There she slowly undresses him, their two forms outlined against the glowing red coals of the dying fires. She lies back on the elder's platform and pulls him on top of her.

After what seems like hours, she totally exhausts him. He lies with his back against the smooth wooden planks, catching his breath while the dim outlines of the thatch roof above him spins in a slow, clockwise circle. He doesn't know what words to say. He wants to tell her she is beautiful in her own unique way, but the language eludes him, so he just kisses her lightly one last time and wearily heads back toward the long house, dragging his clothes in one hand.

He thinks she was sleeping, but she rises and comes after him. "Come back here in a few more hours! I will meet you here! There is much time before dawn!"

"I - uhhh, yeah, sure, okay....", He remembers she doesn't speak English, "Oh - *vung, vung*!" She is insatiable. Even with that promise, she clings to him, feeling him with her hands, trying to get another rise out of him. But he is too exhausted. He has to push her hands away and walk on alone to the long house. He promises he will come back and see her after he'd caught a little shut-eye. It is the last thing he thinks of before his head sinks back on his cot.

And then he wakes and it is bright morning. Larky sits on the edge of his bed, listening to the rain and the thumping in his brains. He shakes his head slowly from side to side, but the beat continues, "Somebody's beating a drum", he mutters, feeling stupid and slow. He sees his socks are on, so he starts to pull on his boots before

43

realizing his muddy fatigue pants are lying on the floor.

He's just about got his pants on when Beale runs in, "Hey, Larky! You're missing it!"

"Ong Be, please - I hear a drum...."

Beale grabs a water pitcher and pours it over Larky's head, "It *is* a drum! They're drumming somebody out of the village!"

Larky reaches for one of his boots. "Beeee.....*please* don't talk so loud. Who's drumming who out of where?"

"Come *on*, you've got to see it!" He grabs Larky's remaining boot in one arm and pulls him out the door with the other. Larky blinks in the too-bright light, sitting down with a thump in the doorway and trying to figure what's going on while he pulls on his other boot. Beale gets him up and they walk over to join the other Americans, who have gathered under the thatch roof of the central meeting place. The only sounds are the crackle of the common fire, the drip of water off the eaves of the meeting hall, and the deep, steady *boom, boom, Boom* of the drum, which comes from the nearby temple.

Larky sees the chief elder is standing near where he had made love to his mysterious lady the night before. The old man's wispy, white beard flows in the breeze, and he looks frail as a dandelion seed. Villagers stand about whispering to each other, and one tall, thin man is carrying a coil of heavy rope.

Beale whispers enthusiastically, "Isn't this neat?!"

Larky is feeling cold fingers around his testicles, "I ain't so sure....what's this all about, Old

44

Buddy?

But Beale has no time to answer as the village elder calls out in a high, ceremonial pitch. For a moment nothing happens, and then Larky feels a sudden chill. For out of the house he had approached last night steps his mysterious lover, the beautiful lady of his midnight adventures!

"Ohh, shit...", he whispers, feeling guilty and afraid.

The woman is dressed in a filmy *ao dai* of pale peach silk. She is as attractive in the daylight as she had been the night before. She walks nervously to a place before the elders, and stands not ten feet away, looking boldly at Larky.

Larky makes such a fuss trying to scrape some mud off his pants leg that Ranley turns and glares at him, "A little respect here, Larky. Important ceremony...!"

Larky nods. It is all he can do to keep from making a mad dash out the front gate.

The elder calls again in his thin voice. Larky stands frozen to the ground. After an endless moment, a burly man comes from the same doorway where the woman had appeared. This man is completely naked. He looks strange and out of place. Head bowed, he slowly approaches the group. Rain dribblesdown his broad chest.

"W-who's *that*?" Larky asks..

"The village smithy," Ranley says.. He got caught porking the lady over there, *not* his wife."

As the smithy walks along, one old woman spits at him, the gob of orange betel juice dribbles down the black curls on his stomach to nest in his dark pubic hair. A brief cry of satisfaction goes up from a group of middle-aged *bas*, but it is quickly

45

hushed by angry looks from the elders and the monks.

The thin man with the rope steps forward and shouts, his angry words tumbling out too fast for the Americans to understand. With one violent gesture, he rips the silk *ao dai* from Than-An's back. She tries to cover herself with her hands. The village men chuckle and the old *bas* hiss like geese. The thin man begins to bind the couple together, tying the left leg and left arm of the woman to the right leg and right arm of the burly man. The woman begs and pleads but the thin man only shakes his head and binds her more tightly until his coil of rope is entirely used up, firmly knotting them together.

The drums now take on a new beat, *ba-BOM-ba, ba-BOM-ba, ba-BOM-ba.* The elder silently points to the couple, and then to the gate.. They turn from him and begin to walk, steered and pushed by members in the jeering crowd. They stagger and fall on the muddy ground. No one moves to help them up. Than-An seemed to think the fall is her partner's fault, and she beats at him with her free hand until he catches it in his own and squeezes. She yells and lashes out a vicious kick at him, only succeeding in pulling them down in the mud again. He grimly holds her fist, crushing it until she stops attacking him.

Larky can't stand it, "Whut's going *on*, Ong Be?"

"I *told* you - *that* man got caught in bed with *that* woman, *not* his wife....Larky, are you alright? You look white as a ghost."

"Uhhh.... don't we have to be somewhere?"

"You won't see this once in a lifetime!"

46

As the couple marches toward the gate, the beautiful woman looks back and Larky is sure she is looking at him.

Larky moves over next to Ranley, "Ahh, what's going to happen to her?"

"The new couple can marry and stay in the village to live down their shame."

"They won't do that, looks like."

"Or any other man can claim her."

"Nobody looks like they're stepping forward."

"Now's your chance. Don't you want her?"

Larky's face blanches, "Uhhh, sarge - ain't we supposed to *be* somewhere?"

"Right, nug - Black Lady Peak." Ranley is still looking at Larky. Finally his battered face breaks into a grin, "She wasn't that good then?" He turns away before Larky can think of anything to say. "Come on, Boy-Dimbo-Wonders -- we're headed for Nui Ba Den!"

CHAPTER SEVEN

Once they were on top of Nui Ba Den, the Dimbos sat on the tails of their ponchos in a small circle around the smoky little trash fire Charley built in an abandoned 55-gallon drum shitter, started fast and easy by squirting a can of lighter fluid on some damp cartons and old packing crates. They were safely behind the sandbags and thick accordion rolls of barbed wire. Ranley was nearby in the tiny, rat-infested radio shack, trying to contact the 114th RRU in Tay Ninh. Intercept being a seasonal game on Nui Ba Den, the American Radio Researchers had unstrung their wires so the natives wouldn't steal them, and pulled out for the season.

There is nobody else at the outpost except a half-dozen ARVN privates left in the hands of a jittery corporal who tells Beale in broken English that he'd been studying pre-med two months before at Saigon University.

"Wish Ranley'd hurry up," Charley says uneasily.

"He's only fifty yards away. You could hit him with a rock."

"Not much of a mountain", Mad Denny grumbles, "I'd call it more of a hill."

"Just another black pimple on the topographic face of Asia", Beale recites calmly.

"Did you make that one up, or steal it from Old Joe Conrad?", Charley mutters.

"You don't like the bush - don't take it out on Beale," Mad Denny says, shifting his weight on his damp poncho.

"You'll never know, Charley", Beale replies loftily. "And when I write a best-seller, I won't *give* you a copy. You'll have to buy it off the shelf, just like I don't know you."

"The day you get something published will be legitimate excuse for a book-burning."

They had hiked back to Long Chu that morning, and then driven their jeeps to the base of Nui Ba Den. A primitive road had been bulldozed to the top, but it was washed out and overgrown with brush so that only a footpath remained, and Ranley had insisted they all make the climb.

Beale had slugged along happily, his mind at rest, a silly nonsense jingle going over and over in time with his steps

Nam is south
Nam is south
Nam is south
... Of Bac!

Charley had insisted on bringing along a heavy pack. Once they reached the top, he enlisted Larky to collect camp debris, and started his fire. The day dragged on, and the rain that had never left them since they started diminished to a chilly mist. The light was fading, but from their vantage point around the fire they could still see a wide and gloomy panorama of rice paddies, sandy marshes, and sluggish waterways looping to the south and east.

"Red Dog better hurry back. I don't want to spend the night up here." Charley breaks out a second can of lighter fluid and sprays the fire, causing it to flare up with a big whosh.

"Don't even *think* about it, Ol' Buddy. Might bring bad luck!"

"There is no such thing", Beale says, crossing his arms with his hands under his armpits to stop his hands from quivering.

"Well, it *is* your goddamn fault, Ong Be", Mad Denny says, starting up after nobody had said anything for several minutes.

"Yeah, sure. It's always my fault."

"Well, it *is*, sheep-dip! If it wasn't for you and your war-itch, Charley would be back in D.C. right now, drinking cherished 'Melican beer Budweiser, convincing the lovelies he's a spy and screwing up a storm. Of course he holds you a grudge."

"Don't tell him that!", Charley waves his hand in disgust, "He's fucked up enough as it is."

"Wait a minute." Beale feels uneasy. "What are you talking about, Denny?" The other three Dimbos are outlined against the fading light of the evening sky, looking like three grim judges ready to pass judgment on him.

Larky finally speaks up, "Awww, Christ, now somebody's *got* to tell him . . . When we was back at Meade, Charley convinced Nelson and James that you was going to blow Drunk-Sarge's amazing and untimely demise to the newspapers."

"But *why*?"

"Ol' Charley here rightfully figured they would ship your ass to Nam like you wanted, jest to get rid of you. But don't feel guilty -- it isn't *really* your fault, Jack. The Bugger from Bayonne here just outsmarted himself -- he didn't realize once all that fear set in, the folks back at the Puzzle Palace would figure they had to get rid of *all* the

50

Dimbos...."

"Yeah," Charley agrees with an unhappy little chuckle. He fishes in his sack and comes up with a hard salami, which he begins to carve with a switchblade. "It seemed like a great idea at the time."

Beale fumbles inside his poncho, feeling around for his cigarettes with trembling fingers. They'd hinted at this before, and true or not, he had accepted the notion it was his fault the Dimbos had all ended up in Vietnam. He didn't like to think about what kind of responsibility that gave him, and he was grateful when Larky shifted the subject, "Hey Denny, remember drunk-spick Rafaelson falling into the pulper..."

"Course, dip-shit." Denny's voice is calm. He seems at peace with himself.

"What was you thinking when you saw him go in?" It is a good question for that night; something in the way the wind moves over the old mountain echoes the savage moan of the pulper blades and makes Rafaelson's grisly end fresh in their minds.

Beale finally gets his hands around his Marlboro hard-pack. "Anybody want a smoke?"

"We don't smoke", Charley says pointedly. "And you never used to. *Bad for the wind*, you used to say, back when you was perfect."

"Leave the poor feller alone, Charley", Larky says. "You made your own bed...." His mind is still on Rafaelson, "You didn't *know* he was going to fall in *for sure*, did you, Denny?"

"Sure I did", the calm reply comes out of the rainy darkness. "He was too blotto to do anything else. And it was him or me...." There was a long pause before he continues. "None of you was

51

close enough to see, but for a moment that night it was *me* going in that blender...."

"You're shitting us..."

"No. True. When Rafe dove for the controls, he shoved me and I lost my balance. I had to grab him to save my own ass."

"But how do you know for sure you couldn't have saved him?" Beale asks in a small, shocked voice.

"I just know it."

There is a long pause. "Don't think about it, Ong Be", Charley offers. "Have a piece of Tuscano."

"I don't want your goddamn salami! Denny, suppose it was somebody else; you know, not Drunk Sarge, but somebody worth saving maybe..."

The fire is almost out again, but Charley makes no move to revive its dull glow. Again Denny's voice comes out of the dark with a calm certainty, "I'd have done the same thing."

"Naaw, you wouldn't have..."

"Christ, Beale!" Charley's voice is thick with sarcasm, "Nobody wants to die!"

"In a time like that, Mister Be, you'd push your own mother in. You don't think, you just do it!"

Charley laughs. "There you have it! If it had been *you* instead of Drunk Sarge, dear Ong Be, Mad Denny would have grabbed you too, but it wouldn't have done him a damn bit of good!"

"Why not, Charley?", Beale shoots back, his voice now full of anger.

"Easy. You'd have fucked-the-duck by hanging on -- and *two* guys would have been blended right up to the great mix-master in the sky!"

Beale is frozen into silence. His hands refuse to unwrap from his Marlboros to find his matches. *After all, hadn't he done the same thing by hanging on to the three of them to get his deepest wish, to get over to Nam?* Now they were all in his blender. And his was an even finer sort of guilt; there had been no case of life-and-death, just his uncontrollable itch to *see the real thing*. He didn't have to have night vision, he knew Charley was staring across the space that separated them with that knowing grin of his, thinking the same thing. *Some friend he turned out to be!* Beale gives up fumbling for his matches, grateful no one can see the bothersome tic in his eye, or the way his hands are crushing his cigarette pack as if they have a spastic life of their own.

The rain-laden wind sobs endlessly as it moves over the face of the small dark mountain on its timeless and inexorable way east across Asia. Countless cycles of seasons, of wind and rain, of dust and wind, of birth and struggle and pain and death, have not broken the Black Lady's basalt shoulders; Nui Ba Den will endure.

CHAPTER EIGHT

The ARVN privates take turns cranking the wireless until somebody finally answers Ranley's call, "This *is* the 114th Rock-and-Roll Unit!"

It is the next morning after their arrival at Nui Ba Den, and after spending a night in a bunker crawling with rats, Ranley isn't in the mood for joking around. "Okay, Smart Guy", he explodes, "where's the C.O.?"

"This *is* the C.O., Smart-Guy-Yourself. Have at it."

"Where *are* you people? Black Lady is manned by a half dozen Zip teenagers, and I've been trying to ring you since yesterday!"

"Red Dog! Captain Nordoff said you'd be calling! We're at our rainy season headquarters, down in Tay Ninh."

"Nobody told me."

"Well, we are. Got a small theater, too, just like the 3rd. Now playing Catch 22 and looking forward to the Green Berets."

"Nelson'll have your nuts!"

"We don't work for civilians, Red Dog! And our team only got one weak fix last three weeks before we pulled out!"

"You even bother to follow it up?"

The voice on the other end of the line stiffens, "Don't get your balls in an uproar, sergeant. We got the fix."

"Has anyone been out there since?"

"We aren't *complete* turkeys here in your beautiful but remote 114th! In fact, we got the fly-boys to paste it with a few iron bombs. Hey, if you like, I'll hang on to **Catch-22** an extra day or two for you."

"No thanks. There are enough crazies in *this* war...."

"Suit yourself", the crackling voice comes over heavy with sarcasm, "by the way, if I ever need brain surgery, remind me not to ask you, okay?"

"You'll never need it, sir." Ranley signed off quickly, before the man had time to think about it.

CHAPTER NINE

Two hours later when they were still about 5 miles outside of Tay Ninh Ranley pulled over to the side of the road. He spread his map on the hood of his jeep while the Dimbos huddled around him. The overcast was thinning, but the countryside still lay shrouded in fog, pierced occasionally by a shaft of pearly golden light. Ranley points across the deserted farmlands that now stretched fallow and neglected away as far as they could see. They once were grazing fields rather than rice paddies; now they were overgrown with waist-high saw grass and scrub trees.

"About 200 yards that way, in plain view of the road, if the fix is any decent...." Ranley sounds preoccupied, like a man talking to himself.

"We're going to get soaked walking through there", Charley says.

"That's a fact." Ranley grins, "And muddy. Who's going to stay with the jeeps?"

"I will!", Charley, Larky and Mad Denny say as one voice.

"You," Ranley says, picking Mad Denny. "The rest of you guys follow me. Walk in my footsteps so you maybe don't get blown up."

Ranley starts from the road, plunging through a culvert that is knee-high with scummy water, and moving quickly away from them. Beale follows next, followed by Charley, who mutters, "At the rate my debt is growing for the joy and wonder of all these experiences, I don't know how I can ever pay you back, my dear Ong Be...."

The grass is higher than it looked from the road, and soon they are struggling through reeds and elephant grass that obscures their vision. Larky slings his rifle upside down over his shoulder and draws his .45.

Beale gives Ranley about five paces, but Charley is right behind him, so close that each time he raises a foot, one of Charley's replaces his footprint in the mushy ground. After about five minutes, Ranley motions for them to stop. Beale stops immediately, and Charley runs into his back. "Jesus Christ, Beale!", he says angrily, "give me some warning!"

"We're just about there. Look!"

The muddy earth in front of them is chewed and blasted for several hundred yards in a long, roughly rectangular pattern. There are dozens of saucer-like depressions, each with a shallow pool of muddy water at its bottom.

Ranley gingerly makes his way across the rough terrain. The fog has lifted, only to be replaced by low clouds that again threaten rain.

"Shit," Charley says, "We could be gunned down from any side!"

Ranley stops and brings his AR-15 to the ready. They all see it at once; four splintered logs rimming a dark hole in the ground.

"Daring bastards. In plain view of the road."

"Yeah," Ranley says, "But last week you could have walked right over that hole and not even know it was there - the trap door would have been covered with dirt and live grass." He speaks casually, but the muzzle of his gun never leaves the dark opening. He pulls the pin on a concussion grenade with his teeth and drops it through the opening, "Fire in the hole!"

Beale expects the grenade to come spinning back out like it sometimes did in the movies, rejected by the enemy. He can see it in his mind's eye: The smooth olive ball turns slowly end-over-end, slow motion and growing big as a balloon and then big as a blimp until it explodes suddenly in mid-air, killing them all. He shakes his head, \wondering what simple trick of time made a thing like that take so long to happen. Just then in reality the grenade down there in the hole went off with a little shock wave, sending a spatter of dirt and a cloud of dark gray smoke boiling out of the entrance.

Ranley moves cautiously to the lip of the hole, "Who's coming with?"

He turns and Charley is standing right there. Without a moment's hesitation, Charley says, "Beale is, sir."

"You're volunteering him?"

Charley gives Beale a wicked grin, "He *wants* to go, for the experience!"

Beale nods, "Yep. I'm it." He pushes back a crazy feeling that Nam, *his* Nam, is reaching out for him with white, bony fingers, fingers that come up out of the muddy ground to wrap themselves around his neck. He shakes his head to get rid of the image. "He's right, Red Dog. I want to go."

By this time Ranley has lowered himself almost completely into the tunnel. "Okay. Just follow me. And don't touch anything." He has brought a few road flares from his jeep. Now he lights one by twisting off the top, and slowly inches his way out of sight.

Larky lowers Beale over the side. He jacks a

cartridge in the chamber of his .45 and hands it to Beale, "Take care, Ong Be. An' remember, she's been filed down for a kind of easy pull, so don't keep your finger on the trigger."

Charley, who has managed to drag along his nylon goody-bag, pulls out a small pocket flashlight and hands it to Beale, "Yeah, here. Take care of yourself, Ong Be...."

"Sure. I know you really mean that."

"Hey, lighten up - are those the last words I've got to remember you by?"

"Oh, fuck off, Magnolia!"

"Much better - a more spirited last farewell!"

Beale is able to give him a rueful grin before he clicks on the light and moves out of sight.

The tunnel smells of earth and underground rot, and something else -- the sick-sweet odor of death hangs heavy in the air. *There's a dead guy or two down here somewhere*. Beale moves slowly, feeling his way with his feet, his flashlight barely able to poke through the heavy smoke from Ranley's flare. The notion that Ranley is somewhere up ahead comforts him. *Nothing could happen with Ranley along. Good old Red Dog Ranley.*

Beale bends under low ceilings lined with heavy timbers. There are places where the dirt has caved in, and he has to crawl over mounds of cool, damp earth.

Ranley, who has moved on about twenty yards ahead, calls back, "Dead man, Beale."

As Beale moves forward he sees the man is bloated and stripped naked.

"Don't touch, he may be booby-trapped,"

59

Ranley says, his voice reaching Beale from somewhere up ahead. Beale gingerly steps around the body and is about to move on when he makes the mistake of looking directly into his face. He's never seen a dead face before, outside the mortuary presentation of his dead grandmother. This face is puffy green-gray and twisted like a Halloween horror mask. He thinks he sees the mouth twitch, and he jerks back when he sees it is dozens of white maggots crawling around the blank eyes and lips. He feels the thin, rotten air rushing in and out of his lungs. He looks around, he doesn't want to be here. *He couldn't go back - he couldn't go forward!*

The tunnel takes a turn to the right up ahead, and Ranley has moved out of sight. Beale forces down the vomit rising in his throat and moves past the body. His back touches the wall to stay as far away as he can possibly get from the corpse. He is moving slowly, stiff with fear, when he hears a scraping sound. He freezes instantly, sweeping the weakening beam from Charley's flashlight to search the area. He finally sees it - a grenade buried in a tin can at the bottom of the sidewall behind the dead man! He realizes his foot has snagged an almost invisible black thread strung an inch above the floor, a thread that runs to the grenade. Ranley must have stepped over it without even seeing the thread - but he, Beale, for all his carefulness, has caught it!

The grenade totters at the edge of the rusty can. Beale gapes; another ounce of pull on the thread, and it will pop out of the can. He eases his foot back from the thread, knowing the pin has been already pulled, and all that holds the handle is the rusty circumference of the can. If that grenade comes out, he will have three seconds.... maybe less.

"Ranley!", he calls, not caring that his voice sounded like a bleating goat, "Ranley!"

"Just a minute, Beale." There is a light sawing noise from around the corner, like a man cutting a cord with a knife, and then something heavy slams into the side of the wall.

But Beale doesn't have a minute; reacting to the impact of whatever hit the wall, the grenade teeters, and then falls out onto the floor!

"Grenade!!" Beale shouts, and he does a diving tuck-and-roll over the bloated body. He just manages to get around the corner behind the protecting wall of earth when the grenade goes off with an ear-shattering explosion.

Ranley still holds his flare, and Beale his little flashlight. The two men look at each other, shocked and dazed by the blast, and coughing from the acrid smoke. When the dust clears enough so they can see, Ranley puts an arm around Beale's shoulder, "They almost got us." He points to a punji stake contraption which, driven by powerful springs, has slammed long wooden spikes into the wall.

He has Beale describe exactly how and where the grenade had been placed. Ranley nodded, "Smart. We see the grenade and dive around the corner into the punji stakes!"

The tunnel behind them is illuminated by Charley's little flashlight. A grotesque horror of spattered flesh meets their unwilling gaze. All they can see left of the body is the bloody skull, which has lost most of the flesh from its face. It grins up at them with shining white teeth as if they share a great secret. Beale digs around in the loose dirt on the floor until he finds Larky's pistol. He'd dropped it when the grenade first came loose. He moves on after Ranley, who is continuing along the corridor beyond the bend.

Ranley has lit a second flare, and is working to dismantle something else. "Bouncing Betty. Give me some time." After a few minutes he motions Beale forward again, "Okay - I got the trigger and the spring. Just give it room when you pass."

They enter the main room, a low, timber-supported area big enough to hold a half dozen or more people. After searching the work area and the bunks, Ranley decides the place has been stripped clean. "Shit. All this for nothing. You okay?"

Beale nods. He feels numb, as if his monster has deserted him, if he ever had such a thing. "Yeah. Can we go now?"

"Sure."

They sidestep past the disengaged Bouncing Betty and make their way back the way they'd. Beale shudders as he sees the skull still grinning up at him. A few maggots move around in the mushy, half-filled eye sockets, continuing their grim work. He moves to catch up with Ranley. His light is much dimmer now, and the sergeant is getting too far ahead. Beale tries to speed up, but trips and falls forward and Larky's gun fires with a tremendous roar.

Ranley senses the bullet whistle by him in the tunnel. He hits the dirt, then comes back for Beale, "What happened?"

"I'm alright. Just a little embarrassed." Beale

62

kicks the dirt pile that he'd stumbled over - revealing a small packet of muddy papers.

He leafs through the packet, "Looks like personal papers - Wait a minute!" He kicks more of the dirt aside with his foot, "Something else here!" Digging in the loose soil, his trembling fingers bring out a logbook wrapped in a Viet Cong flag.

Larky and Charley help pull them out of the tunnel, their relief obvious. "We didn't think you were ever coming back out!"

Larky, remembering the helmets and swords his dad had brought back from Okinawa, asked, "Hey, kin I keep the flag?"

"Nope", Ranley says. "It's Beale's. He earned it." Ranley thumbs through the codebook Beale had found, "*Oh boy*, did he earn it!"

Beale lifts his right elbow, and Ranley stuffs the stained cloth of the flag under his arm. Beale couldn't do any better than that for the moment because his shaking hands were busy, trying to get a Marlboro going.

Larky takes over driving Beale's jeep the rest of the way into Tay Ninh. After going a few miles in silence, he glances over at his passenger with a triumphant smile, his round face lighting up with pleasure, "So, you found yore monster again, didn't you Ong Be - jest about like I said you would!" He speaks as if they'd only talked about it yesterday.

"I *think* so, Larky. Or maybe he's found me."

"Yup. Sometimes that's the way she works . . . " After a while Larky nods and smiles again like

63

a proud big brother, "Yore doing real good, Ong Be. Real good. You should ought-a be proud of yourself."

That was all he said, but it was enough to lift Beale's spirits. He was finally able to light up another smoke. As they continued on down the road he found himself wondering if Larky was some sort of *idiot savant*, an innocent saint, a clever fool who saw more clearly because he didn't have to reason every little thing through. There was no way Beale could think of to be sure, or even to explore the possibility any further than he had. It didn't matter anyway, he finally decided. Larky had an uncanny way of *knowing* how he felt, an almost spiritual *something*, and with his understanding, he could fix things. *His true calling was that of a mystic healer, not a preacher, though maybe they were two aspects of the same thing.*

Beale decided he'd probably never know any more than that about it. *Better to simply accept,* he thought to himself, *than try to dissect the reality. Get into it too deep, and maybe it just goes away.* He didn't want that. He needed Larky, and he probably needed the other Dimbos as well. What was it Charley had said about the four of them and their symbiotic relationship? Beale was the head, and the head represented intellect, reason, and analysis. Charley described himself as the feeling, the emotion, and the compassion and - of course - the hot sex drive. Mad Denny was their vital, devil-may-care energy, their *fuck-you* on the army and its narrow, closed-minded ways. *And Larky, poor unassuming Larky, was what? Their spirit? Their innocence? Their connection - like the*

64

hippies believed - to some higher cosmic plane? His, Beale's, own bridge to survival? Again, he feels too close to some ageless wisdom, like he is about to start cutting up real truths. *Leave it, Beale*, he tells himself, *Ahlou. . . Ahlou . . . Ahlou . . . leave it be, be, be, Ong Be.*

He butt-lights another Marlboro and starts to wonder what Tay Ninh is going to be like.

CHAPTER TEN

Going to Nam had been Beale's goal. He'd thrown away a scholarly career to see a war, as (he told himself) had his hero Ernest Hemingway. Although he might deny it, he couldn't help but be encouraged by the early 1960's notion that he was fighting Jack Kennedy's brushfire war to defeat communism and save the peoples of South East Asia from communist oppression. He had argued that way with Mavis before he signed up for his three year tour in the army. The only problem with his choice was that the real world was a lot more chaotic than he had imagined. The local people running the show – the South Vietnamese government, the Buddhists, the ARVN soldiers, even the people on the street – didn't seem to want or need to be rescued

In his desire to *see the war for himself*, Beale now found himself in an unexpected world of violence, personal greed, army politics and complex ancient foreign animosities. He didn't know it at the time, but he'd done one thing right, if only by accident; he'd signed up early, before the buildup of American troops, before the war turned massive and ugly. At this time, there were less than 20,000 American advisors in South Vietnam. The quaint objective, simply stated, was to keep the South Vietnamese soldiers from shooting their own feet off until we gave them enough weaponry and training to fend for themselves.

Anybody can see there is still a stubborn

66

civilian French presence, and the atmosphere is more Terry and the Pirates than G.I. Joe. Beale guesses this is why Ranley choses to billet his troopers for the night at Anna's Place on the highway outside of Tay Ninh proper. Nordoff declines with a volley of threats and expletives, choosing to stay at a shabby hotel in the center of town.

Anna's Place never appeared back in the States in any movie, or on the nightly network's war news, either. It is a border refuge, a centuries old roadside bar-restaurant, motel and road house featuring a gang of eager young waitresses who double as prostitutes, a thriving trade they can use to become wealthy and return to their native villages for a life of dignity and respect.

Ancient Asian Pear Trees hang over a swaybacked broken-tile roof shaded emerald green with clinging moss. The heavy wooden double doors in front are battered and worn. If they could talk, they would tell unbelievable stories of decades of river pirates and crazed Cao Dai religious sects, of Montagnard murderers, and lonely and frightened Frenchmen, of Mogok rubies and Japanese hoards of reddish-bronze gold bars, and of sweet, innocent love lost and found and lost and found again.

The doors are thrown wide to the warm evening rain that brings with it a flood of chatty ARVNs and an assortment of rough-looking border Mekong riverboat men wearing go-ahead slippers made of old truck tire rubber, and tattered gray shirts and ratty pants from which the original dye has long since worn away. There are haggard traveler-merchants, intent on selling watered-down antibiotics and their own snake oil inventions. Tattered refugees huddle in one corner of the room; three young boys try to hide deeper in the group as they take frightened glances at the ARVNs. Recognizable by the neater cut of their clothing, several Saigon Cowboys can be seen in another corner of the main room, hoping to avoid the draft by slipping over into Cambodia and on to the attractions of Thailand. The girl waitresses move through the crowd like last Friday's flowers, stopping to chug Vietnam whiskey like the tea it really was and to beg *you buy for me* just one more little drink.

Beale has set aside his ever-present ball-point pen and notepad and is enjoying a pleasant Ba Muoi Ba buzz. He sips his warm beer and stares happily at the unexpected diversity jostling each other in the crowded room. He is thinking he has found it again, his *real Vietnam*. Ranley and the other Dimbos are playing five card jacks-are-wild poker with some Vietnamese rangers, and the Americans seem to be winning more than they are losing.

A one-eyed Vietnamese comes over to Beale's table. He wears a tattered T-shirt that had once been tie-dyed, and \ a pair of bright blue bulky bib overalls that look almost brand new, and his missing eye is neatly sewed shut. "My name is Tan-oi," he says in broken English, adjusting his large red bandanna cap so it sweeps dramatically down on his forehead, not quite covering his right eye.

"Beale," Beale says, indicating with one hand that the man can sit at his table if he wants to.

"You Melicans not can drink good," Tan-oi says.

"And, like most Vietnamese, you are too impoverished to prove it," Beale replies. He has come to that stage of intoxication where gravity and reflection are required. He beckons to his bargirl, using the hand gesture scooping towards himself that he had learned at language school, and he speaks in Vietnamese, "Hoa, keep the Ba Muoi Bas flowing for Tan-oi and myself here…and a whiskey for you, I presume."

Tan-oi tips his beer bottle to his lips, hesitates, and then speaks in Vietnamese. "Hoa is a very lovely name," he says in a crisp Northern dialect.

"It is the generic name for flower," Beale tells him. "And you know as well as I that it is not her real name. In fact, it is the most common bargirl name in all of Vietnam."

Than-oi nods, "She seems attracted to you."

"Where did you get those pants?" Beale asks.

"From the local Christian charity. A Lutheran minister."

A wave of excitement runs through the large room and an excited cry, *Nguoi Moi!* goes up from the ARVNs.

"Montagnard," Beale says.

Tan-oi shrugs, agreeing, as a tall, dark-skinned man enters. The man is over six feet tall, towering above the rest of the Vietnamese in the room. His shiny, black hair is cut in a pageboy from which peeps one iridescent green feather. His features are harsh and angular, more like an American Indian's than those of a man from Asia. He is wearing a red-and-blue silk shirt open in front, a red-bark loincloth, and necklaces of alternating

69

gray-green jade and ancient yellowed bone beads. He carrys a wicker bird-cage in each hand.

"*Nguoi Moi*. Doesn't that mean *Monkey Man*?" Beale says.

"Sure," Than-oi grins. "They live in the mountain jungles like monkeys."

"What are they like?"

"You not let your daughter marry to one."

"No...I guess not."

The Montagnard stalks solemnly to the bar and sets his birdcages on the counter. A few of the ARVN soldiers gather around him, shouting friendly insults, shoving and waving fistfuls of piasters in the smoky air. The montagnard stands with quietly confident dignity, head and shoulders above the shouting crowd, arms holding the bird cages, and doing nothing else.

"Ahh, too bad," Tan-oi says, shaking his head in regret. "No cock fight tonight. No one will bid against the champion."

For the first time Beale takes an interest in the birds inside the cages. In one there is a big, ugly rooster, clearly the champion, while the other contains a somewhat smaller contender. The Ba Muoi Bas were having their effect on him and he wants to see a cock fight.

"Aren't there good odds on the little bird?" he asks.

"Well, yes...ten-to-one, maybe fifteen. But no fool want to take the risk."

Beale fumbles in his pockets for the fat wad of 200 piaster notes that is there. Mad Denny had exchanged $100 of his car money on the black market for over three times its official value. Beale stands to get a better look at what's going on. He pushes his way through the bodies crowded around the birds in their rough bent-bamboo cages while Than-oi follows close behind him, carrying their fresh bottles of Ba Muoi Ba.

"You know," Beale says, "I feel really lucky today." He divides his thick lump of folded-over paper money roughly in half. For a moment he seems lost in the multi-colored bills of red, purple, green and blue.

"Monopoly money," he says, almost to himself. Never stopping for a minute to think Than-oi might simply vanish with the piasters, he takes the beers and handed the money across to his new drinking partner.

"Here," he says, "You place the bet and we'll split the profits. Bet on the little bird."

Than-oi blinks his one eye; he seems startled that the American might so quickly trust a complete stranger, "But why you waste your money like so?"

"Lucky hunch," Beale said. "The little chicken is blind in one eye, like you! A lucky sign!"

Than-oi gives him a skeptical look, but he takes the bills and waves them over his head and pushes his way through the crowd to the bar. He dickers with several shady looking characters and two of Anna's burly bouncers and in a matter of a few minutes has Beale's thick wad of piaster notes in the bottom of one box behind the bar while a second box is piled high with opposing bets.

Beale joins Than-oi in front seats next to the makeshift ring that is being erected on the sawdust floor, a waist high barrier of sheeted tin reinforced with plywood, the scratched and battered metal

71

sheets printed on one side in labels identifying Green Giant peas, Princess sweet potatoes and La Contessa tomato paste.

Ranley and the Dimbos leave their poker game and push through to join them.

"What the hell did you do, Beale?" Charley asks.

Beale grins like he's pulled off the coup of the century. "We bet on the little chicken."

A momentary shadow of doubt crosses his face. "Right, Than-oi?" he asks.

"Vung, Monsieur Beale!"

Charley laughs, "You never gambled on anything before, did you. Stupido? And then a shadow crosses his own face, "Except on Nam…" He shakes the thought from his mind, "What the hell, *stugatz* – that money you got for your car is burning a hole in your pocket! Look, sucker, that chicken's blind as a bat!"

"Only in one eye, Charley."

Charley finds he is interested in spite of himself. "What kind of action did you get?"

"Ahh, I paid 4,000 p…" From the way he hesitates, it is clear he doesn't understand.

"No, Dummy-Dimbo – what ODDS did they give you?"

Beale confers with Than-oi for a moment.

"We got mostly 16 to one. Some at 18. A little bit at 20."

Charley shrugs, "Could be 100 to 1 on a blind bird. You're going down, Beale!"

Beale stubbornly shakes his head. He pulls out his second wad of money, setting two 500 p notes aside and then counting out the rest, which is in purple 200's.

72

"If I save this 1,000 for expenses, I could still bet you…2,000 p." He squints at Charley across the smoky ring, "At a hundred to one, you would owe me 200,000 p. That's roughly a thousand dollars."

"Get serious, Ong Be, nobody would do that."

"You chicken?" Beale makes a purple fan out of his 200 p notes and waves them in Charley's face.

"Screw you, I'll take your money, idiot! Twenty to one."

"If you lose, you owe me $200 *my kim,* that's cold hard American dollars."

"I got it right here, kraut-head," Charley says. He digs a small roll of money out of his sock top. The money, which is in five and ten dollar bills, looked soggy and worn, like it has been through a washing machine.

Beale insists Ranley hold their money, and Charley makes a big show of handing his American money to Ranley. Beale nods and hands his ten purple notes to the sergeant as well.

There isn't much ceremony to start the event. No one else wants to bet on the small blind challenger, so the two fighting roosters are dumped in the small ring and the fight is officially on. The montagnard is ready to shove them together with a long stick, but the champion doesn't need any prodding. The bigger rooster ru*ffl*es his ratty brown-and-green feathers and circles the smaller bird. He suddenly dashes forward, flapping his wings, pecking his horny beak and slashing with his left leg spur.

The smaller bird has retreated to one corner. He stands quietly, weaving on his legs. His neck is already spotted with his own blood, which is running down his breast and spotting the sawdust on the floor. His head swings back and forth as he tracks his strutting opponent with his good eye. That eye shines like a black bead in his face. Beale takes it as a good sign. *Lucky, lucky, lucky Beale!* But as he has bet alone against the odds and against the crowd, he is also alone in his belief that the smaller rooster has a chance. The crowd shouts, looking for easy money and an early kill.

Anna pushes her way through the crowd to stand next to Ranley, who puts his arm around her.

"Anna! My nug bets the farm on that little pecker chicken! What do you make of that?"

Anna smiles, "A *Trung Hoa* wager…"

Beale knows what that means. *A Chinese gamble. Long odds, big reward.*

Ranley gives her a second look, "But…"

"Shhhh…" Anna put her fingers to her red lips, "I have stack of piasters next to his big one."

"You what?" Ranley can't believe his ears.

Her eyes are wide and innocent, but her smile grows broader, "Twenty-to-one…who could resist?"

Charley shouts across the ring, "Hey, Ong Be! You better put a tourniquet around Little Blindy's neck before he bleeds to death!"

Beale butt-lights a new Marlboro from his old one and gives Charley a sour look. "It's not over yet, *paisano*."

"All over but the funeral…which will probably be conducted with chicken stew."

The champion rooster struts and stalks, walking back and forth in an aggressive half-circle. He dives forward without warning, and again the air is full of claws and beaks and pounding wings. Again the smaller challenger seems to do nothing but take the beating. He is now visibly weaker. He walks in a tottering circle in the center of the ring, and blood flows from his tail feathers in a small stream. The crowd laughs and cheers, urging their champion on for the kill.

The bigger rooster struts about, taking his time. When he is sure of his victim, he flaps his wings and rushes toward the smaller bird. The smaller bird flaps his own wings and rises in the air, actually climbing over the champion in what looks like a desperate last attempt to escape. He is trying to get out of the way...but one of his spurs finds the champion's neck, and blood spurts from a deep wound.

The larger bird renews his attack, coming on in a furious frontal assault, but Beale's little challenger retreats to his corner, dodging and running, darting and dipping as he does his best to weather the storm. And after thirty seconds, the champion begins to wilt. He staggers and finally topples over on the sawdust.

The rangers hiss and boo, calling insults in Vietnamese. "Phony! Fraud! The *Nguoi My* fixed it! What does a rich and ugly foreigner need with our money anyhow? Ugly American! *Nguoi My xau!*"

Anna's bartenders take stout wooden clubs from underneath the bar and bang on it until the crowd quiets down.

"Fair fight!" Anna booms in her hearty, loud voice. "The American wins! You foolish warriors should not bet so much of your monthly pay if you are not prepared to lose it!"

The grumbling continues as she brings Beale the box filled with his winnings. She signals her head barman with one hand in a crisp down stroke. The man strikes a loud gong hanging from a wooden ceiling beam. The ARVNs grumble, but they don't want the bar to close down for the night so they slowly drift back to their poker and their *Ba Muoi Bas*.

CHAPTER ELEVEN

Beale sits with the Dimbos, dividing his money with Tan-oi. The piles of wrinkled and multi-colored bills take up half the table, and threaten the poker game, now getting underway again.

Charley elbows a pile of the money aside, "God's sake, Beale, take your monopoly game somewhere else!"

"Don't be a sore loser, Charley."

"I am not a loser!"

Ranley nudges Beale from the other side of the table, "Oh, oh. Look sharp. Looks like we got trouble."

Two ARVN lieutenants and a captain stand before them. As the captain speaks, the Americans can see every Vietnamese wearing a uniform has turned to watch the action. "These men do not make so much money as you. We szink you owe us ze chance to get our money back."

Ranley leans back in his chair, "You were willing to take our man's bet when it looked like easy money . . . "

The captain's face flushes beet red, "You *owe* us zix one chance. It is ze custom in Tay Ninh."

Ranley gauges the mood of the crowd and shrugs, "Hey, we're your kind of people."

One of the lieutenants spits on the sawdust floor, narrowly missing Ranley's boot, "I serious, doubt that."

"What's your poison? Five Card Stud? Blackjack?"

The captain shakes his head, "No. Ze test of manhood. We bet your lucky Ong Be cannot beat our man to drink ze *Chet Dan*!" He pushes a four-inch high stack of piasters into the center of the table and indicates a pudgy corporal who is looking them over with a superior smile.

Beale looks uncomfortable. "Black Death? What's that?"

"Forget it." Ranley shakes his head. "It would only make you sick."

Anna, who has been listening from the bar, speaks sharply to the ARVN captain, speaking so fast that Beale can't understand. The man shouts back at her.

"What are they saying, Red Dog?"

"Anna says he should pick on somebody who knows more about Vietnamese customs. And the arrogant ARVN *Dai-uy* over there answered back he thinks you have a monkey-dick."

"A monkey-dick? Well, piss on him - let's do it!"

The Dimbos cheer him on, led by Mad Denny's call, "Fuuuuuck the AAAAAAARRRRVVVVIIIINNNNNS!"

The captain has some knowledge of English; he spins around and points his finger at Mad Denny, "*You* ze number 1 smart guy - okay, you take his place for ze *Chet Den*!"

Denny shrugs and raises his glass, "Why not? - But I pick you, pussy-lips. A personal dare, just me and you, *hai nguoi* against the *Chet Dan*, whatever the uck-fay it is."

The captain tries to back away from the challenge, "No, we already have pick our champion."

78

Mad Denny grins and folds his arms, "No guts, no glory. Go for the *hoan ho, Dai-uy*!"

The Dimbos start a chant, banging their fists in time on the table, "Hoan ho, Dai-uy; Hoan ho, Dai-uy; *Hoan ho, Dai-uy!*" Anna and the bargirls take it up, and soon the room is rocking with the jeering chant.

The captain has no choice; he reluctantly takes his place across a wooden table from Mad Denny. One of Anna's men brings a wooden holder from behind the bar with half-dozen large eggs in it.. The eggs are old, so old they have a grayish-black cast. The bartender places a large beer mug in front of each of them. Anna herself selects two eggs, holding them up to the light, and then cracking them into the glasses. Black fluid runs down the side of the glass and collects at the bottom. Something solid follows with a sick little plop and the putrid smell of sulfur hangs heavy in the air.

Mad Denny's eyes widen at the sight. "What is it?"

Anna pours a half a beer in on top, but the fetid mess in the glass stays solid black. She takes a pair of chopsticks and stirs each glass, but all that does is turn the entire liquid black. "Don't think about it."

"But what is it?"

"Old duck egg. Buddha say it is good for you; help you to father many male children." Anna gives him a hug and whispers in his ear, "Hold your breath. Drink it down fast, in one gulp.

The ARVN captain leans back in satisfaction, crossing his arms and grinning at Mad Denny. Ranley counts out piasters from Beale's winnings and pushes a second pile to the center of the table.

Anna sets a new beer next to the foul smelling mug and speaks with a sharp bark, like a mother demanding her kid finish his vegetables. "Quick now! Then wash it down with this!"

The glass goes to Mad Denny's lips and he swallows it all, even what remains of the vile little lump at the bottom. "Ahhh, Vietnam", he says with a burp. "How about seconds?"

The captain manages to get his down too, glaring across the table at Denny. He gets up and walks around while his men slap his back and shout, "Hoan HO

After a few moments, he returns to the table. There are shiny circles under his eyes, and he looks uneasy.

Mad Denny tries to put on a good show, "You look a little pasty, fella."

"I am fine," the captain says..

Mad Denny claps his hands, "*Chet Dan! Mot lan nua!*"

Anna inspects two new eggs and hands him one. Mad Denny cracks it in his glass himself, eyeing the captain, "My mother never was much of a cook," he says. "Her eggs tasted worst that this." He pours in half a beer and stirs the black mess, "That's why this is such an improvement!" He chugs the contents of the glass and quickly downs the chaser while the Dimbos cheer him on. He burps and manages a smile, "Ahh. *Et vous, Dai-uy?*"

The captain stops halfway through his drink, clearly in trouble.

Mad Denny grins, "Here's the old Glass-eye Trick; maybe it will help." He grabs at one eye, then closes the lid and shoves his hand in front of his mouth. He uses his tongue for a lump, rolling it around to look like he is eating his eyeball. It's a simple kid's trick, but the captain gets the idea. His cheeks go full and he bolts away from the table, losing it and vomiting before he is half way to the bathroom.

"Ucking-FAY ANTASTIC-FAY!", Mad Denny cheers, reaching for the piasters, "Another round for the Dimbos!"

The Dimbos divide their new stacks of play money and go back to poker and drinking more Ba Muoi Bas.. Another half hour passes before Ranley calls out, "Arvin Alert! Definite sour feeling on the horizon."

Mad Denny looks up, "Ahh, *Dai-uy. Vous avez retournez.*"

Beale grins, "*Thua ong manh gioi, khong?*", the Vietnamese translating literally, *Do you have your strength, good sir?*

The ARVN captain's eyes glitter and his lip curl. "*Vung. Toi manh lam.* This time, we go for real...."

"What is it?", Ranley says. Larky watches him cross his arms, his one hand over his second hide-out gun.

"You will see!" The captain claps his hands, like he is calling for a servant, "*Nguoi Moi! NGUOI MOI!*"

The tall montagnard comes to their table. After a brief, whispered conversation, he disappears out the side door, only to return with a second man. This one is wearing a multi-colored woolen poncho, and a wide-brimmed, bright green cap with a sagging brim and red-and-yellow bird feathers stuck around the rim. Apparently he has been waiting outside in the rain, for the water is dripping from his rough clothing. In appearance he seems a strangely mournful figure, for all his wildly colorful garb, but the oddest thing about him is the flock of little birds that sit all over his shoulders and the front of his poncho, clinging to the woolen cloth with their tiny claws. They are gray, finch-like birds with oversized red beaks and puffy white jowls. They seem at ease and make no attempt to move about or fly away, even though there is nothing to prevent them from doing so.

The Dimbos stared. "Christ," Beale whispers under his breath. "A new act in the circus."

"The Circus of Life, Ong Be," Charley says. "You getting all this down, scribe?"

The captain produces another pile of piasters, this one as damp as the dollars Charley had gotten out of his sock. He puts he money in the center of the table and plucks one of the birds from the montagnard's shoulder. He sets the bird on Beale's shoulder, then on Larky's head, then on his own arm. "Such gentle creatures! So trusting! See?"

He holds it up for all to see. Then, in one snake-like motion, his hand moves up and his head jerks forward and he bites off the little bird's head, which he spits out on the table in front of them. He holds the shuddering little corpse high, crushing it with his hand and drinking the blood that runs out from the severed neck. A dribble runs down his chin, and the Dimbos see blood on his yellow teeth as he grins at them.

"*Ngon lam!*", Mad Denny mutters dryly. "Very tasty."

One by one, the other Dimbos back away from

82

it.

The captain laughs, "You must put up a champion or give our money back!"

"Or get the shit beat out of us," Beale mutters, "Shall we give them the money, Red Dog?"

Ranley leans back, undecided, "Tough one to call, Mister Beale. In a free-for-all, the buzzards get the pickings."

Tan-oi put his hand on Ranley's arm. His good eye flicked from the birds to Beale, "The finches have sharp beaks. In the moment they feel threatened, they go for your tongue. The man who quits has to from bleeding."

"Not worth it," Ranley agrees.

Tan-oi smiles, "I will do it." The little man hitches Larky's belt around his shoulder. "It will add to the story I will tell my sons."

"But if they can bite your tongue..."

"I am the champion in - in my home town."

Ranley takes him slightly aside, speaking softly so only the two of them can speak without being over heard, "The discipline of a *Bac Viet* against a corrupt ARVN officer."

"Why do you call me *Bac Viet*?"

"You talk like a Northerner trying to talk like a Southerner."

"*THEY* accept me." Tan-oi indicates the ARVN soldiers with a little hand gesture, twisting his wrist as if the group wasn't worth much more than that. He shrugs, and gives Ranley an amused grin, "And I *could* have come down in '54...."

"No. A man like you would not waste his time in Tay Ninh. He would have found his way to Saigon. But no matter, Than-Oi. This is Chez Anna, and you are the champion for the hated *De*

83

Quoc Xam Luoc My, the American Invader-Gangsters."

The little man nods, "It is a strange world."

The contest begins with Than-Oi and the captain each dispatching a bird and tossing the crushed husk over his shoulder. The Captain is drinking *Ba Muoi Ba*, but Than-Oi washes his birds down with Budweiser, which he calls in French with a slight German accent, "*La Biere Roi des Americaines.*"

Beale takes his own beer and cigarettes to another table. Hoa trails after him, and asks an old *ba*, who seemed to never tire,to bring them two bowls of fried rice laced with crabmeat from the kitchen.

After a while, Charley joins them, shaking his head in disgust. "Whew, man - I can't watch that." The two girls he'd been talking to all afternoon both join him at the table

"It's getting late, Charley."

"We'll spend the night, my dear Ong Be. What's wrong? You getting a sudden virtue attack?"

"The last time I got involved in one of these spur-of-the-moment things, the girl practically ate me alive."

"What's so bad about that?"

"A spooky, mean black lady. Try it some time. Take a walk on the voodoo side."

"No kidding?"

Beale shrugs, "I just don't want things to get out of hand."

"Hey - you're the scribe. Just write your way out of the story."

"Very funny."

84

his spine. "Buddha only know how high I climb."

"The dragon rolls the dice."

"Yes."

They stand on the floor until a new record falls into place, the soft syrupy harmony of a slow waltz floods him with undergrad memories of black bow ties and cummerbunds and pale blond girls in stiff, swirling skirts

Going to spend an evening / in the salt-sea air

Quaint little villages / here and there

You're sure to fall in love

with old Cape Cod....

He holds the pretty Tay Ninh prostitute, swaying gently in the smoke-filled room, and it is odd trying to remember other girls halfway around the world, and exactly what any of them looked like or what they had said to each other.

She kisses him on the ear; "You come see me *tanh pho* Saigon?"

"I can't unless I know your real name."

For a moment she stiffens in his arms. She stares deep into his eyes. "My name Night Lark."

"And do you have a lovely voice, Night Lark?"

Again she hesitates, just for the briefest of moments, " . . .. Yes . . . promise you come see me?"

"Sure I will." He tosses his promise off without a second thought. After all, it is impossible they will ever see each other in Saigon, simply because she will never get there. Although well paid, Anna's bargirls are little more than indentured servants. Hoa probably started ten years ago as a peanut girl of six or seven, and

87

chances were she still owes Anna another ten years. She might get to Saigon sometime in the future - as a middle-aged, wealthy and respectable *ba,* bringing her own young brood to marvel at the 9 story tall Caravelle hotel, the bustling, packed streets and the eager peddlers hustling on the busy streets of the capital.

Than-oi and the *Dai-uy* were allowed a short intermission when they ran out of birds. The two original montagnards left and returned with a third, an emaciated old man in a battered poncho who was weighted down with a new batch of finches, but the contest ended three birds later when the *Dai-uy* took an unlucky bite that left his maimed tongue spouting blood in a thick, gouty flow. He insisted on dispatching the bird, but it was plain he wouldn't be able to continue.

He lay down on the table with his head sideways so he wouldn't choke on his own blood, while one of the older bargirls dipped a needle and thread in a tumbler of whiskey. He gulped half the whiskey down, and stuck out the bloody mess that had been his tongue and the girl calmly stitched him up with the coarse, black thread.

The Arvins mill around in a surly bunch, but Anna's barkeeps catches their attention by rapping their sticks on the bar. Ranley offers 50 P each to tide them over until the next payday, and they agree to settle when they see Anna come up with her short barreled scattergun.

After the Arvins leave, the crowd thins out quickly, and the Dimbos find themselves counting their stacks of piasters, surrounded by the chattering girls. Larky sits in one corner with Tan-oi, teaching him his favorite song. Tan-oi sings as best he can

> Za ya-lo ro-za Tec-Xa
> She za o-ly gir' pho me

Ranley and Anna, who have formed a giggling twosome over a pitcher of hot wine, take their stacks of piasters and leave for the back rooms. Mad Denny looks after them, "He's a great guy, but I don't know about his taste in girls."

Hoa glances up from her position, resting in Beale's arms, "You don't know so much, *Dinky Dao* Denny. Anna is plenty good famous love doctor. She best lover in all Vietnam."

"Whaat?"

"You believe it, G.I. Rich men come to her from Bangkok, from India, from Phnom-Penh, from *Bac Viet*!"

Denny looks down at his own girl, "But she's so.... fat!"

"That only make her more great in her powers." Mad Denny's girl grins mischievously, "And she taught me all what I know."

"Yeah? How much is that?"

"More than too much for you, Crazy G.I." She pulls Denny to his feet and they wander off together. Larky and Tan-oi pick up their piasters and two girls and dance for a while to an old French waltz before they also disappear.

That leaves Beale and his huge pile of piasters and Hoa, and Charley and his two girls. The barmen start stacking the chairs on top of the tables. Soon there will be no place left to sit.

Beale is past nostalgia, nonsense and numbness; he's drunk so much that the room keeps spinning off to his left. He concentrates, gets a lock on it, and it stops spinning for a moment. But the moment he thinks he has it, his world begins a drift to the left again.

"Come on, Ong Be." Charley staggers to his feet, none too steady himself, "I got a double, so you can witness my incredible performance with the other sex. Life *is* a Circus, you know." He takes Beale's arm, "Beale?"

But Beale is out like a light, pockets stuffed with money and head down on the table. Charley and Hoa take him by his arms and lead him, walking on legs as responsive as rubber stilts, to their room.

"Tell her, Charley", Beale slurs as they half-drag him along. "I'm saving myself."

"Sure, old buddy! By the way, your Zip being a bit more precise than mine, how do you say 'soaring on joyous clouds of passion?'"

"Come on, Charley, I'm serious...." But serious or not, eternal vows of celibacy are unnecessary and promises of greatness are impossible to fulfill; for on reaching the bed, Beale collapses sideways across it and lies there motionless, out like a light.

"" Magnolia sits on his bunk, thinking matters over, "Hoa . . . I couldn't help overhearing you on the dance floor, saying how nice it would be to meet Ong Beale in Saigon."

Half-joking, she waves a scolding finger in his face, "Old Vietnamese saying, Ong Cha-Le - 'Careful, you'll catch your nose in your ear'."

"Yeah, well, I'll watch out for that. But look, what I was thinking is, Beale has so much money in all his pockets he doesn't even know how much,

90

and he really likes you and he's so lonely down in Saigon, I don't see how he could possibly mind if you took enough to buy yourself back from Anna . . . "

She shakes her head and makes a scolding sound, "Ong Cha-Ly, that would be stealing!"

"Okay, but he told me just the other day he wished he had a nice girl he could teach English to, you know, like Professor Higgins in MY FAIR LADY?"

"Lights out for you, Cha-Ly!" Hoa blows out the candles in the room as the two other girls grab Charley from behind and begin to undress him. She waits in the darkness until the threesome's wild laughter becomes somewhat more subdued.

A thin line of light finds its way under the door from the ornamental electric light in the hall, and after a time she can make out the outline of Beale's body. She sits on the edge of the bed, taking off his clothes and carefully folding them on a chair, hesitating as she sees the piasters bulging from every pocket. She sighs and turns back to Beale.

Hoa trails her fingers in the hairs on his chest, making tiny circles that slowly move toward his nipples, then away again, then circling the nipples again. It is too dark to know for sure, but she imagines those hairs are golden brown, like the light hair on his eyebrows, and his nipples would be pink, not brown like her own. Finally she brushes the tips themselves, and is rewarded to feel him stir and give out a little moan.

She stands and takes off her clothing. Standing naked in the darkened room, she caresses her own pert breasts in the same way as she had done his, feeling her own nipples come hard.

"It not stealing to trade love for money," she whispers to herself.

Hoa sees Charley and his two girls are off in their own world. She lies down next to Beale, again running her fingers lightly over his chest, his belly, and his thighs. She whispers in his ear, blowing softly as she had done on the dance floor, "Dance with me, my dear Ong Be. Just a little dance with me...."

He is on the threshold between sleep and waking. She thinks he is a strange man – distant and scholarly, and yet attractive. She knows that if he wakes completely he will probably get sick and everything will be ruined. "The dragon rolls the dice....", she whispers to herself. "We are just the players."

She lifts herself to her knees over him, moving carefully and gently down on him until his full length is hard inside her. She bends down and forward to let her hair brush his face, and kisses him lightly on the lips. She finds it satisfying to make love to him like this. She has rarely been in control before, the rough-and-ready up-river men more often throwing themselves on her like drunken pigs.

She tells herself she is the mistress, his beautiful but mysterious stranger. She fantasizes they are living in one of the pulp-romance novels the bargirls love to pass around until they are threadbare and come apart at the seams. He has met her in a Saigon Cafe called Le Swan in the middle of his most dangerous mission; he is some sort of top-level diplomat for the Americans and she is the husky-voiced oriental singer who alone holds the key to his happiness. Reality and fantasy merge, and it is a time she wants to last forever. She tries to be restrained and in control as Anna has insisted all the great courtesans of the world throughout history had been, but she finally cannot fight back the trembling passion that surges up inside her, and she begins to come in great, swelling waves. She holds herself on the edge and comes over and over. Still, he stays hard inside her and she moves a little more freely on him until he trembles and shudders and they finally climax together.

Beale is in his own dream world. He has taken Mavis out to Leo Carillo Beach, twenty miles north of Malibu, a less frequented series of rocky coves with little sandy pockets above the surf line. In his dream it is early January, a raw, blustery day with a distant, cold sun. The place is deserted and they find a sandy, sheltered place away from the water. It is suddenly pitch-black night and they are making love when he realizes the woman he was with isn't Mavis after all. She has changed to someone else, to some *thing* huge and far more dangerous than a black mistress, and at the same time more alluring and attractive. In his dream Mavis fire-blossoms into a great, shining dragon. The dragon-lady devours him, tearing his back with her claws, and he doesn't mind, he is on fire, driving into her, driving into the center of a dark unknown essence that he wants to make his own more than he'd ever wanted anything else in the world. His love finally bursts in a blue-white shower of phosphorescent shrapnel, and he feels a temporary peace flood through him like a benedictal truce.

After, he curls up in a ball like a little boy, and she holds him as the last incredible tremors of their lovemaking still vibrate inside her.

"Your little Night Lark will never fly away and leave you, my dear Ong Be," she whispers. "*Never!*"

Sometime later, when all is still in the room, she rises and briefly moves over to the table where she'd left Beale's clothing. She sings softly to herself as she goes through one or two of his pockets. And then she gathers her shawl around her and, singing an old central highlands ballad about love and money, leaves the room.

In his own bed not five feet away, Charley hugs his two sleeping mates and smiles at no one in particular. Charley is sure Ong Be hasn't been right in his head since he got to Vietnam; Ranley had mentioned something about a bad incident when Beale's plane first landed at Tan Son Nhut. More than a few times, Charley has winced at the involuntary tick in Beale's left eye and turned his head away when the *stugatz* fumbled with his matches and his Marlboros. *The girl was a young innocent, but there was nothing wrong with that. Chances were, Ong Be would be less up tight if he got a steady lay - and that would be good for all the Dimbos! It was worth the try. After all, a man in a war zone ought to be steady enough to light his own smokes, and he was sure good old Ong Be would do the same for him if the situation were reversed.*

That starts Charley thinking about the fat, stubby little whammy of Laotian Gold he'd picked up earlier that night. He still is wearing his shirt after a fashion, open in front and crumpled up

94

around his neck, in fact it was the only thing he still was wearing, the rest of his clothing strewn around the room where his playful friends had tossed it. He manages to dig the toke out of his pocket and get it lit without waking the girls, a major feat in itself. And, in spite of the logy, downer effect of the beers, in ten minutes and three long drags he leaves the girls, Beale, the room, Tay Ninh, South Vietnam and all the wretched rest of Southeast Asia far behind as he goes over the top - up, up and *Away!* into the outer stratospheres of his mind.

CHAPTER TWELVE

Ba Muoi Ba is not a bad beer; there are old South East Asia hands who swear by it and claim to miss the somewhat medicinal formaldehyde tang and the buzzing after-burn. Some will only drink it warm, while others have become accustomed to the Saigon street-cafe practice of letting it cool with a big chunk of ice floating in the glass. But a *Ba Muoi Ba* hangover ranks with the best of them - a Tijuana Sunrise, a Bronx muscatel resurrection, or even the glum Inca morning after a long night of Pisco Sours. All of which meant Beale became aware of the dull, thudding ache behind his eyes long before he dared wink one of them open. And when he did, there was his friend Charley in the other bed, lying naked, hands behind his back, being ridden by one of his girls.

"Beale! Get my watch off the floor somewhere. I'm going for a record here."

"That's really gross, Charley . . ." Beale's voice is one long groan.

"No, no, Ong Be! It's life and nature, *and* a possible personal best! We were up to 25 minutes, about the Italian average, when I dropped my watch, and I naturally can't get it -!"

Beale swings his legs over the side of his bed. He puts his head between his hands.

"How can you be so damn *cheerful?*"

"Me? You're the one should be smiling. Celibacy is a heavy cross to bear. Maybe now you'll be more of a happy camper."

It is about then that Beale discovers Hoa on the bed behind him, stretching her arms in a graceful yawn that makes her bare breasts look even more pert and lovely. She leans forward to kiss him gently on the cheek, and then ruffles his hair.

"See you in Saigon, Ong Be. For now, I get you hot *pho thom*." She wraps herself in a light silk robe and hurries away.

"Now *that's* a contented woman!" Charley says. "Off to rustle up a little hot soup for her man's breakfast!"

"But I didn't - I don't remember...."

"You were *fabulous*, Be. We all saw it."

"You *saw* me?"

"Played her like a maestro attacking his grand piano."

"I feel like warmed-over *Chet Dan*." Beale rubs a hand over his bleary vision. He wanders out the door, dragging his pants in one hand, looking for the bathroom and not caring that he is leaving a trail of piasters behind him. There is nothing he can do about Hoa or Night Lark or whatever her name is anyway. He will just have to sort it all out later.

Outside Chez Anna the morning is bright and glittery, with the sunlight glaring off the previous night's raindrops dripping from the palm trees into the puddles in the rutted parking lot. Ranley is up bright and early, dickering with Anna for an assortment of Budweiser, Miller High Life, and Schlitz, twelve bottles in all, which she packs in ice in a yellow plastic milk-carton.

By the time the Dimbos, dressed in their rumpled civvies, drive their jeeps back to the

114th, Captain Nordoff and Toady are loading their gear.

Sergeant? This weather's not going to hold forever, you know."

Ranley nods, squinting at the sky. "Should rain about noon, sir."

"Well, we'd better be shoving off then."

"You are aware we've got to make one stop, sir..."

"No, *I didn't know that!*"

"Security check. Perhaps you should go on ahead, sir."

"I'm not traveling out-of-convoy!"

"Then we'll be ready in 15, sir. Just have to change to fatigues."

They drive along the bumpy road to the fortified hamlet at Long Chu. Parking their jeeps in the muddy compound, they turn down an invitation from the strange little commander to inspect his new latrine facilities and Ranley leads them in a silent line through the path in the rain forest toward the hamlet of Thong Nhet. Beams of sunlight fall through the high umbrella of trees overhead. Monkeys chatter and small parrots angle swift flights through the dappled light. The captain and Toady unhappily bring up the rear, swinging their M-14's to cover every rustling noise in the path-side brush, Nordoff constantly muttering that this trip had better be of the utmost importance. Ranley knows the officer wouldn't stop them; since Beale uncovered the Tay Ninh Liberation Front papers, they would be Puzzle Palace heroes, at least for a couple of weeks, and that would mean they could do no wrong.

None of the Dimbos brings along any gear

except for their rifles, and they practically skip along, eager to once again slip into the timeless way of life of Thong Nhet. Mad Denny and Larky switch off carrying the yellow plastic container with the beer in it. As they go, Larky narrates to an unbelieving Denny the lurid details of his hot midnight romance in the village, and Beale's thundering headache begins to subside as he sweats out his hangover.

They cross the laughing brook and break out into the clearing. But the timeless village of Thong Nhet is no longer there.

Ranley stands like a tragic statue, staring at the blackened poles and charred ruins.

"Looks like napalm," Nordoff says with a professional air.

"Yep. Napalm", Toady echoes.

Ranley says nothing and the captain impatiently clears his throat, "Probably an accident. You know, they've got to dump it somewhere."

Ranley turns slowly around in a complete circle, as if he is in a daze. "Torched," he says, "somebody torched this place."

"It could have been the VC just as soon as us!"

"Yes, it could have. Napalm or a few cans of gasoline. Makes no difference, does it. . . " Ranley speaks in a crazed, booming voice, addressing the blackened and deserted village, "Yes, my people, we've saved you in the name of freedom and democracy - or liberation of the masses, we're not sure which! Unfortunately, good sirs, ladies, and little children, we've had to utterly and completely destroy you to do it!"

No one answers. The monkeys stop chattering

99

in the trees. There is a long silence and they hear the wind through the palm trees and somewhere a slow drip of water.

Nordoff continues to look around, "Ahh, Sergeant - Ahh, *Sergeant Red Dog*, if there's no other reason to be here than to look at a burnt-out bunch of shacks, we really should be going..."

Ranley looks past him as if he isn't really there, talking to the Dimbos, "Fellows, believe me. There once was a time when some of us had hopes and dreams and ideals. Not all of us. I mean, we had dick-heads and ignoramuses, just like now. But some of us *really thought we could make a difference....*"

The captain shifts impatiently on his feet, his eyes darting to the nearby jungle and back again, "I don't know what you're talking about, Sergeant - but you can't run a war that way."

"That's what we're doing, isn't it... We're taking charge, making it *our* war, going to do it the All-American Way...."

"You think those slope-head dinks back there at that Long Chu pigsty could do it without us?"

"We'll never know."

"Well, then?"

"That makes us lingies an outdated species, Captain. You don't need to talk to them anymore." He turns to Beale, "Dinosaurs, that's us."

Beale's mind is in a whirl. Vietnam has him going like a yo-yo - from killing madness to wonder and ecstasy, and back again. It is inconceivable that the centuries-old hamlet can have been wasted overnight. This new destruction, superimposed over the violence since his arrival in country, takes away his newfound confidence. He doesn't feel much like Lucky Beale any more. And the road he'd chosen yaws before him open-ended, a long, dark tunnel that goes down and down into blackness without end.

"*Dinosaurus Lingus*", he agrees without really thinking about it, "Sub-species Dimbo."

Nordoff throws his helmet on the ground, "Christ's sake - what are you men talking about? Don't go dink on me now!" Seeing no one answers, he retrieves his helmet and puts it back on his head.

Toady tries to get things moving, "Ahh, fellows, I think what the Captain is trying to say makes sense that this *obviously* isn't a secure area, and we really *have* to be going."

"Go on ahead. We'll be along." Ranley takes one end of the bright yellow carton and heads for the ruins of the central meeting hall. Beale runs up behind him and grabs the other end. The Dimbos trail after, followed after a moment of hesitation by Toady and the Captain.

They set the carton on the low platform where the village elders had stood, and where they had enjoyed their fine evening with the peasants of Thong Nhet. Ranley numbly takes out a beer and stares at the familiar red-and-white-and-black label. He flips off the cap with his Swiss army knife, and tips the bottle. The beer forms a foamy pool on the damp ground.

"Christ! That's a *Bud*!", Toady yelps.

Ranley's looks at him, and his eyes are hard and glittery. He doesn't say a word. Toady backs away, looking to his C.O. for support. The Captain shrugs, saying nothing. Toady walks away, flinging his hands in the air, "Will

101

somebody *please* telleth me what in God's Name is going on?"

Beale selects a brown bottle of Schlitz, simply cracking the head on a square limestone block and pouring the golden liquid on the ground. "For the spirits", he says, looking at Charley.

Charley hesitates, then takes a beer bottle and cracks the neck off on the whitish rock. He puts his arm around Beale's shoulder and pours the beer to the ground. "For the spirits."

Larky takes a bottle and emptys it, "May the Lord, thy God, the Eternal Spirit keep thee."

Mad Denny joins in, and they quietly pour all the beer until it is just a foamy puddle on the ground.

They walk away from Thong Nhet without looking back, feeling the tree-line is full of eyes watching all of them. They hustle along, worried they might have played out their welcome. Reaching the grubby little strategic hamlet at Long Chu is a relief, and they quickly climb into their jeeps and motor away in single file, heading east along the lonely stretches of blacktop.

None of them feels like talking. The rain starts at noon and they drive back to Tan Son Nhut in silence, with the mechanical *flup* of the windshield wipers and the whine of the jeep engines loud in their ears.

CHAPTER THIRTEEN

The water-soaked logbook Beale had tripped over in the slimy underground tunnels of Tay Ninh contained three handwritten pages of cryptographic codes, together with instructions for weekly changeovers to confound the listening *nguoi My*. Of these, one single code, tagged simply *Bac* or 'north', was of the greatest significance, causing a subtle shift in listening throughout Southeast Asia, and ending in intercepts of transmissions about troop and supply movements from the north that in turn became an angry *point-in-fact* in stiff diplomatic correspondence between the United States, the Soviet Union, and Red China.

The lesser notes Beale and Ranley uncovered, plus personal entries footnoting the logbook, indicated that the damp and deserted hole in the ground had been the provincial headquarters for the Tay Ninh Liberation Front. A few letters were stuck in the tattered and stained book. These were from North Vietnam; the man who had carried them was a low-ranking officer in the regular army of the Democratic Republic of Vietnam. This evidence as well, though circumstantial, pointed toward direct intervention in the affairs of the South, at a time when worldwide communist propaganda had been glorifying the war as a popular people's uprising.

Of course the war goes on. This is just a small battle won on the all-important propaganda front, a small victory in the war of words. More than change anything in South Vietnam, it shapes the nature of the international squabble for a while. The North Vietnamese and the communists in general know that eventually they are going to have to fall back to another line of reasoning; if, indeed, the uprising in the South were simply the *glorious awaking of the masses*, it would surely have been already mangled and crushed by the South Vietnamese military might and the massive help pouring in from the Americans. And the counter-effort was going to involve a quiet but massive infiltration of supplies and North Vietnamese regulars.

Beale and Ranley had inadvertently laid bare the most brazen of lies, perhaps from the communist point of view a year or two prematurely. Faced with proof positive, the Russians and the Red Chinese will find it more and more difficult to defend arguments that the struggle in South Vietnam came simply from within, and the endless debates in the United Nations and the international community will have to shift to the more shop-worn ideologies of communism versus capitalism, where the communists will argue to justify their involvement in terms of the old Marxist-Leninist cry for world liberation.

The press was not informed directly or indirectly of any of this by the Puzzle Palace; to do so would have raised the Six Pesky Questions: *Who, How, What, When, Where and Why*, bothersome flies the agency was not particularly prepared to swat. A major coup had been scored, and the Fifth Column would just have to pick up on it from the shift in the winds.

As for the more mundane aspects of the success, Harris was granted the raise and the promotion he'd been after for some time, and a few others in the section got commendations. Ranley was talked about as the Player of the Week, an unofficial title attached to nothing but scuttlebutt.

Jack Beale knew little, if anything of this. Real good news rarely drifts down to the enlisted in the army, particularly not if they've got a clearance, because the general rule for spies and spying -- even electronic spying -- is that the fellows on the bottom should know as little as possible, actually should know nothing at all if that was possible and they still could function. Beale's Spec 5 promotion came through, and the rainy season deepened. He was officially put in charge of the lingie section at the White Shack, reporting to Ranley, the same job that he'd been handling all along. There was a short but important directive that from now on it would be less important *to prove* the North-South link while still of *vital importance* to intercept, decode and translate all covert messages; and look for any and all evidence that North Vietnamese might be deciding to move swiftly.

Nelson sent Beale a short note on an otherwise blank sheet of paper, saying he'd always expected great things, and was glad to see his instincts rewarded. Dirty Old Mary mailed him a crumpled, empty pack of Lucky Strikes, with the short note:

Wanted to send you these, but smoked them first. – M.

The hubbub, if it could be called that, among

this highly select little group quickly died down, and Beale found himself doing exactly what he'd been doing all along, decoding and translating whatever messages came his way. And it being the deepening of *The Season of the Wet*, no matter what the urgency from the Puzzle Palace, fewer and fewer intercepts crossed his desk.

The other Dimbos are taken off-guard by his promotion, and it takes a while before they learn to live with it. After all, until this happened they'd always been promoted together. For a few days they talk of little else as they walk their daily half-mile along the runway through the rain to the White Shack, cursing their moldy boots and their luck, which has tossed them in the same pot of *pho ga* with Beale.

"Beale, a Spec. 5! We've got a case here of the blind leading the blind", Mad Denny grumbles.

"Could be worse", Charley shrugs.

"Uck-fay! He never had an original idea in his life! Do-it-by-the-book-Beale."

As usual, it is Charley who sees the light first, "Hey, come on, get the big picture here, fellow. With one of our own running things, we can sluff off a little more, get him between us and the army bullshit."

"I guess."

"I *know*. Beale will never turn a Dimbo in. And he'll do all the work for the section. What more could you ask?"

Mad Denny and Larky both chuckle their approval. Larky nods along with the gang but he doesn't say anything. He is secretly pleased for Beale.

The days drag by as the *Season of the Wet*

thickens in beat and intensity, ever deeper and deeper shades of gray. The morning sunshine becomes rare; now the heavy, warm rains pour down all day, only to stop sometime after midnight and begin again before sunrise. On weekdays the Hueys still lift from their pads next to the 3RD, but now they have to wait for the dawn light and by that time the morning shift is already up so their pulsing racket only annoys the night shift who swatted their netting and turn in their bunks, pulling damp pillows over their heads as they drift back into their fragmented, testosterone-laden dreams of personal heroics in moments of bed and battle.

With electronic intercept down to almost zero, Beale lives up to Charley's prediction; he has his department caught up two days after they return from Tay Ninh. The Dimbos work from four in the afternoon to about seven in the evening. The rest of the time they read or write letters, or while away the hours at the favorite army card game of pinochle. They blame Beale for getting them stuck in an eternal rainstorm and fantasize what the girls of Saigon will be like -- if they ever get out there to see for themselves.

Beale spends much of his off-duty time in the pseudo-Bavarian decor of the lifer's section at the EMC, a whiskey on the rocks in one hand and a Marlboro dangling from the other, listening to the sergeants and warrant officers swap old adventures. General Westmoreland with his fierce eagle eyebrows has replaced General Harkins as the commander of MACV, and now General Maxwell D. Taylor has been named ambassador. Now the escalation has begun in earnest, and there are over 30,000 troopers in-country and nobody's pretending they are *advisors*. The optimistic common opinion is that mop-up time is at hand.

Still, some things remain the same. "What War?" an E-6 hard-striper named Taters Johnson grouses, "I fill out a fricking form before they let me load a clip in my carbine!"

A voice from the bar is heard, "Westy - *and* Taylor, in the same dinky, one-by-six country. There isn't room for those two brass-balled egos *and* the Viet Cong, is there?" Lieutenant Boudreaux and his fellow pilot Lieutenant Jackson, regular guests in the enlisted men's club as the 3rd didn't have enough officers to have their own place, pick up their glasses and join the group near Beale. Boo-boo has, as usual, brings an elegant bottle of *Chateau de Pape Neuf* along with him. The bottle is always just half-empty, but he's been spotted refilling it from a big jug of Gallo burgundy. Now he gazes into the ruby red depths of his glass, "Wyatt Earp and Bat Masterson both show up for the County Frog Hop!"

"Whatever that means....", Taters mutters, with that instinctive reaction non-commissioned lifers have for young officers.

"It means, my good fellow," Boudreaux says as he twists the neat end of his little waxed moustache, "that nitro and glycerin abound, and all you need is a little shake-shake-shake...."

"And what's *that* supposed to mean? Christ, can't you just talk *Uh-MURican*?!"

Ranley looks around with a casual glance, clearing the room to make sure none of the native help was around, "Anybody looked at the operations map lately? Seventh Fleet's working intercept way-the-fuck up in the Gulf of Tonkin."

Jackson takes a sniff of his fellow-pilot's wine glass and wrinkles his nose at the bouquet, "Got our nose up the *Bac Viet's derriere* again."

"Pretty far up. Christ, the Turner Joy practically steamed into Haiphong a couple of times!"

Beale had heard the ugly and persistent rumor when he was stationed back at Meade that the army needed an incident to *legitimatize* the fighting. "Think we're trying to instigate?"

Ranley shrugs, "How would you feel if you saw a Russian destroyer a hundred yards inside the Golden Gate?"

Boo-Boo thinks it over and then shakes his head, "Naaa, that's too dumb, even for the Pentagon. The people would never swallow it!"

"If we were going to try to pull off a poor man's Pearl Harbor, we'd be smarter to get them to attack us down here...."

Taters snorts in his beer glass, "Sure, Uncle Sam's going to frame Uncle Ho by bombing Saigon! This here is the U.S. of Uh-MURica you're talking about, chum! We're the *good* guys, remember?"

"I keep trying to....", Boudreaux says with a sad look on his face. "I keep trying to...."

"Me too", Ranley says. Beale catches his eye, and knows he is thinking about the shattered bamboo bones of Thong Nhet hamlet, the ashes cooled now, the rain drumming in where once there had been warmth and food and a place out of the wet.

The conversation shifts; somebody has gotten a San Francisco Chronicle in the mail and they pass it around, amazed at the incredible close-up photos Ranger 7 was sending back from the moon.

Beale loses interest and drifts along to his barracks, hoping Larky has stood mail call, but there are no letters waiting for him on the taut wool blanket of his bed. He sits on his footlocker and gets out of his damp fatigues and boots. He shoves his toes into the webs of a pair of rubber go-ahead slippers and trots naked through the rain to the centrally located washrooms, with his towel and personals kit held over his head. After a chill shower, he brushes his teeth in the brackish, chlorine-tasting water, and then dashes back to his barracks.

He sits on the edge of his bunk under the fan, hoping it will dry the perpetual damp that has settled into his skin. Finally he gives up and applies talcum powder over his entire body.

The tip of his Marlboro is a small, red bead in the dark as he lies awake in bed, stretched out naked under his double-fold mosquito net, listening to the frustrated buzzing of the mosquitoes and the weird chittering of the moist-skinned lizards that cling to the walls and skitter about. *When was he going to get down to some serious writing?* Ever since he could remember, he'd scribbled his impressions of everything he'd seen or felt or done, but now when he is surrounded on all sides by the incredible and the outrageous, he can't seem to write anything longer than a few broken lines.

Sleep won't come and he lies awake until sometime after 2 A.M. The fans hum overhead, pulling the reluctant air through the barracks full of sleeping men, and the last of the night's rain drips from the eaves outside. The white radiance from a distant, falling flare sends bars of slanted light through the open-air slats of the walls in a pattern across his bunk.

There is a firefight somewhere to the southwest. He listens as Ranley has taught him, and is able to pick out the sharp voices of the M-1's, the lighter ping of carbines, the angry-dog bark of a Browning. This is his world now. The States are so remote as to be practically non-existent.... they are another reality, something he can set aside like a book of old photos.

His mind wanders and he thinks about Mavis, remembering first her curved, tawny body and the way she pounced on him, a tigress for love. How cruel and strange she had seemed just a few short months ago! Mavis doesn't visit his dreams any more. He still has nightmares, great twisted gristly visitations that leave him drained and ill, but they aren't about her. He isn't sure what they are about. When he wakes, he can't remember.

CHAPTER FOURTEEN

The road that leads to Ranley's unconscious body lying smashed and twisted on the airport restaurant floor while sirens whine and some other wounded guy wails *God, GOD, why me, God?* - that long and twisted road began several months before with an angry black man and a frustrated scooter-bus driver.

The scooter-bus driver's name was Nguyen Tu Giang, and he drove one of the dozens of little, painted white people-carriers that ferried the peasants and *nguoi My* back and forth to their homes and barracks along the rut roads that crisscrossed the massive Tan Son Nhut airbase. Giang's was a dented, white bus with the number 183 painted on the side. He was about 35 years old with a wide, toothless grin, and he made enough money for his family to get along in a sagging roof, dirt-floor shack in the southwest corner at one end of the large air base.

One night when it was close to curfew time Giang picked up a load of drunken *nguoi My* returning from town. They sang loud and off-key, rasping out beer-inspired melodies in their harsh, barking *tieng My*. They shouted at Giang to get going, and a huge black man stood on the side of the driver's cab and slapped his cone hat every time he let up on the gas.

Giang had no choice but to continue. The other men jumped off the back of his bus one at a time as he drove along the route, and so far no one had paid. The last one left was the unpredictable

112

black man. Though dressed in army fatigues, he was also wearing a conical peasant's hat, and carrying a large, wooden nutcracker shaped like a naked woman. He sat on the tailgate with his legs hanging over the back and said sullenly, "124th Airborne Barracks."

"That no good!", Giang protested. "One-Two-Four was long ago before now! That one of first stop by Main Gate!"

The black man grunted, jumped out of the cab, and pissed on the roadside. After he finished, he started to walk down the dark road the way they had come.

And Giang made the mistake of his life by running after him. "You owe me 16 P!", he shouted, "You tell all else that you pay! Others not pay! Now you owe 2 P, each man - You *not* pay, you *number ten bad man*!!"

"Hey, Jack - git away from me!" The American brushed the slighter man off with a one-handed swat.

Giang should have let it go, but to him 16 piasters was a lot of money - it would buy a meal for his family, or half a pack of cheap *Phap* Basto Rouges or an entire week's *nuoc cafe* steaming with milk and loaded with raw sugar crystals the way he liked it for breakfast while he squatted on a dusty street-corner just outside the Main Gate with his fellows. Giang ran after the black man, and took hold of his shirtsleeve, "Please! Stop! You pay - you pay - *right now* - 16 P!"

The black man unexpectedly turned and swung a wicked blow with the heavy nutcracker. It connected with Giang's head at the temple. There was a hollow *thunk* sound, and Giang sank

113

to the ground without a word.

The American stared down at Giang. He muttered, "Oh, shit...." He looked around; the road was dark and deserted. The ever-present rain pelted down as if it would never stop. Somewhere a few blocks away a dog barked. The black man took a last look at the motionless body on the road, and started away at a fast walk toward his barracks.

The incident was never unraveled. No one contacted the black man, and it was even suggested that Giang may have accidentally fallen from his truck and struck his head, in spite of the fact that all the drivers knew his bus had been parked in neutral with the engine running and the hand brake on. This whitewashing theory met with howls of protest and was quietly dropped. Still, the final outcome was simple, if not very satisfactory: Giang was dead, and there was a war to run.... no one seemed to have time to press into what might turn out to be an ugly affair for the Americans, not for the sake of one insignificant and impoverished scooter driver. And that was the beginning of the trail that led to Ranley.

Giang's widow was only thirty-two, but she looked fifty. Her face and hands were wrinkled and worn from worry, work and malnutrition. What teeth she had left were coated black from chewing betel nut, and her body was pear-shaped from childbearing.

Of her husband, she only remembered the little things that now were missing: The burned-out stubs of his Basto Rouges, the rubber thongs he used to leave by the door, his laugh coming unexpectedly from outside in back, playing with the children.

They had no savings, had never heard of a pension plan. She sold his interest in the scooter-bus for enough to bury him, and then began to take in laundry from the Americans who lived next door at the 3RD RRU. To her surprise, this went well - so well that in a few months she was making much more than Giang ever had. She hired two young girls from the neighborhood to do the heavy lifting and ironing, and once again had time to go daily to the market just outside the Main Gate to buy fresh vegetables, fish, and occasionally a small piece of *thit bo* or a flapping winged *ga* so she could cook real beef or chicken *pho*.

Giang's widow looked like any of hundreds of other peasant women. She wore thin, white cotton blouses and baggy, black silk pants. Her face was nut-brown under her conical hat. She chewed and spat the orange-red gobs of betel juice because she was addicted to the menthol-like sensation in her mouth, or smoked Kools when she could get them. But she was in one way different; since her husband's death, Giang's widow would do anything to hurt the Americans.

Her contact was made at a ramshackle banana stand not a few blocks outside the Tan Son Nhut Main Gate. There were over thirty types of fresh bananas at the stand, all brought from the countryside in huge bunches, large and small, sweet ones and those bland and good for frying in peanut oil, red and rust, green and gold and yellow bananas.

Each market-day Giang's widow bought bananas. They were always ready, four or five in a brown paper sack. But instead of moving on to

115

another booth, she would chat for a moment with the sales woman, and then ask to use the toilet facility in the small, tin-walled back room.

Back there it was rank smelling and close, for there was no window, and the only light came in through cracks in the tin walls. The toilet itself was a large, porcelain-coated metal pail. While squatting over this, she would reach in between the bananas for a gray tube of soft putty about the size of a fat cigar. This was carefully wrapped in American Saran Wrap. Taking a small jar of petroleum jelly from a dusty shelf, she would quickly grease the tube and slip it far up into her vagina. Then she carefully replaced the jar and pulled up her baggy pants. After thanking the lady for the use of her room, she would put the bananas in her webbed plastic shopping bag and head back for home.

At the gate, the sleepy guards occasionally pawed through her groceries and poked at the bound-legged hen tied upside down to her wrist. Once, after an explosion at a *Ba Muoi Ba* and Buffalo-burger stand, she had to file through a dressing room with the other *bas*, strip naked, and have her clothing inspected. But they didn't body search anyone, and so she passed through with nothing more than a bad case of nerves. Biting her lip to keep from screaming, she pulled her clothing back on, picked up her shopping bag, and made her way to the tiny grocery store on the street where she lived. Here she again borrowed a bathroom, and left the soft, gray tube lying on the dusty floor in the corner, covered by a roll of stiff toilet paper that nobody ever used now that incredibly soft *My* paper was so easily lifted from

116

the bath rooms of their friendly allies.

The trail continues, the gray putty on its deadly way. The people shepherding it along rarely, if ever, think of the individuals who will be maimed or killed as beings very much like themselves, with similar problems to their own. They only think of their own injustices, their own hurts, and their own causes. It has been a long, long war, counting the French invaders and the Chinese before them, and the list of injustices, hurts and causes is truly endless.

Some of their reasons are matters of life and death, as is Giang's widow's. Others are foolish things, misunderstandings or trivial matters that might have been prevented with a little thought or consideration.

For instance, this small store where Giang's widow left the putty had once been a source of intense pride. Before it came into being, the shop keep's wife had always stockpiled extra food in case of emergencies. She was thought a little daft, because there was *always* food in Saigon - after all, they lived in the center of a rice bowl! But one bad rainy season there had been real shortages, and the neighbors, knowing she kept huge extra bags of rice, came begging. Her husband was happy to sell at a big profit. Shortly after that, he quit his job as a dock laborer, and they opened a store in their living room, and later built a storage shed in back. The store had expanded again, gaining another small storage room and a few feet extra in the front when they put up some large fold-up metal counter windows so the customers wouldn't trail mud and dust into the house.

To the Americans it was the most god-awful

117

ramshackle place, and since they sold no beer, nobody ever went there. But they passed by on their way out to the Main gate, and they made jokes about it. One wag who worked in supply had a big, blue sign beautifully stenciled with neat white letters *PIGGELY-WIGGELY MARKET*. He presented this to the shop keep, who proudly hung it above his front door until another American, this one well meaning, stopped by to let him in on the joke, that 'Piggely-Wiggely' meant 'Sloppy Mess'.

The shop keep pursed his lips and quietly removed the sign. He had lost something important in front of his friends, his customers, his wife, and his children. So when Giang's widow timidly asked if he could store something that would not necessarily be helpful to the Americans, he had agreed.

He had stored hundreds of the tubes in the bottom of a large flour bag when a scooter bus driver came for them. The shop keep never knew exactly what the tubes were, and the bus driver hauled the flour sack away without offering any explanations.

That night an average-looking half-Chinese man with rotten teeth was smuggled on base for one eight hour shift using the credentials of a cleaning man who had gone to Da Nang for his mother's funeral. This man's name was John Vincent and he was born and raised in Hanoi. He lived in Saigon, rotating quietly between a number of safe houses in and around the city, but in earlier times he'd been all the way to Peking where the enterprising *Chung Hoa* comrades had enrolled him in a course in plastics explosives.

Early in the morning after John Vincent's

guest appearance, the same scooter bus driver who had picked up the 250 gray tubes drove through the rain to deliver a flat, heavy package wrapped in water-resistant butcher's block paper to a cleaning man who waited outside the airport restaurant. This man, it goes almost without saying, was a friend of Nguyen Tu Giang.

The cleaning man's instructions were very clear: all he had to do was use a ladder and gently place the package out of sight on top of one of the concrete ceiling beams. There was one moment of panic when, all the way up the ladder, he felt his arms might not reach high enough. He wavered, thinking he was going to fall and be blown to pieces. But he just was able to slip it up on the girder. He finished his clean-up work, setting out fresh napkins at each table and refilling the sugar, salt and pepper shakers. He carefully locked the door behind him as he left, just as he always did.

By this time the cyclo-bus driver had putted his slow way from the scene toward the Main Gate, filling his bus as he went with *Bas* intent on the morning's shopping. Giang's widow had been told that there would be no little gray tubes for some weeks, as it would be too dangerous to carry them for a while. And John Vincent was also safe and well, reading a stack of local newspapers while he lay on a moldy bed in a rats-nest hole in Da Cau.

119

CHAPTER FIFTEEN

"You see, your *country* hooker", Charley says with the serious look of a real expert, " will have more heart, while these *city* bangs will have more art."

"Nope. A painted woman's a painted woman." Larky shakes his head. "They don't got hearts."

Beale looks up from the lone intercept on his desk, "I don't see how, with all the culture and history of Saigon out there for the taking -"

"Oh, Beale, can it, you *stugatz*!"

Beale has convinced the Dimbos to come in early because there is incredible news -- MACV has lifted all restrictions except the midnight curfew, and Saigon is no longer off-limits! Beale has badgered the Dimbos to put in some kind of effort so they can leave the White Shack early and sign out for town before dark, and they are so excited at the prospects that for once they have listened to him, at least, after their own fashion.

Charley stands on the table, "Thus spake Pizarro to his men: My pizanos, you concentrate on the gold and jewels, and leave the sinful loins of the native women with their bizarre and outrageous sexual customs for me - as your leader - to handle!" He manipulates his fingers like he is turning two huge radio dials while Larky and Mad Denny cheer him on.

Beale grumbles, "Piss on your pizanos of Pizarro...."

That was when Ranley walked in waving three partial broken intercepts. "The entire day's work, guys; the war's crawling to a halt before your very eyes.... at least on our side...." He tosses the sheets on Beale's desk. "Who's for lunch?"

"Buffalo-burgers again?", Mad Denny says.

"Yeah, what's wrong with that?"

"Airport Restaurant again?", Larky chimes in.

"Yeah. Why not?"

"In-di-GEST-ion is why not!"

"Come on, you nugs - you'll never regret it - the grapevine says Judy Joy's coming in today or tomorrow!" They know by now that Ranley doesn't care what the food is like. He likes rubbing elbows with the itinerants, the photographers and the newsmen, the minor show-biz singers and hoofers, the civilian Peace Corps and government AID types who come and go through the civilian terminal from that far-away mythical place called Stateside.

Beale leans his chair back against the cement-block wall and sticks an unlit Marlboro in his mouth, patting his pockets for matches, "Okay, I'll bite, Sarge - who's Judy Joy?"

"You're damn right you'd bite if she spread it! *Miss April*, you schmuck, that's who Judy Joy is - the one on the leather couch with the fire going!"

"Red Dog meets Judy Joy," Mad Denny mutters, his sparkling eyes giving away his otherwise dark look, "is it sodomy, bugamy or simple incest?"

Ranley rustles through a stack of old magazines. "Judy Joy has a pair of fantastic forties!" He finds a weathered Playboy and triumphantly opens it to the centerfold and holds it up for them to see.

Denny studies the photo gravely, "I don't

121

know.... I personally think this woman's a fraud. Looks like she has about a pound of silicone in each jug."

"Ridiculous! Those beauties are as natural as the day she was born!"

Beale is already working on the first of the three new messages, "Why don't you bring us something back? I'd go, but we're trying to clean up the shop so we can get downtown."

"Modern science", Mad Denny continues, as if talking to a convention of plastic surgeons, "is so advanced that you could have your hands all over her and never know for sure if she was real or not."

Charley gives the picture an expert nod, "Looks like she had a nose job too, doesn't it...."

"Screw you guys! I'll go myself!"

Ranley drives the company jeep across the tarmac. The rain has briefly let up, and he is able to roll back the plastic side flaps for a little fresh air. The wind, whistling through the half-open cab, makes a hollow little sound as he bounces along.

Word was, the airport restaurant had been designed by a famous Eurasian architect in *Vietnamine Moderne.* It sports a graceful, pre-stressed concrete frame ceiling with bamboo walls and plenty of open air.

Ranley sits at one of the tables where he can look out the window at the passengers leaving the terminal building. There are about sixty people in the restaurant, and dozens more milling around the wide concrete sidewalk outside.

Sometimes he'd see one of the regular reporters he recognized from Time or Newsweek. He'd been there when Westmoreland had landed, all-fierce with those snapping dark eyes and heavy black brows under his gunpowder gray hair. And he'd seen General Nguyen Cao Ky, the dashing ARVN fly-boy general who wore purple scarves and twin army issue .45s in black holsters and drove a Ford Falcon convertible raked low like a West Coast hot rod, the snappy little car painted purple to match his scarves and featuring a white top and a glittery chrome spare tire mounted in back. That was fun, because Ky put on a great show, the straight pipes on his Falcon rumbling as he pulled out in a column flanked front and back by jeeps with manned .50 caliber machine guns. Ranley had also watched Robert McNamara hustling through the terminal surrounded by bright boys, striding efficiently along in a crisp, lightweight suit, slim leather case holding the war in his left hand, defying any moisture to gather on the lenses of his wire-rim glasses.

On this day, there are no big, attention-getting arrivals; few ARVN officers strut by, on the way to Hue or Da Nang. There are no round-eye women; this is late summer, and since January American officers have no longer been allowed to bring their wives along. A few nuns sail by like plump, black pigeons with stiff white wings around their passive faces. Bald Buddhist monks in orange robes float by, equally as calm as the nuns, followed in turn by plain, brown-robed novices carrying their wooden begging bowls.

There are three or four oddly dressed European journalists, and a few Australian soldiers in their rakish bush hats, secure in the knowledge that they are the real jungle warfare experts.

Short, pudgy Vietnamese move in excited

little clumps, the wealthy upper class in Hawaiian sports shirts and their women in expensive *ao dai*, wide French sunglasses clinging perilously to their sweaty little noses as they return from extended weekends in the mountain resort of Da Lat or from their beach houses on the coast at Cap St. Jacques. Young Scandinavian and Dutch hikers gaze about in soft-eyed wonder, everything they own in the knapsacks on their backs, intent on their a mad plans to bicycle through the war from Saigon to Phnom Penh on the first leg of their journey west to Bangkok and on to Burma, India, Afghanistan, Iran, Iraq, Turkey, Greece, and so back home.

American businessmen gab as they stride along all shout and bustle in their polo shirts and polyester pants, their sports jacket and ties tucked neatly in their small suitcases, smelling new enterprise and fresh fortunes in the thick air. Here and there Ranley spots a lone Japanese businessman, moving fast and yet cautiously, aware of the special contempt the Vietnamese reserve for them since World War II. And still the occasional Frenchman stalks by with blood-shot eyes and a disdainful look for every bit of it. And there are turbaned Indians, known locally as the 'Jews of the Orient', on their way to fabric deals in New Delhi or Hong Kong.

Ranley's hamburger is tough and dry. He loads it up with ketchup and orders an iced tea from the pretty little *co gai* waitress. The girl is barely five feet tall, and can't weigh more than 85 pounds. He finds himself thinking about the American wives, no longer allowed in country with their officer husbands.. He misses them. American women are more substantial, to his taste there is just more to them.

A commotion over by the terminal entrance catches his attention. He fumbles in his fatigues jacket pocket for his little Minolta; he'll show those Dimbos! He stands to get a better look, but still can't see through the crowd. He makes up his mind to go over and get her autograph at least, and maybe snap a picture as his proof that he'd really met her. He stares out the door, but at that moment the group thins, and he sees it is just some big-cheese ARVN general. He shrugs, disappointed. That is the game, you never know who you are going to see.

He thinks about the cold, cardboard-like half of a hamburger waiting for him, and starts to walk away. Then he remembers his iced tea.

As he goes back inside and moves toward his table, there is a huge ball of fire from the ceiling. He is picked up and lifted easily over several tables. While he flies through the air he sees in a flash of slow motion the tumbling bodies of others pushed around as if slapped by giant hands, and he thinks *Well, they finally got me, the sons-of-bitches! That's what I get for staying too long!* His shattered eardrums hear no sounds. There is no rage, no bitterness, and no more time. The wall comes up and slams into him, and he sees only blackness.

CHAPTER SIXTEEN

A wide-eyed Boo Boo Boudreaux brings the news, breathless from a run across the tacky asphalt tarmac in the mid-day humid wet. The Dimbos take it about as expected, the three newcomers showing alarm while Beale is intent on the details.

"Well, is he *okay*?", Beale keeps asking.

"He's got all his limbs, plus his sight and almost all of his hearing...."

"Well then, he's okay.... I guess...."

"Yeah, sure, he's *great*, you *stugatz*," Charley says.

The officer lets this exchange pass and is almost out the door when he pauses, "You can go see him, you know. Actually, Beale, Taters said he thought Red Dog asked for you . . . "

"Me? What for?"

Boudreaux shrugs, "Who knows? Technically, at least, you're next in command, aren't you?"

Beale sat alone, chain-smoking for about a half-hour. Finally he can't stand it any longer, "We're all caught up with our work - let's get out of here. I'm going downtown. You guys can come along."

Charley shakes his head no, "This *ep plastique* shit cools my lust considerably, Ong Be."

"Well, stay in the barracks - whatever you want, I don't care."

The Dimbos eye his retreating figure. "Hey, *stugatz*," Mad Denny yells after him, "who's going to keep you out of trouble?" But Beale doesn't answer. Charley waits until he is out of the hearing, "I don't like this . . . "

Larky's face wrinkles into a look of disbelief, "Shoot! We going to let Ong Be fornicate with all the women of Saigon by his lonesome?"

Mad Denny looks at the other Dimbos, "I think good old Ong Be has more on his mind than a trip to Saigon General."

Charley is still against going, "He's already got us in a mess of trouble."

"Come on, *meatball*, that's ancient history. They were going to send us to Nam anyway, sooner or later."

"And *what* are we going to do, now that our feet are in the soup?"

Mad Denny gives him a playful shove, "I don't know, Larky. Turn into noodles?"

Charley sighs, "Okay. Come on fellows, let's go see what old Lemonlips has up his sleeve!"

They catch up to Beale and the four of them change to civvies and sign out under Toady's watchful eye. The greasy little clerk eyes them as he popped a big zit on his left cheek, "You know, you really should reconsider your plans - there's a *lots* of explosives floating around town."

"No", Mad Denny waves a finger back at him, "the V.C. used it all up at the Airport Restaurant. The *real classified scoop* - which I shouldn't be telling you as you have no clearance and absolutely no *need to know* - is it wasn't a terrorist bombing at all, it was a response to bad food. The V.C. held a base-wide contest - we came in second last."

Toady's voice increases in intensity and he

waves a warning finger back in their direction, *"Into a fool's heart you can put no wisdom."*

Larky gives him a curious look, "Where's you get that quote, fool?"

"From the holy bible!"

"You wouldn't be referring to Exodus 31:6 . . . *In the hearts of all that are wise hearted I have put wisdom."*

"God's *meaning* is quite clear."

"I wouldn't know - them *ain't* his words. If you're going to quote it, you got to get it right."

Toady isn't used to being called on the exactness of his quotes. He arches his eyebrows to mask his sudden nervousness, "The bible tells us *Wisdom is more important than diamonds or furs."*

Larky scratches his head and his smile widened, "Seriously, now. You better get your biblical shit together, friend. As a nearly, almost-minister, I can tell you you're mouthing unholy, made-up gibberish. Maybe you mean *Job 28:15, The price of wisdom is above rubies."*

Toady angrily pounds his fist on the table, *"Wisdom builds the house on a solid seven pillars!"*

" That would be Proverbs, 9:1, *Wisdom hath builded her house, she hath hewn out her seven pillars."*

Toady's voice cracks into a crazed falsetto as he shoots back, *"Beware! Fools laugh at things a wise man would consider carefully!"*

Larky leans forward, resting his elbows on the shoulder-high sign-out desk, "I kin go bible with you all day, fool. I was *fed* bible morning, noon and night since I was a baby. What you *mean* is, *The heart of the wise is in the house of mourning;*

128

but the heart of fools is in the house of mirth! Ecclesiastices, 7:4."

Toady endures a general round of jeers from the Dimbos, as they whistle and shout and clap Larky on the back. Charley raises Larky's hand, "Declaring our new winner and biblical champion -- Chaplain Larky Larkspun!"

Toady grits his teeth, "Laugh at God's Word if you want, but I'm warning you just like Captain Nordoff warned Ranley a hundred times -"

"Warned him *what*, dip-shit?", Mad Denny growls.

"Warned him to abstain from *native* places!"

"They're supposed to be our allies."

"Don't you deceive yourselves! A lot of us don't go downtown at all anymore! The Colonel himself only goes once a month, to get new issue stamps from the post office for his kids back home."

Larky waves his hand in a magnanimous gesture of acceptance, "Finally got one right! *Deceive not yourselves,* Jeremiah 37:9."

Charley reaches in the open ammo case on the desk and fills his pocket with prophylactics.

Toady angrily jerks the ammo case away, "You can*not* take so many rubbers!"

"Why not? I got the dago hots - I'm going to need 'em!"

Beale nods, "It's an old family curse...."

Larky pipes up, "Now you should *know* this, Toady -- Joshua says clear as a bell, *Sanctify yourselves against tomorrow,* an' Ezekiel advises *Be thou prepared!*"

"Like to see for yourself?" Charley starts to unzip his pants.

129

"Get out of here!"

Toady watches the four of them march out the door and down the gravel road to the 3RD's gate, chanting *Sai-GON BOUND*! Sharp barbing thoughts of hatred and revenge roil through the chubby little clerk, and his face is flushed and purple. Everyone in the company puts him down, and he likes to think he bears that kind of indignity as Job did his boils -- but he is a serious Jehovah's Witness, and nobody, *nobody* calls him out on bible texts! *The sense of the bible was what was important; anyway, not the exact words as this or that scholar had imperfectly copied them!* Toady had found that most people went along if it sounded biblical and if he tagged a chapter or a verse number on the end, and sometimes he made up things for fun and that was okay, too. The few who might know the difference and be offended had sense enough to realize he had access to their files. He could make R&R magically disappear and work days and detail rosters appear in their place. He'd even extended a few tours of duty by several weeks; little mechanical errors involving lost paperwork and blurred entries. *Saigon Bound, indeed! If that's what the Dimbos wanted, the four of them were going to find themselves bound hand and foot to their beloved dens of iniquity! They'd be lucky if they EVER got out!*

Toady settled back in his chair and began to run over the possibilities. One thing was sure as judgment day - he'd think of something, and it wasn't going to be pleasant.

The Dimbos caught a cyclo-bus outside the 3rd, and in twenty minutes were showing their

130

I.D.s to a bored M.P. at the Main Gate. And then they were walking through, to the other side.

Outside the main gates of Tan Son Nhut it is a different world, a colorful madness of commerce and excitement. Native taxi-drivers yell from a row of battered blue-and-cream Renaults, *"Anh, Anh, Anh - ANH, OI!!"* The wide, circular street is congested with Vietnamese riding bicycles, pedicabs, scooters, motorbikes, motor pedi-cabs, cars and trucks. The sidewalks themselves are masses of movement as cone-hatted peasant workers and olive clad ARVN soldiers come and go through the main gates. People hurry away from the base, or sit hunched in the warm rain as if they don't care, chatting and drinking *nuoc cafe* or *nuoc the* and chop-sticking down *pho* noodle soup they buy bowls from little portable soup kitchens set up on the sidewalk.

To the right, Beale sees an old cemetery with white limestone slabs crowded together in crooked little rows. The cemetery has a ceramic wall with a strange, floating dragon, and stylized, puffy white clouds in a light blue sky. A cab driver comes up to him, taking his arm and speaking in rough English, "You go downtown?"

"Yes, yes - downtown. Tell me," Beale points to the odd ceramic, "what is that over there?"

The cabbie is middle-aged and lean, with skin tanned a deep brown. He eyes Beale through lids narrowed to a squint, and then shrugs, as if it is of no importance, *"Nguoi Phap* - you know, Frenchmans soldier, subtlety," Mad Denny mutters. "Give us a quote, Ong Lar-Ky."

Larky shrugs, "How about Numbers, Chapter 14: Verse 29 . . . *They shall lie down alike in the*
131

dust, and the worms shall cover them."

Charley gives Beale a long, measured look, "Well, that's sobering. Nice place for a warning, right outside the Main Gate. "Can we go back now?"

"You're not serious? We haven't *gone* anywhere yet!"

"I mean back to Number 1 Stateside, G.I."

The cabbie beams at them, his grin carrying from ear to ear, "Oh, you first-time see Saigon!"

"That's right", Beale tells him..

Charley gives him a shove, buried over there. Too dead to go home."

"Typical Vietnamese

"Don't *tell* him that! That's like telling a New York cabbie you're from Peoria! You're going to end up with your throat cut, dumped in some swamp somewhere!"

Several men and women gesturing and shouting to them from a group of tin shacks in the mud next to the cemetery catch Beale's attention. "What the hell do they want?"

The cabbie takes his arm again, steering him to his cab, "No, no, no. Bad place! That Hundred-P Alley! No good for you! Very fast, very cheap, very *Number 10* make you sick! You want downtown girl!"

"Vung", Beale says, experimenting a little, *"Toi muon di thanh pho Saigon. Saigon General ho-pi-tal. Di di, mao len!"*

"Ohh, you speak Vietnam!"

Mad Denny claps him on the shoulder, "Congrats, Ong Be - you've sent us to Hanoi in a crate!"

The Dimbos laugh but they crowd into the taxi

132

and the cabbie soon has the fender-dented little car racing madly through the rain-drenched streets, heading down Ngo Dinh Khoi street and across an arm of the brackish Song Thi Nghe estuary, and on past the high, mossy cement walls topped with barbed wire, on the other side of which they see glimpses of tall green trees and huge old French Colonial homes.

At the hospital, Boo Boo meets them outside Ranley's room, "Beale - he *has* been asking for you. But don't expect too much, they've got him doped to the sky. Come on." The lieutenant leads the way, followed by the wondering Dimbos.

Ranley isn't looking good. He has a bandage over one eye, another around one arm near his elbow, and a big one across his abdomen. There are literally hundreds of fresh gashes torn in his face, arms and chest.

Boudreaux whispers, "The pepper marks are from concrete fragments. They had to take most of them out with a tweezers. He's got a bigger chunk torn out of his arm, and a fragment they had to pull from his abdomen. He's lucky he didn't lose his eye; they had to take some small fragments and grit out, but they are calling it abrasion. His eyes are badly crossed -"

"What's *that* mean?" Larky says.

"Means he's probably fucked up in his gourd," Mad Denny mutters.

"Red Dog!" Beale takes his limp hand, "You going to be alright?"

Ranley's good eye pops open. "Yep. I'll - be - back."

Boudreaux, who is standing out of Ranley's line of sight, shakes his head, "No, Rans. You're

133

being airlifted to Manila, first break in the weather."

Ranley looks around wildly, almost desperate, until he can see Boo Boo, "I'll - be - back! Can't-keep-me-away!"

Boudreaux pats the hand Beale is holding. It is the only place on the sergeant's body not dotted with angry scabs, "No one's trying to keep you away, my dear Red Dog. I assure you, our mutual military friends will welcome you back here with open arms! Just get a little R&R with the mama's of Manila for a few months." He gives the Dimbos a brisk wave, "Ta-ta! I have to be running along now. Don't stay too long, the nurses will shoo you out."

Ranley's good eye wavers over to take in the Dimbos, finally focusing on Beale, "My apartment - on Truong Ming Giang - paid for rest of year - yours - here's key - " With a major effort he hands Beale an envelope with an address scrawled across the front of it. He reaches for a handful of Beale's shirt and pulls him close.

"Take it easy," Beale says. "It's not important now."

"*IS* important! Books! Take care - my books! Guns - under loose board - behind books - okay to use." Ranley is gasping with the effort, sweat beading on his forehead, but he insists on continuing. He pulls Beale closer and speaks softly so only he can hear, "Chest - under bed - gold bars - hide gold bars!"

"Gold?" Beale's eyes go wide. Americans were barred by law from owning raw gold, which was the standard of the U.S. dollar, pegged in value at $35 an ounce. He remembers Ranley's

134

fascination with gold - he always wore a heavy golden neck-chain, a golden dragon ring, and a massive wristband on his watch.

"A little - I never - go anywhere without it -!" Ranley is sweating. His hand relaxes on Beale's shirt. He's running out of steam. After several tries, he manages to gasp, "Finally - Em Tuy."

"Em Tuy?"

Ranley nods, gathering enough strength to crane his head around, his one eye looking at everything and nothing at the same time, "Cherry Bar. Downtown. Tell Tuy - what happened." Again he pulls Beale close to him and whispers in his ear, "*DON'T* let Tuy - go to apartment. She has – her own place."

He is running down now, and as he drifts off to unconscious, Beale gets a last instruction, "Tell her – my place is - booby trap....or she'll steal everything."

The Dimbos stand in the twilight gloom on the steps of Saigon General, watching the lights of the busy traffic flow past them. Ranley has affected Beale more deeply than he wants to admit. In the short time they'd worked together, the moody sergeant had, at least for him, come to symbolize the few things that were right about the army and the war effort. Red Dog had ideals that dated back to the beginnings of American involvement. He believed the Americans were the Good Guys, and that the ARVNs could win; or rather, that they could win with American help. Beyond that, Ranley was living proof that an ordinary person from the States could survive for years in Vietnam and keep his mind and his sense of humor fairly together. Ranley's principles appealed to the liberal Democrat in Beale; even caught up in the flap and bustle of daily life in Nam, he had thought he could ignore much of what he felt, and coolly push down the unrest in his mind somewhere, way down beyond thought so he wouldn't have to deal with it. The monster that had come to him on his plane ride into Vietnam returned more easily as the weeks went by, came quickly and unbidden, and each time claimed its prize. When others who knew him less would call him remote, unfeeling or cold, the Dimbos would shrug and say it took time to really understand him. And they were right. It was harder and harder to get to know Jack Beale, or even for him to know himself . . . because one aspect of his monster was *denial*.

But now, standing on a street corner near Saigon General after seeing the pepper-shot and spent Ranley, Charley looks accusingly at Beale, "Christ, Ong Be - we almost went with him today!"

Beale shrugs, "Hey, man - when your time is up, it's up."

"What the fuck is that supposed to mean?

"Well - fatalism, I guess...."

"And where do you want to take us next, *Mister Chet Dan?*"

It took a lot, but Beale finally is angry, "Christ! Why don't you just turn tail and go back to the base - run back to Toady Zit-face and his kind?! Go ahead!"

Charley thinks about Beale's sudden outburst and then nods at the other Dimbos as if to say, *Here it comes, fellows.* He grins skeptically at Beale, "And where are *you* going?"

"*Somebody* has to tell Em Tuy about Red
136

Dog...."

Larky scratches his head in an imitation of a rural idiot, "*Em* Tuy - *Little Sister* Tuy? Who's that, anyway, Ong Be?"

"Probably some little peanut-girl that old Red Dog befriended," Mad Denny snickers. "Nuts for sex favors."

Charley pretends to ponder, rolling around the little street Vietnamese he knows, "Wait a minute.... *em* also means 'honey' or 'sweetheart'?!"

"Yeah, sometimes...."

Charley nods, feeling a little better. There are only two things about Saigon that attract him; the food, which is supposed to be first class, and women. The cuisine he could investigate any time, but for now, the girls seemed to be everywhere, mysterious and doe-eyed, gliding along the streets in their silky *ao dai* with their colored umbrellas tilted against the rain, peeping at him from the doorways of neon-lit bars, smiling as they passed by in cabs and old, black French Citroens - the delicious, willowy-slim *co gai* of Saigon, at last within reach! He points an accusing finger at Beale, "Ohhh, you sly dog!"

"What?"

"Don't play innocent with me, Ong Be! Let's all go see this little peanut girl you're trying so hard to keep to yourself!"

"Oh, Beale, how could you?", Denny says.

Larky chuckles, "*Withhold not good from them to whom it is due* . . . How *could* you, Ong Be, after we've all saved yore miserable life by coming to Nam and keeping you from eating a buffalo-burger an' getting blown up for lunch!"

Beale protests, but nobody believes him.

They wave down a cab and pile in, once again chanting the old Dimbo team cheer, Sai-GON BOUND!

CHAPTER SEVENTEEN

The cab took the Dimbos to Hai Ba Trung Street and dropped them off in the middle of a bustling nightlife scene. Beale hands the driver a 20 piaster note and the Dimbos dash in the front door of the Cherry Bar, ducking the half-dozen assorted peddlers and beggars pleading like hungry dogs, *"Anh, Anh, Anh, ANH!"*

When their eyes adjust to the dim and softly lit interior of the Cherry Bar they see it is decorated in rich shades of burgundy. The tables are crowded with American men, mostly in civilian clothes, attended by young girls wearing heavy silk brocade *ao dai* or expensive-looking western style dresses that are tight fitting, low cut, and slit along the side of the skirt up the thigh.

A middle-aged woman appears at their side. She slurs softly in English, "Prease, come zis way . . ." Her face is heavily made up and her jet-black hair is teased in an elaborate coif.

"Uhh-uhh-uhh-what heavenly bodies!" Larky sputters, looking around at the girls.

Charley waves his hands, *"Vung, vung, VUNG!* Paradiso Magnolia!"

"You like Amelican whis-ky?" their hostess asks.

"Ba Muoi Ba."

She shrugs, "All same plice: *Ba Muoi Ba,* Amelican Whis-ky, Sai-gon Whis-ky, all same, 100 P."

"Oh well then, 'Amelican' whiskey," Beale shrugs.

"Naw, I'll stick with the *Ba Muoi Ba*", Magnolia says. "You ever notice you drink too much, Ong Be?"

"*You* ever notice you've constantly got your nose in my life?"

Several of the girls extricate themselves from other tables, and glide up to the Dimbos. One wraps her arm around Larky's shoulder and whispers in his ear, "You buy for me one Saigon Whiskey, and we talk-talk?"

"Why shore!"

She signals with one hand, and a lean barman dressed in a white shirt, a black vest and black string tie brings her a small glass of what looks like whiskey.

"One hundred P", he says, looking at no one in particular. Larky digs in his pockets and handed the money across.

The rest of their drinks come and are passed around. Beale sips his whiskey and studies the girl who has wrapped her hands around Larky's arm. She looks like a teen-ager, though he couldn't tell for sure through her heavy make-up. He reaches across the table and taps her shoulder to get her rapt attention away from Larky, "Pardon me, but we're looking for *Em* Tuy...."

"Ahhh.... you know *Em* Tuy . . . ?" It is a statement said as a question. The long hair curls in waves around the girl's pretty face, and her mascara-darkened eyelids give no expression.

"No. We have a message for her - from Sergeant.... from Red Dog."

"She not know any Red Dog."

"Perhaps she knows him by the name Ranley."

"Ahhh, *RAN*-ly. *ALL* girls know Ran-ly!"

140

The girl promptly gets up and goes to another table.

"Thanks, Ong Be - Just when I was scoring, too. You're going to owe me 100 P for this one!"

But a minute later Larky's bargirl friend returns with another girl. This newcomer has the delicate features and classic symmetry of a true beauty; she is just over five feet tall, but her thin *ao gai* suggests an ample body for a Vietnamese. Barely a teenager, she gazes at them with a look of wide-eyed innocence. Charley moves his chair over, making room for her.

She gives him a pathetic look, and pouts unhappily, "I cannot stay.... unless someone buys me one Saigon Whiskey. It is a rule."

Charley agrees and passes over a hundred-piaster note.

She looks over the Americans, "Who has the message for me from my Ranley?"

Beale notices she speaks better English than the other girls. Her pronunciation is measured and careful, like one who is at least conscious of the difficulties of the language.

Mad Denny reaches over and sips from her glass before anyone thinks to stop him, "Huh, Charley - you paid 100 P for tea!"

"Course it just tea!", Larky's girl scolds. "No girl drink whiskey all night. Get too drunk, not be friend to G.I.!"

Beale holds up a hand for silence, "Tuy. *Em* Tuy. Ranley has been in an explosion at Tan Son Nhut."

Tuy gasps, her hands fluttering to her breasts in a gesture of helpless dismay.

"Nice going, Beale," Charley mutters, "All the

sensitivity of the master-race at your disposal, Goering couldn't have done it better...."

The young bargirl looks helpless, an overly made-up waif overwhelmed by tragedy. Beale thinks of a schoolgirl play-dressing up in mommy's finest who is interrupted with the sudden crushing news that daddy is really dead. One trembling hand goes to her perfect oval lips, and she says, "Is he - alright?"

"I'm afraid not. I mean - he's going to be alright, but they have to ship him to Manila, to get him better."

A small tear runs down her cheek, making a line through the heavy mascara under her eye. "He was my friend.... my close friend." She breaks down and begins silently sobbing in her hands.

"Atta way to go, Beale", Charley says.

"*Some*body had to tell her!" Beale reaches across the table and awkwardly pats Tuy's hand, "I'm sorry. We're all sorry...." He has an inspiration, "Look, we can take you to the hospital to see him!"

"No," she says quickly. She casts her glance down on the table, daubing at her eyes with a small handkerchief, "That would not be proper."

Mad Denny grins, liking the idea, "We could probably pull it off - dress her like somebody else!"

"No!", Tuy says again, this time with a hint of an edge to her voice. There is a pause while she seems to compose herself. "I - I not bring shame to my Ranley. But.... there is one thing you do for me."

"And what is that?"

"I have leave some few of my things by my

Ranley apartment. Just some little, personal things - but of great importance to me. You will take me there?"

Beale hesitates, remembering Ranley's warning, "Well, actually he'll be back in a little while. A few months at the most - and then you can pick up your stuff."

"A few months!!" She sounds suddenly indignant. "That will be too long!"

"Well then, you can tell me what the stuff is, and I'll get it for you."

"No, no, no...." Her head is buried in her hands again, and she sobs heavily.

Charley glares at Beale, "For Christ's sake, since when did you get to be such a hard-ass?"

Beale's face flushes bright red, "Goddamn it, Charley, he said specifically she was not to go into his apartment!"

"You sure of that? Those were his exact words? Any of you guys hear Ranley say that?"

Mad Denny and Larky shake their heads.

"He was talking personal to me."

"Maybe.... and maybe he was so doped up he didn't know what he was saying."

"You know, I'm tired of you people not listening to me. I know you don't think I'm smart or that I know anything, but I'm not going along with this!" Beale gets up so swiftly the chair falls over backwards behind him.

"Aww, sit down. You're always getting upset about something."

"You'll see I'm right! Ranley *warned* me about her!" He points a shaking finger across the table, "That woman will turn out to be trouble - real trouble for all of us! Don't forget I said it!"

143

Magnolia sighs and runs his fingers softly along the back of Tuy's hand, "Don't pay any attention to my friend. He had a bad experience with a little *co gai den* back in *My Chao*, understand?"

"A *black* girl?" Tuy raises her eyebrows as if she can't believe it, "White American G.I. not date black American girl. It not the custom of *My Chao*."

Charley shrugs, "*Believe* me, he did it anyway."

"I can't tell you *anything*!" Beale gulps down the rest of his whiskey and leaves their table, knocking over another chair and pushing past the waiter as he leaves.

The night air is thick with the smells of cooking food and motor exhaust, but it is fresh compared to the stagnant nicotine and alcohol atmosphere in the bar. Beale throws his raincoat over his shoulders and takes in a deep breath. The street is busy with traffic. He looks for a cab, thinking to go directly over to the apartment and hide Ranley's gold. Maybe it would fit behind the books with the hidden guns. But the cabs all have their little top-lights off, indicating they are occupied, and so he walked on down the street, hoping to pick up a ride at the next busy intersection.

He passes bars and tailor shops, and portable cigarette lady stalls with their Nestlé's chocolate bars, Double-Bubble and Wrigley's gum, their Crooks and Owl cigars, and a wide variety of French and American cigarettes, all arranged in large, slanted trays in jumbled quilt patterns of color. A young man with a slimy grin and a missing leg gestures toward some florescent paintings of garish sunsets over beaches and mountain ranges. When Beale shakes his head, he lifts a dirty canvas aside, revealing a row of erotic silk paintings done in the same technique, the vacant-eyed girls naked in their vampire-pale skin, stringy black hair and blood-red nails and lips. A thin old man hobbles up to Beale on crutches, holding his hand out for piasters. Peanut girls run by, shoving the little rolls of used newspaper in his face until he gives up a few piasters and buys some. A man at his side pulls his sleeve, "*Anh, Anh, ANH!* Here! Number one cock book!" He shoves a soft-covered copy of Little Angel, Big Screw in Beale's hand.

"No thanks." Beale pushes the book away, "I've had enough paper fucks to last a lifetime.... ask anybody who knows me."

A tall, gaunt montagnard who reminds him of the bird-men at Chez Anna walks up to Beale with a tray full of flutes, whistles and crude string instruments. He has a pile of thin ceremonial robes around his neck, embroidered with bright and intricate patterns, as if the Navajos had gotten into neon dyes.

"How much?" Beale selects the most colorful of the robes.

"For you - 800 P!", the man says in a thin, singing voice.

"Too much." Beale shakes his head and gives the robe back.

"Wait - wait! *Anh, ANH!*" The man sprints after him as he walks away. "For you, only 600 P!"

"It is not very well made. The threads will

come apart."

"Very much good made! It supposed to look this way!"

"Khong phai..." Beale gives him a sideways glance and a negative shake of his head, and again walks away.

"Anh, ANH, ANH!!" The man is right behind him. "You speak Vietnam. You speak Vietnam good! For you, 400 P - no, 350 P!

"200 P."

"Good, good, good."

Beale wanders down the street, wearing the robe around his shoulders. A merry voice over his shoulder speaks in Vietnamese, "You pay too much, Ong Be. You should always ask me first. I could get such a marriage robe for you for only 100 P!"

Beale turns around, surprised to hear his name in the crowded city. Before he can do anything, the girl who has spoken pulls one end of the robe around her own shoulders, steps up to him and lightly brushes her lips against his, "The montagnard peoples believe we are married now. It is their true and ancient custom. Is it so in America?" He just stands there and gapes. It is Hoa, the girl he'd met at Anna's Place!

"Night Lark! What are you doing here?!"

"I came, thanks to you! I took a few hundred P extra from your pocket to buy my freedom from Anna! I knew you would want me to - you were too tired to think of it!"

"A few hundred?"

She stands before him, full of confidence, a little gamin telling her sins and hoping to be spanked, "Actually, it was about - pretty close to -

146

almost - well, exactly 12,665 P! A pretty good deal, yes? You get me for that cheap price!"

"But I don't...."

She puts a gentle finger to his lips, "I know - you didn't even notice the money was gone. You made such a huge pile that night." She steps back and studies him, obviously pleased at what she sees, "So, a girl takes a chance, and here I am!"

"But - what do you do?"

"I out of the whore-girl business. I work there at night, and take singing lessons, too." She points to a neon sign about three doors down a small side street. The sign says Hong Kong Bar. "Now I a respectable Saigon bargirl. Plenty talk, plenty tease, but no action!" She comes closer and looks up at him, "Soon I sing in nightclub, you will see!" She smiles and kisses him full on the lips again, "See how your little Night Lark miss you!"

She takes his hand and pulls him toward the bar, "Come. Buy me one Saigon Whiskey to satisfy my boss, and we make our plan."

"*Our plan?* But - I can't right now. I - I'm supposed to go to a friend's apartment."

She is thunderstruck, and he sees tears starting in her eyes, "Friend? You have new girlfriend?"

"No, no, no, no, no. Nothing like that."

Rather than explain the whole thing, he goes with her. They ended up at her tiny apartment in Da Cau. He'd drunk too much, as usual, and it takes a long time before he comes in spasms of hot, dreamy joy. And then he holds her until she drifts off into sleep.

Suddenly awake, Beale sits up on the edge of the bed. Dizzy and exhausted as he is, he knows there was something he still has to do. It is cold and clammy, strange for Vietnam, and he can hear the rain drumming on the tile roof overhead. There is a bare light bulb hanging in the hallway, he remembers it from when he and Night Lark came in. Dim light filters over the walls of the little room, which do not go up to the ceiling, and he looks around while the whole world drifts off to the left in its customary fashion.

There is just the one room. He figures the bathroom must be down the hall, if the place even has one, and not just those little night-pots. He wants a shower. Hoa claimed she was his, but there was no telling what disease she might have picked up since he last saw her. Staggering to his feet, he finds a big bottle of rubbing alcohol on top of her dresser, which is the only piece of furniture in the room other than the sagging bed.

Without giving it a second thought, he unscrews the cap and cups his hand, pouring out as much liquid as he can hold, and then washing himself. He takes a second handful and rubs it in, and he was screwing the cap back on when the burning started. It mounted swiftly, fire on fire, doubling him over until he thought he had to scream. He gritted his teeth, setting down the bottle, and then went down to his knees, clinging to the rickety dresser for support while the pain went up and up, beyond sheer pain to some pure, white light area where agony blinded his every other perception. He gasped, grinding his teeth and rolling his eyes, and still refusing to utter a sound while the alcohol bathed him, branded him, seared the core of his being. At last, after an endless time, the fires slaked and he could breathe normally again.

He slowly got to his feet. He felt shaky, but his head was clear again. He remembered he had to get over to Ranley's apartment! He glanced at his watch - quarter to midnight, he still had 15 minutes until curfew. Hoa was sleeping like a baby. Moving quietly, he pulled on his clothes and left the place.

He'd lost his raincoat, but he still had plenty of money. Without any idea of his exact location, he walked back out along the narrow alley-like street until he came to a wider road, and followed that until he found an intersection. Five minutes later he had successfully hailed a cab, and was rocketing over to Ranley's apartment, on Truong Ming Giang Street about a half mile from Tan Son Nhut.

It was a neat little town-villa of white stucco, with a tile roof and purple flowered bougainvillea bushes growing up the sides. To the left, as one faced the house, the single, weed-overgrown spur of an abandoned railroad track ran past the high-walled enclosure, while to the right the villa was against the walls of another villa built in the same style.

Beale doesn't need his key for the door is already slightly ajar. He can see the marks where someone has pried the door open with a crowbar. His hair stands up on the back of his neck as his mind fills with notions of ambush and booby-traps. *Hadn't Ranley said the place was bomb-rigged? Or had he said to tell Tuy that?* Deciding it was the latter, he carefully pushes the door open and steps into a tiled living room. The place is a mess; books and clothes are scattered everywhere. With a sinking feeling, he makes his way through the study, which has also been ransacked, and into the bedroom. He doesn't have to look any further. The long, flat case has been pulled out from under the bed. Its heavy lock is smashed. He looks into the case, but he needn't have bothered. There were no gold bars.

Beale was suddenly very tired. *The one thing Ranley had ever asked him to do - and he screwed it up!* He sinks to the floor, resting his head against the wall as the room spins before his eyes. The *Ba Muoi Bas* and American whiskey have finally caught up to him. He crawls over to the bed and rolls onto it, pulling a thin bedspread over his shoulders, and is soon asleep.

CHAPTER EIGHTEEN

By the time the cab drops Beale off at Tan Son Nhut the next morning, the base is a beehive of activity. An entire company of ARVNs is protecting the Main Gate, squatting and standing around in full military gear, steel pots on their heads and M-1 rifles in hand. Other Vietnamese soldiers are shoveling sand from a two wheel trailer into sacks and stacking them in circles around heavy machine guns positioned on either side of the road just outside the gate.

Beale ducks in through the gate reserved for American G.I.'s, calling at the same time to the nearest M.P., "What the hell's going on?"

"U.S. passed a declaration of war! Where you been, buddy?"

"Off base."

"Something called the Gulf of Tonkin Resolution! Fuckin' Hanoi dinks tried to torpedo some of our boats, and we're bombing the shit out of 'em right now! The whole base is Orange Alert - you better get to your unit."

"Did we - instigate it?"

The M.P.'s face wrinkles in derision and he looks at Beale like he is mentally retarded, "The U.S.? What the hell would we do *that* for, Specialist?"

Beale climbs into a cyclo-bus as it is pulling out. It is packed with *bas* returning from their morning visit to the market. One woman moves her basket over and he squeezes in next to her. The basket has a live chicken lying upside down, with its legs trussed up. The chicken cranes its neck and eyed him, wondering if it should peck him or not..

There is another G.I. headed for the 3rd, an old E-7 cook named Hensley. Beale nods, "You hear we're bombing North Vietnam?"

"Yep."

Beale tries to rephrase his question as casually as he dares, sure that a lifer would have the real scoop through the army grapevine, "Did . . . did we start it?"

"Shit, no. You joking me, sonny? We *never* do, don't you read your history books? - we *always* give the other guy the first punch! It jist ain't fair! They swing first an' then we got to go in and finish it." The sergeant sinks into silence, the worry written all over his wrinkled face. After a while he speaks up again, "I was in Korea when the same shit hit the fan. The Gooks came pouring down across that DMZ, just looking for throats to slit!"

Beale's face goes white. He can't help it. Guys he'd gone to language school with were stationed at Phu Bai, a few miles south of the DMZ. "Bad, huh?" he manages to say.

"This is *worse*! Then we had *infantry*. Here all we got is *advisors* and *specialists*, no offense meant.... but when's the last time *you* squeezed off on a gook?"

"Well - I never did...."

"My point exactly. Sure makes the States feel far away, don't it?"

Beale thinks about it as they jounce along the bumpy road. Orange is the middle-stage alert; at the 3rd, they will still work the White Shack, but all passes will be rescinded and nobody will be able to leave the base. They will have to wait for the alert to clear – or for it to be moved up to Red. If it ever went Red, the ordnance sarge would open his little blockhouse and start handing out M-14's and live ammo. And they will get out the incendiary grenades at the White Shack.

Beale feels the very strangeness of everything. The old cook was right about one thing; the U.S. had never seemed farther away. Beale's hands start to tremble and he automatically fumbles for his Marlboros. He is relieved when the scooter-bus finally approaches the 3rd's neat barracks area. He jumps off the back of the bus, handing the driver a 5 P note, and walks quickly to the sign-in log.

The 3rd bustles with activity. Details are working in the light rain, sandbagging a position to one side of the small front gate, while others are sandbagging the concrete drains to make them more serviceable as trenches in case of mortar attacks.

Toady, who is acting as an unofficial work-boss, sees him signing in at the guard gate, "Nice of you to join us, Specialist Beale."

"None of your business, Corporal."

"The Captain would like to see you and your dim-wit friends."

"The word is 'Dimbo', numb-nuts."

"Whatever...." Toady shrugs, picking at a sore on his elbow. "You guys are on special assignment . . . " He gives Beale a wicked leer, "With your buddy-buddy, hand-holding faggot native friends."

"I heard you're the closet-queer around here."

"Oh, you're so going to get yours!"

"Not in the ass, I hope."

Beale catches a quick shower, throws on his fatigues, and joins the rest of the Dimbos in the C.O.'s office. Nordoff has his head buried in his papers, and they wait for him to acknowledge them.

Charley leans over and whispers, "Did you get your gold bars?"

"Don't be so sarcastic. Your nice little *Em Tuy* got there first!"

"It wasn't Tuy. She spent the night with me."

"The *whole* night?"

"Curfew until dawn."

"What about *before* curfew?"

"She was working."

"Did you see her?"

"Well, not *every fricking minute*, Ong Be...."

By now they have forgotten Nordoff and are engaged in a full-blown argument. "Ranley *said -!*"

"Screw 'Ranley said'! He was all doped up! And if you were so concerned you should have gone right away. Where *did* you go anyway?"

"Ranley's lay is *TROUBLE*, Charley!"

"Yaa, hooo, look who's the big expert on women now!"

"Yeah, Beale," Mad Denny grins. "Answer the man's question. Where were you last night anyway, that you couldn't go over to good old Ranley's place?"

Beale's face goes beet red, and he looks at the floor without answering.

"Ahh-HAH! The old double-standard!"

"It wasn't just any girl -"

"The respectable man caught in the cat-house again!"

The captain clears his throat, "Ahh-HEM! Must I hear all about your sordid little affairs before we begin?"

"No, sir." Beale straightens up and sits stiffly in his chair, wishing Ranley were there.

The C.O. clears his throat, "Men, I want you to work with ARVN Intelligence on a daily basis. You'll have to work off base, in a secure area, of course, but with no other G.I.'s around. It is my hope that you can gain their trust, maybe learn some things we're not picking up through normal channels."

"What will we be doing, sir?", Beale asks.

"I don't know. They won't tell me. Just *what* you'll be doing isn't the point, exactly. I'll want a report of how they do their intelligence work. Whatever you can pick up."

"They're not going to tell us anything, sir. . . "

The captain leans back and gives him an impatient, exasperated look, "Why not, Specialist Beale?"

"They trust us as much as we do them."

"What about the alert, sir?" Charley is grasping at straws, "I mean, shouldn't we be staying here?"

"Forget it. We're not going to Red. The Air Force just threw a little hootenanny north of the DMZ. Any more questions?"

Charley reaches for one last straw, "Any chance of a transfer to the P.I, sir?

"Only you could say that with a straight face, soldier."

155

CHAPTER NINETEEN

"Nice of them to pack us a bag lunch," Larky says, his voice heavy with sleep.

Charley gives him a gloomy nod, "When I want a peanut butter-and-jelly sandwich for my last supper, I know who to call."

There is a distant, wild call, "FUUUUUCKKKK THE AAAAAAARRRRRRMMMMMMYYYYYY!!"

Beale sighs his relief, "Just in time. Here comes the Grey Snail."

A navy bus grinds to a halt in front of the White Shack. It is an ordinary school bus painted battleship gray, and customized with stiff chicken wire bolted to the windows to keep the grenades out. The bus is about half-full of bored non-coms and warranty officers. Most are dozing while one or two are reading a new issue of Stars & Stripes. One grizzled first sergeant, brows knit, is looking through a month-old Newsweek that has been pawed by many hands.

The road to Bien Hoa is considered secure, so the bus travels alone without escort vehicles, the driver grinding his way through the gears until he finally gets up to his cruising speed of 44 miles per hour. The Snail rolls past wide paddies, all drenched and deserted in the continuing downpour. The bus takes a slow roll through one ARVN checkpoint where grinning ARVN guards wave them on without stopping them.

Beale stares unbelievingly at the countryside. He has little idea what they are doing outside

Saigon, but he doesn't like it. One day before, the Senate of the United States had declared its unfriendly intentions against the North Vietnamese, and yet everything he sees is sputtering on with no apparent change. There is no D-Day, no lightning from the skies, no Hiroshima. It is business as usual.

The usual thick, gray blanket of clouds covers the country. Planes roar into the thick air from Tan Son Nhut or from offshore carriers safe out in the South China Sea, and fly long distances to launch radar-guided rockets at unseen targets. Whenever the fog lifts even a few hundred feet, the HU1B choppers whirl up from their concrete aprons like angry green mantis bugs.

Supplies travel in the same truck convoys along the major roads, heading on Route 1 north along the coast to Nha Trang, then further north to Tuy Hoa, Qui Nhon, Quang Ngai, Da Nang, and finally Hue, ancient capital of all of Vietnam. They also go south from Saigon along Route 4 to the towns of the delta, My Tho, Soc Trang, Vinh Loi, and finally Buan Long at the tip of the Ca Mau Peninsula. Some are attacked or fired on; most will make it to their destination, some will not.. River gunboats, flat-bottomed and fast, speed up and down the rivers, spraying the banks with their daily ration of ammo.

But something is new: The first of 5,000 combat grunts have arrived, the ones President Johnson has promised will put an end to this "outsider aggression on sovereign South Vietnamese soil". Beale has seen a few groups of them near the runway, sitting on their duffle bags in makeshift canvas shelters, confidently cleaning their new M-16's and sharpening the hone on their knives, all gung-ho to get out in the slop. Ranley had told Beale when they arrived it would mark the end of the age of the military advisor. From now on, he'd said, it was kick-butt time. But this only confused Beale more. Nobody on the bus was armed.

The grey snail is almost past a low structure hidden behind some tropical trees and bushes before Beale sees the faded sign that reads ARVN 194th Intelligence Unit. He yells at the driver, who hits the brakes.

"Too Bad, Ong Be", Mad Denny grins, "we were all hoping you'd miss it."

They tumble out of the bus and look around. It's disappointmg: The ARVN version of the White Shack is a tin-roofed Quonset hut sided front and back with whitewashed cement blocks.

"Must be the wrong place - where's the tiger cages?" Charley looks around, half expecting to see a row of the dreaded little cells where – the rumors circulating around Davis Station insist - prisoners are reduced to animals.

A voice answers him in English, a low voice with a halting, hissing French flavor, "Tiger cages in back. Only a foolish fool would leave zem out by road." It comes from a man standing almost out of sight behind a large umbrella fixed next to a fat rubber tree growing in front of the Quonset hut. "Also we have other form of oriental torture, including water-drip on head and burning bamboo splinters, learned from old Charley Chan movies." The man stands at attention, and opens a smaller yellow umbrella over his head. He watches the four young Americans with an air that seems friendly and yet superior and disdainful. "I am jus' kidding", he says in a way that leaves the Americans uncertain, "I am Colonel Phun."

Beale steps forward and introduces his small squad. They have been instructed by their C.O. not to salute. The natty colonel clicks his heels and gives them a slight bow. "Pleeze to meet you."

"You speak English very well, sir."

"I speak *French* very well, having gone to L'Ecole Francaise since a small child."

"Ahh, the French.

"Yesss, ze *French*."

From first glance, Beale sees this is an unusual man, a sharp dresser in his tailored uniform, standing just over five feet tall in his high-topped boots of black patent leather. He wears soft-skinned leather gloves.. His fine, lowland Vietnamese features are plumped out from good eating, and marred only by a huge wart on his left cheek out of which grows twenty or thirty mixed white-and-black hairs that are at least six inches long. Although the rest of his hair is jet black, he also has a small shock of white hairs growing from near the front of his hairline that suggest another, larger growth underneath his hair. He combs these hairs back in a long white streak. "Follow me, pleeze", he says.

He leads them to a single room, isolated from the main flow of business in the Quonset hut. They enter the building through a secondary door that leads directly into the room, crowded with has five bare desks. This room has an inner door, but this is barred shut.

"This is *it*?" Beale asks, disappointment

159

obvious in his tone.

Colonel Phun gives him a small, bitter smile. "We should like, per-haps, to involve you more in our *important* affairs.... but since your leaders chose not to allow us access to your famous 'White Shack'...." He shrugs, his voice trailing off.

"What the devil!" Larky says indignantly, "they let native cleaning ladies go in there - I don't see why *you* can't?

"Even so - this is true, but I do not need it repeated to me....", the colonel says smoothly, chill rebuff clear in his voice. "Here is a stack of messages we have. They await your insight and your clarifications."

"We were told we were going to work with Arvin interpreters."

"Non. Here you will use your famous decoding skills, learned at far-away Fort George G. Meade, at the *encroyable* Puzzle Palace - another zone too busy to entertain my personal inspection." His bitterness hangs in the air like a bad smell after he leaves, carefully closing the door behind him.

The Dimbos huddle uncertainly in a small group in the center of the room. Beale takes a look at the small stack of papers the Colonel has left for them, and Charley finally sits on one of the desks, wiping the rain off his shoes with the napkin from his lunch sack.

"I don't know - I've got a bad feeling about this."

Mad Denny snorts, "You got a bad feeling about everything! We go to the EMC, you got a bad feeling; we go downtown, you got a bad feeling -"

160

"The Half-Moon Bar blew up! We were two blocks away!"

"One bar out of a thousand." Beale shakes his head, lighting up a Marlboro.

"You go to take a shit, you got a bad feeling - somebody might have put a grenade in the john! Let me tell you, Charley, you can't go checking every toilet bowl in Vietnam!"

"Beale can", Larky says. "He's careful about stuff like that."

Beale looks up from the stack of messages, shaking his head, "Look at this mess - Arvin intelligence is just as bad as ours!"

Charley rubs harder at an annoying spot on his shoes, "I bet there *are* tiger cages out back, with men crouched over because they can't stand, crawling around in their own shit!"

Mad Denny hisses, imitating Colonel Phun's French-Vietnamese accented English, "Yessss, I am your tour guide of ze *Oriental Way*. Torture chambers on ze left. An' straight ahead, ze elect'ric dong zap-pair!"

Beale gives Denny a warning glance, "The guy out there's *weird,* Denny, even for a zip."

"He's just an Arvin neo-Nazi. Think of him as a Nordoff in dink-skin."

By this time, Beale has sorted two or three messages from the pile in front of him. He hands the rest of the stack to Charley, "Well, come on. Let's get at it."

"Not me." Charley leans back and stretches with a big yawn. "I'm on strike."

Mad Denny leans back in his own chair and closes his eyes, "Good idea. Me too."

Beale sets the stack of messages back on his

161

desk, "Christ, guys. We've got to make it look like we're doing something here!"

Charley laughs, "Why? You can do in five minutes what takes me two hours. I haven't decoded anything since I got to Nam."

"I'm telling you - that Colonel Phun is strange!"

"They're *all* strange."

Charley shakes his head, "I don't decode for some arrogant Asian dictator who looks like he's trying to make it in an old Bogey flick! I don't do it!"

Larky grins, "Shoot, buddy, you don't decode for *anybody*."

Mad Denny snaps to his feet, saluting an imaginary person in the direction of the locked door, using the old, open-handed French Colonial salute and clicking his heels, "*Vung! Vung! Colonel Phung!*"

Beale gives it a last try, ignoring Denny's clowning and talking to Charley, "Well, you better *pretend* then - we're a long way from home." He is rewarded as a shadow of worry slides over Charley's face.

But Mad Denny isn't impressed. "Awww, tell it to the lifers, Ong Be. These dinks don't know Brasso from a bung-hole." He begins to sing, "There's a Phun-gus/among us!"

Charley has gotten out his yellow note-pad, but instead of reaching for the stack of intercepts, he tears off a sheet of lined yellow paper and begins to build a paper airplane. He joins in, slowly at first, "A Phun-gus/among us, A Phun-gus/among us!" As they sing, he launches his plane, and Mad Denny throws a crumpled up paper

162

ball, trying to knock it down in mid-flight and making a POW! anti-aircraft noise as he throws.

Beale is losing his cool. "Come *on! COOL* it, you guys! Remember, The *Ant does not kick the Elephant!*

"Oh, yeah, ancient Vietnamese wisdom!"

Mad Denny is on another roll, "Allll Riiiiiight, Ladies and Germs, it's the Vietnamese Culture Hour, featuring wise sayings from dink writers, intellectuals, and monks! And here's one for Ong Be!! *After eating soup, piss in the bowl!"*

Charley chuckles, coming out of his blue funk, "Yeah, me too, I've got one for you, Beale! *Where one virgin poops, five flowers bloom!"*

Mad Denny chuckles appreciatively, "Not bad, not bad, sweetheart, but now it's time to go for the big banana - here's my all-time favorite, the saying with the zip-lock on first place: *Heroes are people we fear at first - then come men who only have a piece of cloth for their pants!"*

"Aww, no fair! You just made that up!"

"Nope. Honest-to-Christ, it means something to these dinky-daos...."

Beale isn't making any headway with all the commotion going on around him. He sighs and pushes back from his desk, "This stuff is so garbled it's useless." He holds up the dictionary he's brought with him, "Hoa's can't even make any sense out of it."

"Hurraaay! That's the first sense you've made since we've got here!"

"And these transmissions are *months* old!"

Charley frowns, "Look, Ong Be. These dinks don't want to work with us -- and *we* understand their language, sort of. Can you imagine how it's

163

going to be when the grunt-faces get over here?"

"That's not the point. This stuff is *garbage*!"

"Okay, Ong Be, we believe you. So what? What are we supposed to do about it?"

Beale leans back in his chair, sets his glasses on his chest and rubs his eyes, "I don't know.... it just feels like we're missing something." Stretching like that, he looks up and spots a mike crudely wired next to the ceiling light. "Ohhhhh, fuck....", he whispers, "fuckfuckfuck...." He snaps to an alert posture and waves frantically to the Dimbos, "Okay, guys! Let's all get back to our translations!"

None of them catch on, in spite of his wild gestures. Mad Denny grins at him like he is an absolute fool, "You forget, my dear Beale, we haven't done any yet!"

Beale glares at him, jabbing a finger, pointing at the ceiling, "Look, goddamn it, let's get to work! We've got to help our allies, the brave Arvins, win this war!"

Charley gives him a sad, disgusted look, "You don't know when something's funny and when it isn't, do you?"

"Yeah, Beale - just when we thought you were human, you had to go and get serious about the war again.

Looking around the room in desperation, Beale finds a big marker in one dusty corner. He begins scribbling furiously on his yellow pad.

Charley begins making another airplane. "Yeah, Beale", he adds amiably, "One thing we demand is consistency. If you're going to be a prick, be a prick all the time."

Beale interrupts his writing to soundlessly

mouth the words, "MIKE - IN - CEILING!"

Mad Denny scratches his head, "Well, I'll be a hand-holding faggot dink -- Look, Beale's mouth is going, but no sound is coming out!"

Larky grins, "He must have caught an oral disease on Hundred P Alley!"

"Unless it's anal, working its way backwards through his system...."

Beale holds up his sign, which spells out *WERE BUGGED! MIKE IN CEILING!*, in huge block letters. He waves his note-pad, pointing frantically at the bug in the ceiling.

Charley catches on first, "Ohhhh - oh - oh -" He starts singing, pointing in the same direction as Beale, "Ohhh, say can you see, by the dawn's early light." He drags Mad Denny over and points out the bug. As soon as Denny sees it he joins in, singing along with Charley, "What so proudly we hail, by the twilight's last gleaming...."

Charley has a new idea, as a sudden flush of Vietnamese races through his desperate brain, "*Hang cong Nam he sinh!*"

"Right! The old Zip Anthem!"

"*De choi Viet Nam! De choi Viet Nam! De choi he sing Viet Nam!*" Denny and Charley look at each other, waiting for the next words.

"I don't know any more of their goddamn song."

"Me neither. Hey, give me some of those messages, Ong Be!"

"*Moi, aussi. Hoan ho,* the Republic!"

"Yeah, *hoan ho!*"

For a while they lapse into silence, busy with their messages. Charley leans over Beale's desk, "Hand me that Hoa's, would you? I've got a real

165

pisser here."

Mad Denny plays to the mike in a louder than usual voice, "You know, those dirty V.C. really *are* rotten baby killers. They make me furious."

"Yup, that's right", Larky says as he finally gets into the swing of things. "God an' Buddha are both on our side. That's why I'm so glad to be over here helping with the war effort."

Denny has a thought that makes him break out in a cold sweat. "*AND*", he says,, remembering his scoffing around of a few minutes ago, "the term 'gus', which comes from 'gusto' of course, is a term of great respect."

"Oh, yes - that's right! If we were Japanese, we would call Colonel Phun - someone we *deeply* admire - Colonel Phun-san!"

Denny gives their effort a hollow little laugh, "Ha, ha, ha - that's *right*, but in English, we say Phun-*gus*!"

"Well, I'm just proud to be serving with him in this noble cause, defending the frontiers of freedom, as JFK used to say -"

It is mid-afternoon before Colonel Phun returns. By this time, Beale has deciphered the few messages that could be worked out of the garbled mess they have been given. The Colonel ignores his nervous offering, instead pacing back in forth in front of the Dimbos like he is deep in thought. Finally he pulls Beale aside, out of earshot of the others.

"Ze French....", he starts, clipping off his words with a neat precision. His face works with some vague inner emotion, and then he has control of himself again, "Ze French were always so much better zan us, it was, as you say, a 'big deal' to try

166

to be French. *Mon Dieu,* I learn every zing from zose great, hairy big-noses! Where grows ze best *Bordeaux.* Where comes from ze *mellieur fromage.* Ze name of ze *capital* of all ze *Provencal Francaise.* Why is a German a Nazi. All about *Francaise.* . . " The man gave out a short, unhappy laugh, "And zen zay left us. Not much good now, my *Francaise*, eh?"

Beale shrugs, "I guess not. . ."

Ze *Japanaise* come and treat us like *class inferior* in our own country."

What about the Chinese?" Beale is trying to be helpful, to keep the conversation going, but when he mentions the hated *Trong Hoa*, the giant to the north, the colonel's face goes smooth like glass, "Soooo. . . you study our history. . . "

"Well, sure. . . history, language, culture, art, law."

"And you believe you understand us."

"We're *trying*, believe me!"

The colonel gives him a curt nod, then turns away and renews his pacing. After a short while, he pulls Beale aside again. "You Americans are so - *so full of life!* Everything eez jokes to you...."

"Look, sir - I guess you're not impressed with us. That's your right. But we don't like being bugged. And those messages you gave us were crap!"

The colonel's smooth face takes on a sinister expression, "How good of you to provide zis *information*."

"Yeah. Well, we'd better get cleaned up here if we're going to catch the old Grey Snail back to the 3rd."

"You are not going back transport by zee

Escargot Grey."

"No? Why not?"

"I have personally made *arrangement especial* for your convenience."

"Oh, no thank you, sir!" Beale gives him a crisp salute, "We're *supposed* to take the bus!"

Colonel Phun takes Beale by the arm, his experienced fingers finding the pressure point near the elbow and effortlessly turning him, "You will find zis most *complimentair* for your *education*."

The other Dimbos angrily get to their feet as they see the colonel escorting Beale out the door.

"Hey, wait a minute, Bozo!", Mad Denny says, getting into his karate stance. But an entire squad of ARVN soldiers pours in the open door and there is really nothing he can do. The Dimbos are quickly surrounded and escorted to a half dozen jeeps.

The colonel jumps into the front seat of the lead jeep and snaps his fingers. Beale reluctantly climbs in back. Seeing they have no choice, the Dimbos all squeeze in the jeeps, along with a half dozen rifle-carrying ARVN soldiers.

The colonel gives a short, pig-like grunt as he folds his yellow umbrella. The grim-faced *Quoc Canh*, a Vietnamese military police sergeant with a white stripe on his helmet and white armbands with QC in big, black letters, starts the jeep. Colonel Phun gives a little wave with his umbrella. Gears clash and the jeeps lurch forward, splashing through potholes and muddy ruts..

Beale's fears that they are being spirited to some secret retreat in the countryside are only heightened as the jeeps slide to a halt before a gate that leads directly out onto the Bien Hoa airstrip.

168

Vietnamese guards give them a bored stare, step aside the rusty barbed-wire gate and wave them in.

Beale takes a deep breath and slowly lets the air out of his cheeks. There isn't another American anywhere in sight. It is plain enough for him: the Dimbos are in the deep shit.

CHAPTER TWENTY

An ARVN Jolly Green helicopter squats on its mechanical legs between large and shiny puddles on the concrete apron, seeming to watch its new passengers like a plump water bug while it waits to gobble them up. Its huge rotor rotates on idle, supercharging the already moisture-laden air with a swirling mist. The four Dimbos, led by Colonel Phun and followed by several of the QC, crouch and run for the side door as directed.

The inside is Spartan and unlit. The pilot and co-pilot are in a cockpit up front. The rectangular passenger compartment is ringed with bench seats, with a hole-punch steel floor in the empty center. There are small seats on each side of the door, and the colonel takes one of these. He motions to the Americans to strap themselves in on the bench in the rear corner farthest from the door.

Charley sees that the complicated strapping system, which may have doubled as a safety belt, almost certainly operates on the pulley system used by paratroopers. Fear freezes the trembling in his guts and he jumps up, "Hey, we don't have any goddamn chutes!"

Beale grabs his arm, "Calm down, Charley! Nothing's going to happen to us. Trust me on this one!"

"Some choice I've got!"

The QC's hold their .30 caliber carbines easily, grinning at Charley. The colonel waves him back to his seat, "Of course we have no parachute on zis ship. Zees are not necessaire for *ze friends* of ze

170

Vietnam Republic." He looks them over while caressing the long black-and-white mole whiskers on his cheek.

Charley slides back to his spot between Beale and Larky on the cracked brown leatherette bench, "At least I'll be taking you sad sacks with me."

Mad Denny gets a wild glint in his eye, and starts humming the Vietnamese National Anthem in the same key as the engine whine. Larky nervously taps his foot and looks out the open door.

Beale glances over to where Larky was looking and sees the thick, gray clouds over Bien Hoa slowly part. There is little enough reason for it; just some atmospheric quirk, and yet a tiny spot of blue sky appears far overhead. For a moment, the afternoon sunlight bathes the rims of the fluffy cloud edges in bright gold, and causes a rainbow to hang in the water swirl at the rotor tips. From his square window in the helicopter, Beale sees the landscape transformed into lush greens, and hope rises in his mind. That same sun shines on the far-away U.S., on states like Wyoming where the cowboys roam and California where the surfers ride the big waves, on New York City and the fields of Iowa corn. It can't be such a bad world after all.

But the elements have played their little trick; the light wavers and dims, the clouds close back up, and Beale is again flung down his dark tunnel into the reality of their uncertain future.

They wait in silence for almost an hour until finally a battered, black Ford van pulls up next to their helicopter. Two more carbine-toting QC's escort a group of four Vietnamese teenagers, hustling them along with their gun butts until they are half-running for the helicopter.

The Dimbos eye the newcomers uncertainly as they climb on board. They don't look like hardened criminals, but each has his hands cuffed behind him. They are well dressed for young Vietnamese and look like prosperous Saigon Cowboys in their cheap Hong Kong suits, shiny polyester slacks and bright-colored windbreakers. All four wear sunglasses, and their wrists and hands flash with gold wristwatches and rings. The QC sergeant snarls at them and has his men uncuff their wrists, and then orders them to take seats away from the Americans.

Without further hesitation, the engine roar deepens, and the plump olive craft rises from the runway, heading up toward the cloud level, which is only about 1,500 feet over their heads.

Cold drafts howl and rain spatters in through the open door. Beale shivers in his clammy fatigues, wishing for his poncho. The nearly deafening rotor sound changes in pitch, and Beale sees out the open door that they have leveled off and are almost directly under the clouds.

After a few moments, the colonel breaks his silence, gesturing fiercely at the closest cowboy, "Get this one to stand!" The QC sergeant quickly does as he was ordered.

Colonel Phun looks intently at each of the Dimbos, finally centering his attention on Beale, "Have you ze chill from ze weather?"

"N-no. I'm okay."

The colonel points a calm finger at the cowboy standing in front of them, rubbing his hands together and blowing on them. "Give the

American your wind-breaker!" The teenager sullenly declines, and the colonel gestures to the nearest QC, who smashes the standing youth in the face with the butt of his weapon. "Give him your wind-breaker!"

The teen still declines, and two soldiers roughly strip the windbreaker from the him as he falls to the ground, all the while trying to cradle his broken and bloody nose in his hands. Colonel Phun himself takes the windbreaker from one of the soldiers, "Here. I insist. Allow me." Beale is directed to stand and the colonel helps him into the wind-breaker.. The colonel pats him on the back, "Ahhh. You see, eez over-size for a Vietnamese. Doubtless stolen from ze rack, hard to find a good fit zat way, no?" He beams, laughing at his own joke.

The helicopter leans forward and travels on, still just under the cloud ceiling. Beale sits, hunched forward in his new windbreaker, dividing his attention between the other passengers and quick looks out the window. To his tremendous relief, he sees they are approaching a large city, "Charley - look! It must be Saigon! The old Grey Snail is still back there, probably just leaving Bien Hoa!"

"We ain't in the clear yet, Ong Be. I got a bad feeling about this...."

As Charley speaks, they hear a subtle change in rotor pitch, and then they are hanging motionless in the air, almost two thousand feet over the clumps of tiny toy houses far below them.

The colonel steps quickly across the compartment to the bloody, cowering cowboy who had been forced to give Beale his windbreaker. He shouts at the teenager, his staccato Vietnamese punching in over the noise of the engines.

Beale misses the colonel's questions, but he sees little things he will never forget; the kid is wearing snakeskin cowboy boots and a gold-banded wristwatch. He has on a pink shirt, now soaked from the rain and spotted with blood from his face. He stares at the colonel, then shrugs his shoulders and grins defiantly.

"*Toi khong biet*", he says, twisting his mouth so the words come out like he is spitting.

"You don't know zis? You don't *know?*" The colonel says in English, slapping the kid hard so his head jerks sideways. Blood flies from his nose, and Beale sees angry red lines imprinted on his face. The colonel's voice rises, angry threats filling the air.

"Judas Priest, what's he saying?" Larky whispers.

Beale shakes his head, "I dunno. He's talking too fast."

The teenager with the snakeskin boots is crying, but he manages to snort back his tears, and then he spits in the colonel's face.

There is a finality to the act, and the colonel accepts it without question or further interrogation.. He takes a linen handkerchief from his pocket and carefully daubs the bloody spittle from his own face. He motions to the nearest pair of his men with one hand and then turns away from the teenager, who is now huddled on the floor while blood runs in a steady stream from his nose and soaks into his shirt. One QC casually covers the remaining cowboys with his carbine; two others take the bloody kid by the arms. The teenager might have thought they were just going to move him out of the way, so the colonel could work on one of his friends. But in one motion they pull him the short distance across the compartment and fling him backwards out the open door.

Neither the Saigon cowboys or the Americans are.ready for that, and it comes as the biggest shock of all to the victim. Beale sees the doomed kid's look of astonishment; he finds himself exchanging a stunned glance with the cowboy. Beale has one last glimpse of the western boots falling away from the door. The move is so unexpected that the teenager is gone before anybody even thinks to protest.

The helicopter hangs in the air. Colonel Phun sits back on his seat, casually crossing one leg and looking at the blank wall on the other side of the compartment, as if he is meditating or praying. "We have ze very old *civilization, Specialiste Cinq.* Ze *Francaise* have ze iron maiden, ze hanging, ze dungeon. *Mais,* zay have not been at war *constantement* for over two thousand years."

"You just killed-!" Charley starts to shout, jumping up as if he is going to attack somebody. The QC's swing their carbines around to cover him, and Beale cuts him off with a sharp gesture, "*Quiet,* Ong Nha!"

Larky pulls Charley back to sit by him, imploring Beale, "Lordy, Ong Be, we can't understand him, he talks English like a frog - what's he *saying,* buddy?"

Beale feels the world spinning off its axis, and he tries hard to keep from vomiting. He struggles for the words to explain, "He's teaching us to - to think like a Vietnamese."

"Ohh."

The colonel nods, a faint smile flickering across his face. He says nothing more, allowing the lesson to grow heavy in their minds while the remaining prisoners jabber and whine like dogs, furious at the fate of their unfortunate comrade and frightened for their own lives.

"Silence!" Colonel Phun commands. The sound of his voice cuts the air like a whip, and the three remaining cowboys fall silent instantly, as if he has cut off their windpipes. "I will speak in our native tongue . . . but slowly, for the benefit of the Americans." He turns to the cowboys, "We know of you. You are called the Da Cao Four. You do not do your evil things directly. You buy people who do evil things."

One of the cowboys protests, "No. We not VC."

The colonel smiles, "Who is a VC and who is not a VC? Is one who takes advantage, buying and selling to both sides for profit, a VC?"

"No! We are loyal to the government!"

The colonel looks sadly at his boots, "What a complicated situation. I would like to believe you . . . but you were all seen in the presence of a man we know as John Vincent, also known as Rotten Tooth or The Loner. You delivered several packages to this man, packages we suspect held explosives."

"No! We did not know his name! We delivered boxes of whiskey to him!"

The others quickly agree, "Yes, American whiskey from their PX!"

Colonel Phun shakes his head, still looking at his boots, "We think it was *ep plastique!*"

176

"You can't prove that!"

The colonel nods, "True. Rotten Tooth slipped away with his precious packages before we moved in."

The cowboys take heart and regain a shadow of their old cockiness, "So you have no right to take us like this! You killed our comr - our friend! It was an act of murder!"

The colonel sighs, "It ees not so simple. How we teach our enemies? Are you even able of teaching? Perhaps *non!* Perhaps you are most useful as a lesson to others."

"We will gladly teach them!"

"I'm sure. But here is an idea: Perhaps you can teach both our friends and enemies at zee same moment. At this moment, even as we speak, our excellent pilot positions us very carefully; we must account for the wind, but what a nice lesson if one of the Da Cao Four were to present himself on just the right patio or front lawn – in Da Cao!"

Larky paws at Beale's arm, "We got to stop this, Be! *Thou shalt not kill!*"

Beale stares numbly at his friend, "They're already dead, Larky. Don't be the sacrificial lamb for nothing."

"What?" Larky's startled gaze wavers and drops.

Beale is past the sickness now, in that strange overdrive where truth hangs in crystal shards all around him and every sound rings clear like a bell. "Lemonlips," he says, "know no slips."

"Beale, you're over the edge," Charley says.

"No, I'm not." He stares intently at his friends. "Eight need not die here. Only four - one for each of us."

177

"But - *why?*" Larky wails.

"So we learn our lesson."

"That's crazy! You're just as Godless as he is!" But even as he speaks, Charley knows Beale is right. He blows out an angry breath and slouches back in his seat.

The colonel nods his satisfaction, and the QCs lower the muzzles of their carbines. Colonel Phun runs his smooth fingernails along the white hairs on his head and then points to another of the cowboys and again speaks slowly and clearly in Vietnamese, "Now, Little Scum Number 2, *you* have a chance, your one, single, little chance - I want *information*!"

The second cowboy is wearing a gaudy open-necked shirt of spun polyester. Five or six thin, golden chains show on his bare chest. His face, under the two dark spots of his sunglasses, is gray with fear. He licks his dry lips, "Khong. Khong. Toi khong biet! I don't know anything!"

His voice cracks then, because the colonel has already nodded and in another moment he being dragged to the waiting doorway.

Larky whispers, "Lordy, they can't jest -?"

Mad Denny nods, "Sure they can."

The cowboy, already at the doorway, yells frantically, "The piasters! Dollaire *My kim*! No VC! No VC!"

And then he too is gone, his scream falling with him away from the rush of wind in the open doorway.

The colonel smooths his hair and turns to the next cowboy, "How about you, Little Scum Number 3?"

This one is wearing a light seersucker jacket,

178

cream-colored pants and white shoes, all of which had been muddied and dampened in his hasty transit to the helicopter. He walks to the door, spits in the Colonel's face, and with a quick look of disdain, jumps before anyone can lay a hand on him.

After that the cabin is filled with screams as the last cowboy disintegrates into a gibbering idiot. He babbles about his excellent connections, about specific checkpoints and key meeting places. But the colonel quietly shakes his head after each point he makes, rejecting everything as he recites it.

This one is nineteen or twenty, older than the three who have gone before him. He wears a flashy suit of plaid brown, black and tan, and his plump fingers are heavy with gold rings. His forehead is beaded with sweat; as he argues for his life, his sunglasses slip to the end of his nose, and then fall to the floor.

Carefully retrieving the glasses as the last cowboy rattles on, Colonel Phun thoughtfully studies his own reflection in the mirrored lenses, carefully touching up his wart-whiskers. Then he intentionally cracks the frames in two, and throws the pieces on the ground.

This simple gesture has such an air of finality that a dark stain spreads down the cowboy's pants from his crotch. The colonel shrugs and snaps his fingers, and two QC begin to drag the last victim from his seat. He struggles and kicks while he screams, but their path across the floor of the helicopter is unstoppable, and they are soon at the door itself. As they try to throw him from the craft, he flips himself through some miracle of contortion and lands sideways on the floor with his feet locked in a scissors hold around one of the QC's legs, his rigid body unwilling to fit itself out the door.

In the next instant the scene goes wildly out of control. The QC who is clamped between the cowboy's legs panics and rains short, ineffectual blows on the kid's head and shoulders with his rifle butt. The colonels composure snaps like a violin string and he yells like a madman, *"Chet roi! CHET ROI!!"*

The Dimbos stare; it is like watching a stupid B movie where everybody does crazy, unmotivated things they would never do in real life: From his seat across the compartment from the door, one of the QC's takes careful aim and fires between his companions at point blank range. The shot rings out like a thunderclap and smoke fills the compartment as a red stain blossoms on the back of the plaid suit. Unfortunately, another QC's hand had been in the line of fire, and the bullet went through it, too. The wounded QC whines and grabs his bleeding fingers, leaving his fellows to their own resources. The last of the doomed cowboys is slumped half out the door, a bullet in his back. The wind whips a froth of his blood to speckle the faces and clothing of the Americans and the Vietnamese soldiers left in the helicopter. As the wounded man weakens, the other soldier quickly frees his own leg and kicks him out the door.

The Jolly Green helicopter hangs in the air over Gia Dinh for a few more minutes. Colonel Phun regains his composure, sitting across from the door like an odd little Buddha with his heavy black head of hair uniquely streaked with white,

180

the C.O.'s counterpart at the Shack, fumbles through his orders file and knocks half a chicken sandwich on the floor in the process. He gives up in disgust, "Must have been one of crap-head Nordoff's wild solo stunts."

"Does he have the right to do that?"

"He *thinks* he does, and he's done it before. . . " The captain sounds irritated. Beale can't tell if it is about Nordoff or the sandwich, which the captain scoops up like a softball and throws in his dented trashcan.

Beale goes back to his desk and manages to bully his way through the 3rd's phone system to Clark Air Force Base. He is incredibly lucky; Ranley is in the middle of a "pick-session", three nurses going over him from top to bottom, tweezing the bits of debris from his peppered body and cleaning the infections, but somebody hands him the phone and he sounds to Beale like he is glad for the distraction. He winces whenever the nurses probe deeper than usual, and his sober warning comes clear over the line, "Don't say anything important, Ong Be - land lines being what they are."

"I - uhh - right, Red Dog. You getting back here soon?"

"*Ouch!* Couple of months. They're sending me to Bethesda, and if I'm okay, to the Palace to straighten out Harris who is on another of his god dam power trips. Why, what's up?"

"We got in a little trouble. The C.O. assigned us to ARVN intelligence, and a situation came up and now we need your advice."

Ranley's anger came boiling over the line, "To Colonel Phun? Asshole Nordoff *knows* he's not

185

supposed to send my guys over there! *Ouch!!*"

"Phun put us in a room with a hidden mike -"

"And got insulted at what he heard! Slimy zip son-of-a-bitch always does that."

"Not like this. He gave us a helicopter lift back from Bien Hoa and on the way back he murdered four Saigon cowboys."

Ranley made a strange noise half way between a whistle and a cry of pain, "*Ouuuu!* Tell me more."

"He sort-of interrogated them one-by-one, and then he called them V.C. and his men threw them out."

There was a long pause, and then Beale heard the thin voice start again from far away across the China Sea, "Maybe I know what you're thinking, Beale, but you're not going to nail a man like Phun. The best you can do is back him off."

"You're telling me he's done things like this before."

"There's a dung-heap of evidence that when Ngo Dinh Diem was assassinated, he was there. He belongs to the Vietnamese equivalent of the C.I.A. Spiders and bats feed in the dark. They can do anything they want. You should be ready, just in case."

Beale's blood ran cold, "Ready for what?"

"For *anything*. Chances are, the Americans won't ever hear about this officially. They don't *want* to hear about it. And your only weapon is Colonel Phun won't want them to. He's been up on charges before, he can't stand any more exposure." Ranley paused, thinking it over. "What are the specifics? Anything at all that you remember."

"Well, Phun called the cowboys the Da Cao

186

sitting fat-lipped, tranquil and inward thinking. The three QC's huddle quietly in one corner, jabbering softly as they tie up their f's bloody hand with a dirty rag.

After a while, the colonel addresses Beale again, "You Americans with ze funny, funny ways!" His voice is cloaked in soft bitterness, "Ezz so easy to be happy when you have ze riches, to be brave when you can hide behind ze great power! We are only Vietnamese, zis is only one small but ancient country....yet we humble sons of *Nam Viet* can perhaps teach you one thing, how not to laugh at zat which you do not understand...."

Beale nods and says nothing. He is in the grasp of his old, familiar feelings. His hands tremble so violently that he crosses his arms and tried to hide them under his armpits. The Dimbos don't notice; they are all in shock, staring out the open door, or down at the urine-and-blood spattered floor, or straight ahead at nothing.

Charley looks at his wits end. "Ong Be!", he whispers, "He's just letting us hang up here!"

Beale moves over on the seat and manages to get one arm around his friend, "I'm sorry I got us into all this. Honestly, I'm truly sorry...." Nobody teases him about being the scribe and getting it all down, or blames him for them ending up in Nam. The four of them hunch together in silence while the air whistles in the door, and the helicopter hangs under the cloud ceiling like a kid's plastic toy model on a string.

Finally the colonel gives another hand signal, and the craft swoops down in a long, graceful curve toward the outstretched concrete aprons of Tan Son Nhut.

CHAPTER TWENTY ONE

The Jolly Green lands and lets the Dimbos off at a Vietnamese Air Force compound within walking distance of the White Shack. By the time the four of them have cleared the perimeter of the overhead blades, they are half-running, afraid Colonel Phun might change his mind and try to keep them. They slow once the White Shack is within sight; they are too haggard and emotionally spent to keep up their pace. As they numbly trudge along, they see the Grey Snail pull past in the distance.

Larky stares straight ahead, "Human life means dirt to those godless bastards!"

Mad Denny screams his outrage, "And these are the *good* guys!"

Charley looks back over his shoulder to make sure they aren't being followed and trips and nearly falls on a rough spot on the runway apron. Beale reaches out and keeps him from falling, but he angrily shakes the helping hands away. "I'm never going back there again!" He glares at Beale, "And you can't make me!"

Beale shrugs, "They'll never ask us."

"How you figure?"

"Our Colonel Phun-gus just committed a major war crime. According to the Geneva Conventions, he could be tried and executed. And we saw it happen. That means we're witnesses."

"He might try to bump us off!"

"He's just a little slow. Wait until he figures it out."

"Naw, Ong Be. Not four members of the U.S. Intelligence community - he wouldn't be *that* stupid. . . would he?"

"To him we're just a bunch of crazy lingies. He doesn't know nobody would believe us anyway!"

By this time they are flipping their badges at the bored M.P. sprawled in front of the dark green metal door. "You guys are a *mess*! Is that blood on your faces?"

Charley waves a negligent hand at him, "Naw. Tomato juice. VC threw a grenade in the back end of the mess supply truck."

The M.P. sits bolt upright, "No Shit? I didn't hear anything about it! Were the steaks alright?"

"What steaks? Mess sergeants sell 'em on the black market."

"Ohhh. . . " The M.P. nods like Charley has spoken the gospel, and looks sadly after them, his disappointment obvious.

The first waves of cold air conditioning hit the Dimbos like a dive into an icy pool. Beale shrugs at the guard, who was looking to him to confirm or deny the news about the mess truck.

"Is it any wonder nobody believes us?" Beale says, "You guys *never, never NEVER* play it straight."

The night shift hasn't come on yet, so they make their way back to their workroom without seeing anyone, and wash up as best they can in the small lavatory. Beale goes first, and by the time the others came out he was in Captain Ball's office. It turned out nobody at the White Shack knew about their wild sally into the Vietnamese intelligence community. Captain Ball, who was

the C.O.'s counterpart at the Shack, fumbles through his orders file and knocks half a chicken sandwich on the floor in the process. He gives up in disgust, "Must have been one of crap-head Nordoff's wild solo stunts."

"Does he have the right to do that?"

"He *thinks* he does, and he's done it before. . . " The captain sounds irritated. Beale can't tell if it is about Nordoff or the sandwich, which the captain scoops up like a softball and throws in his dented trashcan.

Beale goes back to his desk and manages to bully his way through the 3rd's phone system to Clark Air Force Base. He is incredibly lucky; Ranley is in the middle of a "pick-session", three nurses going over him from top to bottom, tweezing the bits of debris from his peppered body and cleaning the infections, but somebody hands him the phone and he sounds to Beale like he is glad for the distraction. He winces whenever the nurses probe deeper than usual, and his sober warning comes clear over the line, "Don't say anything important, Ong Be - land lines being what they are."

"I - uhh - right, Red Dog. You getting back here soon?"

"*Ouch!* Couple of months. They're sending me to Bethesda, and if I'm okay, to the Palace to straighten out Harris who is on another of his god dam power trips. Why, what's up?"

"We got in a little trouble. The C.O. assigned us to ARVN intelligence, and a situation came up and now we need your advice."

Ranley's anger came boiling over the line, "To Colonel Phun? Asshole Nordoff *knows* he's not

supposed to send my guys over there! *Ouch!!*"

"Phun put us in a room with a hidden mike -"

"And got insulted at what he heard! Slimy zip son-of-a-bitch always does that."

"Not like this. He gave us a helicopter lift back from Bien Hoa and on the way back he murdered four Saigon cowboys."

Ranley made a strange noise half way between a whistle and a cry of pain, "*Ouuuu!* Tell me more."

"He sort-of interrogated them one-by-one, and then he called them V.C. and his men threw them out."

There was a long pause, and then Beale heard the thin voice start again from far away across the China Sea, "Maybe I know what you're thinking, Beale, but you're not going to nail a man like Phun. The best you can do is back him off."

"You're telling me he's done things like this before."

"There's a dung-heap of evidence that when Ngo Dinh Diem was assassinated, he was there. He belongs to the Vietnamese equivalent of the C.I.A. Spiders and bats feed in the dark. They can do anything they want. You should be ready, just in case."

Beale's blood ran cold, "Ready for what?"

"For *anything*. Chances are, the Americans won't ever hear about this officially. They don't *want* to hear about it. And your only weapon is Colonel Phun won't want them to. He's been up on charges before, he can't stand any more exposure." Ranley paused, thinking it over. "What are the specifics? Anything at all that you remember."

"Well, Phun called the cowboys the Da Cao

Four . . . and he accused them of getting explosives for Vincent John, or somebody like that."

"John Vincent – I think that's the son-of-a-bitch finally got me! *Ow - bastards!* I tell you, Beale, *some day* . . . Anyway, that's good he mentioned that - you guys would have no other way of knowing something restricted like that."

"We're Top Secret", Beale protested.

"Come on, Beale -- you know bands of information are vertical and very narrow. I only know because I used to do the town with a CIA guy. John Vincent is way out of your need-to-know. But what's important here - you have to move right away. Check the local newspapers. Sometimes they'll carry a story like that. You type your own report of what happened and stamp it CONFIDENTIAL. Stamp the newspapers CONFIDENTIAL, too . . . don't classify anything SECRET or TOP SECRET 'cause the C.O. won't be able to read them. But, see, he is cleared for CONFIDENTIAL. *Ouch - take it EASY, goddamn it!* No, not you, Beale. See, Beale, you build a file on Colonel Phun. It's going to be kind-of thin, and you'll have to bluff your way through, but from what I've seen you Dimbos are good at that sort of thing."

"Are we going to be okay?"

"That's up to you. Just remember, you may not know much, but Nordoff doesn't know anything at all."

After Ranley hangs up, Beale explains what is needed to the Dimbos, who get the idea right away. Charley sits at a typewriter and backdates an unsigned report to three days after Diem's death, written with plenty of hearsay, but placing

187

Colonel Phun in or near the Saigon Cathedral at about the time Diem was stabbed to death. They had all heard the rumors, and the general facts were known, so he finds the embellishments easy. Satisfied with his first effort, he starts on a story linking Phun to the notorious Tiger Cages, and using the colonel's casual remarks as quotes. Larky gets out a fat file jacket, and finds a brief case that locks internally and then locks to his wrist with a thin steel cable. Mad Denny takes a cyclo-bus to the main gate for the evening newspapers. And after they've got the papers, Beale sets out to write the main report himself.

The night duty sergeant comes on, swinging a lethal-looking flask of army coffee, "Hey, you guys - Nordoff's looking for you!"

"What's up?" Beale tries to look nonchalant, yawning up from the typewriter.

"Don't know, but you'd better get over there. Some weirdo dink bird is screaming up a storm, says you guys insulted the war effort or something."

Beale shakes his head, grateful he'd had the presence of mind to call Ranley, "Ahh, sarge - Probably some unpaid bar bill or a local lovely swearing we raped her. It's going to have to wait. We've got a Top Secret report to file here."

"Hey, I know what you mean. I had a bitch named Hoa, wanted me to move in with her, too. Once they start, they never quit. *Hey, G.I., buy me radio, buy me hair spray, buy me nylons from your P.X.*"

"Yeah", Beale replies, hardly looking up from his report, "They're all named Hoa. Means *flower*, you know. They never tell you their real name."

188

"Why not?"

"They think once you know it you can steal their souls."

"Is that true shit you're telling me?"

"Yeah, it's kind-a like *three-on-a-match*, you know, bad luck."

Charley can't stand the interruption anymore, "*Will* you stop pestering Specialist Beale - he's working on a crucial assignment!"

"You lingies are really touchy today."

The sergeant flicks the newspapers out of Charley's hands and walked out. As Charley bends over to pick them up he grumbles, "Beale fiddled while Rome burned."

"A lot of good that did."

They were about to get into a full-blown argument when Mad Denny returns waving a handful of thin newspapers. Denny holds up the front page of a paper called *Vit! Vit!* to show a big, irregular white space.

"Beale, we're uck-fayed! The story's been censored! What do we do now?"

All the paper says, in bold letters written in Vietnamese in the center of the white space, *Shocking event in Da Cao censored by Phan Hui Quat government!* Beale studies it for a moment, "Anybody talking about this on the street?"

"The newsboys and cabbies sure know all about it! One of the cowboys landed like a big red cow pie in the middle of Hai Ba Trung Street up near Da Cao. One smacked into the muddy banks of the estuary by the Hai Ba Trung Bridge. The rumor is he screamed from the sky right up until he disappeared in eight feet of mud and they never found him. One fell through a roof, and the other landed in somebodies back yard!"

Beale tosses him the big red CONFIDENTIAL stamp, "Okay, we go for broke. Quote the newsboys - write what they said right on the newspaper in the blank space, as eyewitness accounts."

Denny's look brightened, "All right! You got balls, Beale!"

"You're the balls, Mad Denny."

Charley brings Beale the two documents he's been working on, "Not a lot here, Ong Be."

"Come on, Charley, lack of facts has never stopped a Dimbo before. These are *good*. Now just grab a couple handfuls of CONFIDENTIAL stuff from our general files to flesh this out. There's a report on the Buddhist uprisings and one on the dope smuggling problem, both relating to V.C. exploitation. We know the bastard's guilty anyway; we'll implicate him by inference!"

An hour later and the Colonel Phun file has blossomed into a substantially thick folder. Larky carefully slides it in the briefcase, locks the case, and then snaps it on Beale's wrist. He hands Beale the key with a little oriental bow, "Thou art our hope in the day of evil, oh Great One."

It is late and the cyclo-bus drivers are all signing off, but Mad Denny has shelled out 500 piasters and a coveted Kennedy half-dollar as well, and the driver who had taken him to the front gate is still waiting for them in the rain, parked in the Gray Snail pick-up area. Beale sits up front with the driver, and as they make the last turn, he spots four QC jeeps parked a block away outside the 3rd RRU front gate.

"*Di vay, DI VAY!*" he shouts, and the little

white vehicle slews around in a 180-degree turn. The ARVN jeeps might not have noticed if he hadn't been so urgent about it, but after a moment, two of them spin their tires on the gravel and chase them. By that time, the cyclo-bus is skidding through the first major intersection. Beale reaches across the driver and punches off the lights, yelling, "Left turn, LEFT TURN!" and gives the handlebars a yank at the same time.

"Christ, Beale!" Charley yells from the back, "You're going to get us all killed!"

"Di, Di, Di, mao len!" Beale urges the driver on, directing him to take a path through the concrete blockade at the end of the road. The driver hesitates and Beale smashes his foot on the accelerator, forcing the tiny bus through a shallow ditch and onto the runway apron not far from the Vietnamese Air Force hangers where they'd landed in the helicopter earlier that day.

The Q.C. jeeps come to a screeching halt, one of them sliding sideways into the concrete abutments. ARVN soldiers pour out of the jeeps, leaping across the shallow ditch and running after the Dimbos down the runway, shouting, *"Top, TOP, Nguoi my!"*

The cyclo-bus top speed of 30 miles an hour outdistances them with agonizing slowness, but the soldiers don't give up, continuing to run after the Dimbos. When their bus comes abreast to the backside of the 3rd's compound, Beale has the driver bring it to a skidding halt. Charley, Larky and Mad Denny pile out of the rear end, and they all run for the back of the compound. They no sooner tumble on the rain-soaked tarmac when the bus takes off again in an every-man-for-himself maneuver. The QCs are firing warning shots in the air when Beale leads the Dimbos around the side of the compound and through the secret short-cut Ranley had shown them when they first met. They squeeze through and slam the loose board tight behind them. Larky is the last one in; in his haste to reposition the board, he jerks it too hard and it comes free in his hands.

"*Lord God in Heaven,* let's get out of here!" They make it around the corner of the nearest barracks before the ARVNs can get to the fence, and in another minute they tumble breathless and disheveled past Toady's unattended desk and into the C.O.'s office.

Colonel Phun is standing with a hatched-faced QC at his side, while the C.O. and Toady half-heartedly play a game of checkers on the Colonel's desk. As soon as they enter, the C.O. gestures to Colonel Phun, "I *said* they'd be here pretty soon, didn't I?"

The colonel wastes no time, pointing an accusing finger at the Dimbos, "Zeez are ze men! I have my men arrest zem now!"

Beale speaks up, "Sorry, pal. You *can't* - no jurisdiction where the stars & stripes fly!"

Colonel Nordoff looks like a man out of his element, "I think he's right; I should have *my* men arrest them!"

Toady quickly gets to his feet, "I'll call the M.P.s, sir!"

Beale shoves him back in his seat, and points across the room at the Vietnamese officer, "If anybody's going to be arrested, it's him!"

"Outrage! I cannot accept zis!" Colonel Phun yells and pounds on the C.O.s desk..

Beale feels a rush of confidence flood him like ice water, welcoming the return of his monster, "You have no choice, sir." He taps the briefcase still secured to his wrist, "Security matters."

Charley studies Nordoff and then speaks to him in measured tones, "Our understanding is, sir, that you have a CONFIDENTIAL clearance. Can you confirm this?"

The C.O. is taken by surprise, "Well, yes. . ."

Charley glances at Toady, "Your assistant here?"

"Uncleared."

"Hmmm. Risky, but under the circumstances, we have no other choice."

Colonel Phun angrily motions to the QC at his side, "*Top* this outrage!" The Q.C. frowns and unbuttons the snap button securing his .45.

Captain Nordoff stands, finally indignant, "You can't pull a gun in here!"

At that moment the half-dozen ARVNs who had been chasing the Dimbos pour in and the room bristles with rifles. Colonel Phun's lip curls into an unpleasant smile and he rubs his fingernails through the white threads in his hair, "Zis is *Vietnam*, Captain - not Disneyland, U.S.A.!"

Beale takes a deep breath and clicks open his briefcase, "Don't be ridiculous, Colonel. There must be at least a hundred Americans on the compound, in the mess hall, the showers, the club."

"*Non.* I have taken steps. I am invisible here."

"Don't kid yourself. You may have been clever *here*, but they already know back at the Palace, because I told them. Now we are going to

193

present as much as you need to see, Colonel Phun. Right on top, here's some evidence on what happened when you threw a bunch of teenagers out of your helicopter. "

"Zere is no evidence. . . "

Beale steps forward and begins to lay papers on the C.O.'s desk in neat rows, "We don't want to present all of this, as it is classified, and the CIA finds you can still be a useful tool . . . if you cooperate. Oh, look - here's a document tying you to that nasty anti-Catholic riot when somebody threw all those Molotov cocktails in the Eden Arcade!"

Phun looks worried for the first time, "And what must I do - *pour les cooperations*?"

"Whenever you're ready to quit, just fold your deck and walk out of here. Hey, here's a CONFIDENTIAL document linking you to Diem's death!

Charley pokes the Vietnamese officer's arm; "You could get the chair for that one, buddy! That's a definite war crime. And we got lots more here!"

"O-kay, okay - I szink I see your *argumentation*."

Beale nods, "Yes I *szink* you do. But if any of us ever disappear under mysterious circumstances, this detail pouch on you will automatically be mailed to the Palace."

Charley pokes the Vietnamese officer in the ribs, pushing him toward the door, "Yeah, *automatically!*"

Colonel Phun angrily brushes Charley's hand away and speaks sharply to his men, who follow him as he turns and stalks out the door. Nordoff waits until they are well toward the front gate and then huffs his anger, "Goddamn Zip Dink bastard! I'll have his hide for this!"

Toady reaches for the phone, "I can have the M.P.s intercept, sir . . . "

Beale puts a restraining hand on Toady's sleeve and shakes his head, "Let it go, sir. You'll stir an ugly mess. The Puzzle Palace wants us to handle it this way." He pauses for effect, "You know - low profile."

The Dimbos help Beale gather up the documents he has spread on the desk. The C.O. is still shaken, but now he starts to work himself into a case of righteous anger, "Well, what was that all about? That damn dink came in here with a full head of steam, like he had plenty on his mind. I've known Colonel Phun for over a year, and he's never acted that way!"

Beale snaps shut the brief case, "Security, sir. We are not allowed to discuss it. But we'll all be a lot safer once I get this file back to the White Shack and send some things to the Palace."

The captain flings his arms wide, "But he came busting right in here -!"

"He would have killed us all, sir. You, me, Toady - everybody. Cut our throats and walked clean out of here. Who would have even known who they were? *Seen one dink, you seen 'em all*, you know?"

Beale might have said more, but Mad Denny was pulling him by the arm. They had a moment of panic when they all tried to get out the door at the same time, and then the Dimbos were through the fence and running back along the concrete apron, laughing like crazy fools as they skidded

195

and skipped through the heavy night downpour.

"Oh, Mister Lemonlips," Charley whooped, "You saved our asses that time!"

They ran on and on through the rain, making it half way from Davis Station to the White Shack before they settled down and the grim side of what they'd experienced finally set in. Beale waved his hands like he was asking God for understanding, "Four teenagers are murdered. We see it, and we're just about killed for it!"

Mad Denny takes the pack of cigarettes from Beale's hand and sticks them in his pocket so they won't get wet. "We got to pull our consciences in and get them away from this war, fellows. At least a little."

"What's that supposed to mean?"

"If somebody is knocked off in Janesville, Wis. or Petersburg, Fla., it's murder, plain and simple."

"And those four weren't murdered?"

Mad Denny shrugs and shakes his head, "I didn't say that. But it isn't black-and-white. *Your laws do not apply here, Mister Amelican.* I know my zip isn't the greatest, but that last cowboy wasn't pure – he was confessing all kinds of shit before they shot his ass and dumped him out the door."

"Mob justice, right? We've got to be animals now?"

"No, Ong Be. I didn't say that."

"Well, *what* then?"

"It's like what Ranley was trying to explain to the C.O. at Thong Nhet. It didn't matter *who*

196

crisped it - that village was wasted!"

Charley claps a hand on Mad Denny's shoulder, "For a crazy man, this guy makes a lot of sense. *Think* about it, Beale - we invite ourselves to a war that's been going on for generations. Back in the states we've been learning how to mass-produce hamburgers and do the twist; meanwhile over here these assholes have been inventing ways to send each other off to Buddha heaven. Over here everybody kills everybody. They don't look at it like murder. Half think they're *saving* the republic - the other half thinks they're *freeing* it."

Mad Denny nods, "Right! Why should they give a fuck what we think about it? We were just dumb enough to get involved. That's the true meaning of Colonel Phun-gus' lesson on the effects of gravity."

"Godless heathens. What are the righteous going to do about it?" Larky asks, slowly spinning around and letting the warm rain pelt his face as he looks up in the sky.

"Only thing we can," Charley replies. "Throw a party and forget the whole stupid thing."

"A party?" Beale looks at him like he is nuts, "At a time like this?"

"Yeah. Saturday night. I need it.... Lord knows, *you* need it.... we all need it! Now come on, guys - this was not our fault!"

"But you can't just forget-"

"Well, Nordoff forgot to ground us - that's like God giving us a furlough - and you, Mister Be, are a Spec 5 with rights to a great, big, nearly empty NCO villa over on Trung Minh Giang that is just waiting for us!"

The Dimbos take Beale's silence for assent,

197

and as they talk it over, he gradually warmed to the idea. This Charley is their cheerleader, leading them back from chaos and death to something resembling the good old days. He finally has them link arms; it takes a while to get them going, but at the last they march in step past Maisy and Daisy the 3rd RRUs low flying radio recievers, chanting together, Sai-GON BOUND! Sai-GON BOUND!

Only later, back in the barracks after he finally had his shower and pulled the clammy sheets around his naked body, would Beale's monster leave him. Then, while no one was there to see him, he could finally collapse into a tearful, shivering wreck.

CHAPTER TWENTY TWO

Four *xe-hoi* taxi drivers stand outside the Main Gate in a small huddle. One shakes his head, "We not race. Too dangerous. Lose license."

"Gentlemen," Charley holds his palms out, "We're not asking you to race. Each of you four has been carefully chosen for the way you normally drive, which is like bats out of hell, anyway."

Charley places a second 100 P note in each outstretched hand, and then a third.

"And, of course, since this is a non-race, you will be judged on virtue and good looks."

He handx each another 100-piaster note.

"All you have to do is drive, we won't have a winner."

He waves a lone 500 P note back and forth over their outstretched hands.

"However, the first *xe-hoi taxi* of these four to pull up in front of the Cherry Bar - whether it be Buddha's whim or some random toss of the joss sticks - will be awarded this fine souvenir of the event, a handsome colorful piece of paper which may be suitably framed, or even spent!" He winked at his driver, and they dart for their taxi.

"Hey, wait!"

"Goddamit, Charley, that's no fair!"

"Dirty, rotten, lifer-cheater!"

But Charley's taxi is already rolling, and the remaining Dimbos have no choice but to pile into their own cabs and try to catch him.

Charley loses the lead when his cabbie cuts a

turn too sharply and skids through a fruit-stand, scattering oranges, pineapples and other oriental fruits like *trom trom trop* (lychee) and jackfruit. His driver puts the car in reverse, and spins around to continue.. They drive off as Charley lets loose a flutter of colorful piasters from the window to make it right. But Charley is now in last place, and his driver weaves back and forth behind Beale's cab, trying to pass.

Beale sees a blurred montage of frightened faces, splintered wooden boxes, flying fruit and raised fists, and when things clear, he is in front of Charley.

The little cars zoom down both sides of the boulevard, cutting in and out of traffic, and cutting each other off at every opportunity. They thread between laboring old busses billowing foul black clouds of exhaust, and they cut around startled military jeeps and deuce-and-a-half trucks. Their horns blare and bleet and beep, and the swarms of bicycles, pedi-cabs, motorbikes, scooters, and horse-drawn vehicles scatter like squawking ducks in front of them.

Charley's driver seems to have a faster car, and he is able to nose out Beale. But in doing so, he nearly smashes into another cab that isn't in the race. The new driver swears angrily in a high, shrill voice. Charley winds down his window and shakes his fist, yelling, "*Mange ma gotz!*"

The new cabbie may not have known gutter Italian, but he immediately floors it, cutting Beale's cab off and riding Charley's bumper. Their dash downtown has the same effect on almost every cab they pass, the taxi drivers feeling the outrage at having been cut off, and in effect joining the race, until there were seven or eight blue-and-creams angrily vying for the lead like little bumblebees. Even with this extra competition, Charley's driver manages to get back in front at the last moment and skid to victory in front of the Cherry Bar.

The Dimbos each give their drivers a 500 P note, and Charley passes around a victory bottle of the notorious Algerian Red, everyone swigging from the same bottle. Last insults are flung, and the cabbies disband quickly, driving off in different directions before any white mouse cops show up.

While the rest of the Dimbos go into the Cherry Bar, Beale sprints over to Nguyen Hue Street, the *Street of Flowers*. Carnations don't seem right, so he scoops together a bouquet of exotic Thai orchids, all purples, lavenders, and leopard-spotted white and gold.

It isn't that he is falling in love with Hoa Night Bird or anything like that, he tells himself. He just remembers the old stories his mother had told him about how when she was a little girl at the turn of the century her father had made special buggy trips to town to buy flowers for her mother, shushing the half-protests that they couldn't afford such extravagances with the staunch remark, "A woman should have flowers." Family ways die hard, and coming like that, passed down the generations, buying the flowers is, in Beale's mind, almost mandatory. Beale gives the old Prussian gentleman, who only lived in him as a memory of a memory, a self-conscious and bemused little salute as he leaves the long row of flower stalls with his big bunch of tropical orchids. *Here, I'm not crazy*, he thinks to himself, *in Nam everyone lives close to his or her ancestors.*

CHAPTER TWENTY THREE

It is after midnight in Saigon. Curfew is long past, the noise of traffic outside reduced to the occasional whine of a fast-moving jeep. The sound of the rain is everywhere, drumming on the tile roof, gurgling in the drainpipes, hissing as an occasional drop or two fall into the glowing embers in the fireplace in the big living room at Ranley's villa-apartment.

The Dimbos and their girlfriends have long ago worked their way through the pizzas, which Charley declared "Chicago Style", an amazing find halfway around the world. Half-empty wine bottles and metal trays from the Pizzeria on Le Thanh Ton Street litter the white tile floor.

Tuy produces a big plastic pouch of Laotian gold and rolls fat, stubby cigarettes that they puff and pass around from hand to hand. Charley had gotten into dope in Tay Ninh, but the other Dimbos pretend they were used to such matters, and after a half hour of coughing and pretending, they have finally gone over the top.

They sit in a semi-circle in front of the fire, passing the tokes and listening while Denny softly strums his guitar and sings in his light tenor voice:-

Blowed up at a bus stop / That's paying your dues
Busted an' broken / knocked out of your shoes
That's why they call it...
The Ba Muoi Ba Blues....

Beale watches the glow from the tip of a toke as it pulses in Tuy's lips, then dips and swings in a little arc to illuminate Charley's face. Charley inhales, and then passes to Larky, who starts giggling again, as he's been doing for the last half hour. The bargirls on each side of Larky and Charley look like dark priestesses, calm and smiling, and in a world of their own. Everyone is the same color bronze in the dark, Beale thinks, wondering at the clarity of his own awareness.

Tuy is the prettiest, in a room of pretty girls. *A rose in a field of Brown-Eyed Suzies*, Beale thinks, *a rose with thorns.* He watches her, seeing darkness, brooding melancholy and a grim avarice. He is certain she has taken Ranley's gold, *he is sure of it!*

Hoa sits on a pillow next to Beale, singing the refrains to Mad Denny's blues song along with him. He doesn't know exactly when he becomes aware how remarkably rich her voice is

Lost in translation / The way back refused
Learn meditation....
The Ba Muoi Ba Blues...

She breaks off her singing, smiling at him, "What it like in America?" Her English is getting better and better, now that she practices constantly at the Hong Kong bar.

"Oh, I don't know...." His mind floods with memories of blue and white pom-poms at the Thornton Township high school basketball games, his buddy Ron's battered 50's Desoto at an A&W Root-beer stand with a tray loaded with burgers and fries, the battered aluminum tray hanging from

204

the front window, snowballs arcing through a cold blue Illinois sky at Motlong's Slough, Grace Ann in a ponytail, her ample breasts plumping out her fuzzy cashmere sweater, bottom-fishing for carp and mud-rollers in the shallow Yellowbanks River while his dad stayed back at the car playing poker, drinking beer and eating evil-smelling limburger cheese, the smell of fresh-baked triple-threat chocolate birthday cake, the sound of his mother's voice at twilight, calling him in from the corner baseball lot.

He says, "It all feels very distant, like stuff I read in a kid's book a long time ago."

"Every person very rich there, right?"

"No, not really...." Beale thinks of his own family, scratching all those years to stay respectable while he ground through college and started grad school.

"More people rich there than rich here."

"That's true enough, I suppose. Everybody has more money, but it costs more to buy things."

"I see in the magazine - women all have pretty dress. They get lipstick and hairspray as if it is their right." Tuy has her party favor of Toni hair spray next to her. Mad Denny has pulled a minor-league black-market deal, swapping his monthly ration of six cartons of cigarettes for a carton of hairspray and some decent Italian wine.

Beale nods, "Well, it is.... if they can pay for it."

Tuy speaks up suddenly from across the circle, "Charley say you think I took Mister Ranley's gold."

"Oh, oh", Charley says with an embarrassed grin, "Truth and honesty time."

205

Beale would normally have been set back by Tuy's boldness, but now he feels numb and floating, and secure with his arm around Hoa. *What should it matter that she denied it to his face?* He says, "Yes, I think you stole it."

"You can come and search my house!"

"You could have hid it anywhere...." He tries to change the subject, "Where did you learn such good English?"

"You know already I tell you I was a peanut girl in the bars ever since I want to remember."

"And before that?"

"Before that, I don't want to remember. My family was executed by the V.C. I saw them all in their blood."

"Ohhhh...."

Mad Denny looks up from his guitar, "And how did you meet our man Ranley?"

"In a bar. He broke four bottles of beer over a man's head."

"*Four* bottles?"

"He was a very big man, a *Dai-ui My*, and he was bothering me."

Beale blows out two cheeks full of blue smoke, "An American captain! Is that when you started living with Red Dog?"

Her eyes bore at him from across the room, "I do not see why you do not like me."

"I don't have to like everybody."

Charley gives out an embarrassed little laugh, "Hey now, *em* and *anh*, break it up, huh? This is supposed to be a party!"

Still looking at Beale, Tuy puts one arm around Charley's neck and pulls him over to her, "Ranley was a nice guy, like a father to me. He
206

was not a great lover like my Charley!"

"Will you say that about Charley someday, if he gets blown up?"

Her voice rises, "You don't not say that!"

She is rattled and she drops her proper speech patterns in favor of the more primitive bargirl's Pidgin English. He presses his attack, "Why not?"

"Bad luck! Think of death - it comes!"

The direction of her reply takes him by surprise. "I don't think about it that much...." He reaches for the smoke Hoa holds next to him, thankful for something to stop the trembling that has started in his hands.

"You do so! You don't not think of other thing else!!"

Now Beale feels cornered and a little bewildered. "You can't say that. You hardly know me!"

"My Charley has said." She shows the palms of both hands as if to push him away, "You think it - it comes!"

Charley shakes his head. "Now you've gone and gotten her all excited, Ong Be.... She's a real *Su Tu Ha Dong*."

"Tiger lady of Ha Dong...." Beale thinks it over, remembering his Vietnamese history. *The women of the Northern province of Ha Dong were so hot-tempered they became legendary.* "I can see that." But, looking across the room at her, his mind doesn't see a tiger-lady. Instead he flashes back to the Puzzle Palace and the bloody, howling apparition he'd hallucinated after drunk-sarge fell in the pulper. *Would he ever lose the immediacy of that vision? Why did it come to him now? Was Tuy the embodiment of that witch-spirit?* He tries

207

to tell himself he doesn't think so. *It was just the Laotian gold, and the way she yelled at him.* But he can't stop the run of cold chills up and down his spine, or the prickling goose bumps along his arms. Mad Denny, who has paused for their angry exchange, begins again:-

Gonna go to the C.O. / And tell him my fear
I'm not gonna make it / The rest of the year

"I'll send you to Bien Hoa / To the PX for booze.
To Phu Bai or Chao Duc / You've nothing to lose.
Just forget about State-Side / An' the welcome hurray
Till you nail Victor Charley/In the cold, muddy clay."

So hold tight to your teddies/ And the family jewels
As long as they're playin'....
The Ba Muoi Ba blues....

Charley lurches to his feet and comes over to sit next to Beale. He ruffles his friend's short hair with one hand, "Don't mind Tuy, good old Mister Be." He waves his hand happily around the room, "Shining times, that what we got here - Shining times!"

"Having a good one, huh?"

"A great one! An abso-fucking-lutely great one!"

"We'll have more, Charley", Beale promises. "We'll have plenty more."

It is interesting how easily they pick up the habit of puffing a joint or two. Of course, nobody thinks much about it. It is just the thing to do, and the more you look around, the more you see lots of troopers doing it. It is only later, when Beale is back in *the World*, that this one particular rainy night in the far-away capital of South Vietnam would unstitch itself from the black well that Jack Beale's memory had become and come bubbling up like a howling, noxious gas.

The next morning passes in a haze of lazy lovemaking. They plan another party for the following weekend, and the girls leave for their own apartments, to get freshened up for work. But the next party never happens, because late Sunday night when they return to the 3rd, they find the C.O. has come up with another of his brainstorms. Toady has posted a new duty roster on the bulletin board outside the mess hall, and the Dimbos all are on it.

CHAPTER TWENTY FOUR

"Phu Bai!!" Charley Magnolia yells over the rumble of the truck as if he still doesn't believe it. "Do you know where god dam fricking Phu Bai is?" They have been arguing endlessly whether Nordoff has the right to send them off on missions. Ranley is out of touch, lost somewhere in Hawaii on his way back to the States. Beale contacted Harris back at the Puzzle Palace, but the civilian washed his hands of the matter, saying it was a strictly military problem and he wasn't going to get involved.

Beale went to see Captain Ball, who admitted he felt it was a foolish, unnecessary, ridiculous and silly mission -- but as they weren't busy and he didn't have anything better for them to do, he shrugged and went along with it. They all had the feeling he didn't want to get into an argument with a fellow officer; after all, he was doing the juicy top secret security stuff while Nordoff was stuck with the grind of the day-to-day command of the 3rd.

Beale squints out of the back end of the truck, looking past the rolled-up canvas flaps to where the green-and-gray paddies are drifting away to merge with the horizon behind them. Their tiny convoy is sputtering north along Route 1. In one field, he sees peasants look up and wave their shallow conical hats, cheerfully shouting, "*Nguoi My, Hoan hooooo! Nguoi My!!*"

The moment of spontaneous native encouragement does little to settle Beale's stomach. He feels as uneasy as Charley out here, away from Tan Son Nhut with its comforting bare perimeter, its watchtowers and heavy machine-guns nestled behind three layers of sandbags.

"Yeah, I know where Phu Bai is", he replies glumly.

"I'll *tell* you where it is, *stugatz* - smack up against the DMZ, so close you could spit across the Ben Hai River!"

"Stop yelling like it's my fault! And it's actually a couple miles south of Hue - at least 12 miles from the DMZ."

"Big deal! You know a tank can get there from *Bac Viet* in less time than it takes to get through a carwash!"

"Quit grumping, *Meatball*! It's just a couple of days."

"Hey, can the racket", Mad Denny yells over the roar of the truck, "Larky and me are trying to get a little shut-eye here!" Mad Denny and Larky have found places where they can lie down on the loose ends of the canvas covering the radio equipment; Larky is using his helmet for a pillow and is already snoring like a baby.

Charley has been sprawled on one of the wooden side-benches. Now he sits up and tries to roll a joint. The truck bounces, and the hash scatters on the truck bed. Beale, who is still watching the delta pull away from them, notices what he is trying to do.

"Here, I manufactured these last night." He hands over a Marlboro hard-pack.

Charley pops open the top and selects one of the plump, irregular cigarettes, "Hmmm. Okay, so you're not all bad, Beale."

211

They drive along the coastal route, occasionally seeing the flat, gray sweep of the sea on their right across deserted stretches of sandy beach or on the far side of thatch-roofed villages and patches of palm trees. The joint they share is almost gone before the solid feeling comes and chases the creeps away. Charley puffs out a cloud of blue smoke and grins across at his friend, "So... Hoa moved in on you, huh?"

"Yeah, at the place. A couple of days ago."

"You pay her?"

"500 P a week for food and living expenses. That's what she said she needed."

"She'll keep you broke buying stuff from the PX. Perfume, nylons, cameras, radios - dink broads are like that."

"I suppose...." Beale shrugs, not really caring. By Hoa's standards, they are rich. "Did you ever hear her sing? She's got a great voice."

"Get her a contract with RCA. You know all dink bar-girls want to own bars or become singers. It's in their blood."

"She really does have an extraordinary voice. Even Mad Denny said so."

"This is starting to sound like more than a piece of ass."

"No, it isn't."

"I see it all now!" Charley waves his hand in the air, as if conjuring up the image, "Look, Mama Beale, what I brought home! I met her at Anna's Bar, Grill & Whorehouse in Tay Ninh, and she can warble like Rosemary Clooney!"

"Same-same for you, G.I. Sweet little Tuy meets the Italian bunch! Loving old Mother Magnolia would throw you out on your lasagna!"

"Never happen, Mister Be." He looks at Beale and the merriment brims over until it fairly danced in his eyes. "I love Tuy with a true and honest lust, but I never could marry her."

"Why not?"

Charley leans back and takes a drag from the stub end of the joint, which he holds pinched between his thumb and first fingernail. He eyes Beale with an air of detached amusement, "I told you, I'm already married."

"I thought you were kidding!"

Charley puts his finger to his lips, "Shhh! Jesus, Beale, do you want the whole fricking world to know?"

Beale sits up straight and gives him a pop-eyed stare, "B-but…How? When? Where?"

"Calm, calm, Ong Be. Father Charles will tell thee all. Her name is Beth. You met her a couple times in Monterey."

"But - but you never said anything -"

"Did too. You just weren't listening. You know, the time comes in every international globetrotting spy's life when he's got to settle down, accept his responsibilities and be a man. And, after all, she's having my kid...."

This input is coming too fast for Beale, "B-but…i-if you're married to Beth, then what about Tuy?"

"Come on, Ong Be. No woman expects a man to go celibate cold-turkey – 'specially not a spy in a war zone. That *is* what we are, you know - electronic spies leading an exciting life close to the edge. At least that's what Beth thinks."

"You're not kidding, are you?" It was as much a statement as a question.

"Nope. Dead serious." Charley pulls a thick envelope from his pocket, "Here. I'm not the great poet and author like you, but I spent a lot of time on this. It's a few pages about love through all eternity and that kind of romance shit."

Beale shies away from the letter. "What am I supposed to do with it?"

"Send it to Beth in the event of my untimely demise."

"I - I can't.... nothing's going to happen."

There is a long pause before Charley speaks again. "Maybe, and maybe not, Jack. You just keep the letter for me."

The color has drained from Beale's face, "Why are you doing this to me?"

Charley folds the letter over and stuffs it in the pocket of Beale's fatigue jacket. He chuckles and punches him lightly in the arm, "Because you're my best friend, asshole! I must be really hard-up, huh?"

After a few minutes Charley moves forward along the bed of the truck and finds a place of his own where lie can lie down. Beale sits alone chain-smoking Marlboros and watching the seemingly endless coastal flats unreel behind them.

214

CHAPTER TWENTY FIVE

The trucks pull into Na Trang before dark. The Dimbos spend the night in damp and musty beds in the My Luan, a cheap hotel that contracts rooms to a low assortment of traveling salesmen and government officials, and Beale dreams Beth and Tuy are coming at him with long, sparkling knives, howling deep curses that come out of their mouths like recording tapes played at half-speed.

He wakes in a cold sweat, not recognizing anything in the unfamiliar room. It is four thirty in the morning. He knows sleep won't return; he gets up and puts his fatigues back on. The hotel lobby is deserted; he spends a bored half-hour glancing through some three-day old newspapers from Saigon. One of them features a blank white space on the front, but as it has no caption, he can't tell whether or not it is about the unfortunate end of the Da Cao Four. *Can they cover up a crime like that? Or is that how all tragedy ends, the howl of the victims fading down a time-tunnel as if they'd fallen from a helicopter?* He wanders out into the pre-dawn grays, hunching his shoulders and hunkering down in the chill drizzle. The streets are still deserted, but he buys some *pho* from a woman who has set up her soup kitchen under a sloping canvas on a corner in front of the hotel. The food is hot and laced with watercress and he hungrily chopsticks the noodles around the fish head floating in the center of his bowl.

He talks for a while with the pedi-cyclo drivers, squatting with them in a circle and

215

drinking hot *nuoc cafe* with steaming canned milk and semi-raw sugar crystals. They want to know what cyclo drivers always wanted to know. *How much did an American make? Did they really all have new cars? Could he buy them a radio from the PX, and maybe some Maybelline?*

The Dimbo's ride pulls out of town a few hours later, their small convoy drives steadily north, and they reach Da Nang at three in the afternoon. They stop off at a French sidewalk cafe for newly baked bread and a quick round of Ba Muoi Bas. Larky buys a pack of dirty playing cards from a one-eyed man, and one of the truck drivers comes back from the john grinning from ear to ear that he'd been gummed a quickie by some toothless old *ba*.

From Da Nang the road swings northwest around the Cau Hai lagoon, and on into Phu Bai. Beale wants to go on to Hue for a tour of the Imperial Palace, but the drivers give him a funny look and tell him they have to be starting back before dark.

The 126TH RRU at Phu Bai looks to the Dimbos like it is little more than a landing zone. The heart of the listening post is a circle of sagging wooden telephone poles strung with wire and a group of trailers huddled nearby. It is a desolate camp of portable living-and-work trailers, half-buried under stacks of sandbags, the whole sorry mess on a low hilltop that has been bulldozed flat and bare for a few hundred yards in every direction and then circled with dense coils of rusty triple-dannert barbed wire. For defense they have six big M102 howitzers, and four open-mouthed 81MM mortars, all surrounded by their own neatly stacked

216

sandbag pyramids. Two tanks putter around the sandy trails outside the compound in the only areas firm enough to support their weight. It looks to the Dimbos like they spend as much time pulling each other out of the muck as they do in patrolling.

The Americans consist of the intelligence people, one platoon of infantrymen and the artillerymen, but perimeter defense is left to a company of ARVN soldiers stationed in a tent village of their own on an adjoining low hill.

The Dimbos check in at an underground bunker and are led by a sad-eyed clerk to a sandbagged trailer that has a small window air conditioner running on full blast.

Charley throws his blankets down on a sagging cot and looks over at the rest of the Dimbos, "What the hell are we doing here?" He has asked the same question a dozen times before. So far, nobody can answer it.

Beale thinks he will try one more time; he looks up from his own cot, "I already told you - Phu Bai wants to prove to Meade how impossible their job is. And Nordoff thinks it is *one hell of a fine idea.*"

The air conditioning makes everything damp and clammy. From where Beale is lying, he can see out a lone window rimmed with foggy condensation. All he sees are rolling sand hills that remind him of Fort Ord.

Charley pulls off one of his soggy boots and slams it on the wooden floor, "I could be in the sack with Tuy right now - Goddamn that Toady!"

"Amen to that", Mad Denny growls from the bunk overhead.

There is a short knock on the door and an officer enters. He is short and round, like Santa's ageing kid, complete with twinkling eyes and a bald spot in the center of his sandy hair.

"Welcome to Phu Bai, men!", he says with a jolly laugh.

"Ho, ho, ho....", Denny responds, "....sir."

"I'm Captain Miller. I just wanted to brief you on tomorrow. We'll trek to some of the high points, see if we can pull in some covert from across the border."

"Can't we do it from right here, sir?"

"Not much point. We do *that* all the time."

"You're sending us out there all alone?" Charley looks like he is ready to desert.

"Of course not. You'd never get through the mine field."

"Mine field?"

"Well, yes... Gook suicide squads kept sneaking in on us with satchels of explosives. But we fixed 'em, yes sir-re-bob!"

"So who do we go out there with?"

I'll get you 8 or 9 guys - whoever's not out with the clap at the moment!" He chuckles like clap is the greatest thing, and moves to the doorway, "Chow's at 1730. Don't miss it - we're having gourmet S.O.S.!" He gives them a last merry wave and is gone.

The Dimbos eye each other.

"Gourmet Shit-on-a-shingle?"

"It must be stress," Mad Denny taps his head with one finger and nods, "from living so close to the DMZ."

Beale looks out the dirt-stained window at the grimy camp. He says nothing, but the familiar

218

feelings nibble at his heart like little mice. He has almost gotten used to the idea of street ambush, of hidden plastic explosives and religious riots in the capital. Backcountry Vietnam is a new experience, and in a sense, he is starting all over.

CHAPTER TWENTY SIX

The Dimbos sit in a rough circle with six grunts from the 126TH, backs against the mossy tombstones of an old Buddhist graveyard, hunching in their ponchos and passing the joints with both hands to protect them from the warm and steady rain. It is the afternoon of their fourth and final day in the bush, and in celebration the Dimbos have broken out the last of the hash that Tuy had contributed to their trip.

Over the last three days they had paused to set up their radio reception gear on bare sandy hilltops, in soggy mangrove glades by the sea, in deserted ghost villages of sagging bamboo, and in their favorite outpost, the Buddhist graveyard with its tilted and worn limestone slabs, their mission to find the links to fill in Nelson's precious map back at the Puzzle Palace, and to find the elusive special connections to North Vietnam. No matter where they go, they get nothing but badly garbled messages and static. That is, at least in part, because their knowledge of radio reception is limited to a few hours instruction back at the White Shack at Tan Son Nhut. The rest of it could easily be blamed on the weather.

They have their backs to a shallow wall in the Buddhist graveyard; too tired to even pretend they are listening for intercept. The squad leader looks over at Charley, "You guys really speak dink, or does you fakes it mostly?" He is a 3-striper named Jones, a big black guy from Philly who told them he signed up for four years right out of James

Madison High School. He gives them a sly, gentle smile, "I doesn't means to *offend*...."

Charley grins back, "No - it's okay. Actually, it's a good question. Mostly, we bullshit our way through, except for Mad Denny and Ong Be here."

"They're hot, huh?"

"Well, Beale's almost gone native. He eats fish sauce. Drops his pants and squats on street-corners. Runs at the sound of gunfire. The signs are everywhere."

Beale hands the smoking joint to the squad leader, "Charley's so full of gas, he's going to float off at any minute. The truth is, we mostly translate writing. I'm okay if they speak slow, but if there was a panic I probably wouldn't know if it was rats in the crapper or incoming."

"Man, man, man....", Jones shakes his head, "they's sure a different people." He inhales deeply and passes the joint on to Jose Luis, the only real radioman in the bunch. "I was in the same town with old Medger when he got his ass shot, and I never thought I'd see a place more segregated than Mississippi, but I wouldn't give you nothing for this mess of slope-eye, dwarfy, yellow-skin, honky rednecks.... no offense meant to you fellows...."

"Ethnic purity", Beale nods. "That's one reason why they hate us. And that's why they weren't swallowed up by the Chinese a thousand years ago. They hate everybody who is not a pure *Nam Viet*."

"In the States they were *some* white folks who cared for the black man. Here, blacks get walled out 100%. We got our own bars, our own whorehouses - filled with nothing but half-breeds."

"Half black people?"

221

"Half anything. Blacks, Frogs, Cambodians, Chinks. All the outcasts."

George, the other black in the group, agrees. He is tall and lanky, with sour features that make him look older than his 18 years. "Thrown out of a low-class dink bar 'cause of your skin color - now *that's* disgusting!"

Any novelty to tramping around in the rain-soaked bush had worn off by the middle of the first day. As the days drag by the Dimbos hobble painfully forward on feet made raw by their damp socks and heavy leather boots. The Phu Bai grunts wear new, lighter canvas boots, but the Dimbos are so out of shape it wouldn't have made much difference. The trails they follow are slippery with mud and they sometimes plunge through waist-high streams that can only be crossed with the aid of a rope tied to the first man across. The land is sometimes too open and flat and other times, too brush-choked and hilly, ideal for an ambush either way, and they constantly wait for a bullet between their shoulder blades, or worry about stepping on a mine or setting off a bouncing betty.

Their only relief comes when they pause to try the radio-intercept unit. They have two radiomen, a lean Cuban kid, Jose Luis, who packs the normal unit on his back, and Barf, a strange-looking grunt with a livid pink face, straw-white hair and bottle-thick green glasses. Barf totes a smaller intercept unit that is supposed to be more powerful. The Dimbos spend a great deal of time hemming and hawing over the details of each intercept attempt, working them into half-hour rest stops.

Their little squad moves around in a buffer zone, several miles in every direction from the

126TH. The nearby hamlets have been emptied and bulldozed flat. There is nothing to shoot, not even a stray water buffalo. Occasionally they pass one of the ARVN patrols combing the same hills, responding to the friendly calls of "*Chao, Anh!*" They spend break time talking about the terrain and sharing their coveted *thuoc la My* -- Pall Mall 100's, Marlboros and Kools being the favorites and much harder to come by up here than in the ready Saigon black market.

Charley nervously eyes his watch, sees it is going on three in the afternoon. "Shouldn't we be getting back?"

Jones slaps his knee, "It's under three clicks from here. I'll have you back in mess in under two hours, a steamy goop of S.O.S. on your plate, right next to a cup of army god-awful!"

They finish their smokes and get to their feet. The trail back to Phu Bai is clear, and as Jones promised, they soon have the barbed wire rolls and squatty sandbag pyramids of the 126TH in view. And then George, who is walking point about 40 feet in front of the main body of the squad, steps on a land mine.

"Down!!", Jones screams, "Get down to cover!" But there is no cover. They are a quarter mile from the graveyard, and two hundred yards from the footpath entrance through the barbed wire, in one of those open, sandy areas that has been bulldozed clear.

Beale hears a distant crackle, like popcorn, and sees bullets spurting the sand around him. He finds himself looking at George's body. The lower half has been turned to bloody mush. He has to be dead. It is unreal, like a nightmare dream. Beale probably would have stood there until he was shot, but Jones tackles him, and the two of them find slight cover in a small depression scooped out of the ground.

"Coming in from long distance, or we'd all be dead!", Jones shouts in his ear.

Beale nods, "Single shot weapons."

Jones points to a ragged clump of trees nearly a mile away, "Over there."

Heartbeats later, the Americans behind the barbed wire inside the Phu Bai compound open up, raking massive retaliatory fire over their heads.

"Let's run for it!", Beale yells at the sergeant.

"Can't!", Jones spits back angrily, "That was no V.C. mine that got George! The stupid fucking Arvins re-mined the footpath!"

"Can we crawl around to the main gate?"

"No! Trip-wire claymores run three-sixty! No way to get to there from here!"

Charley buries his cheek as best he can in the damp sod. He'd overheard Jones talking to Beale. He cringes as he hears the soft thump of the bullets in the ground around him. The steel pot slips over to one side on his head, but he doesn't care. He doesn't care about anything. All his premonitions were right; he knows they are goners. *They are all gonna die.*

Someone pat his back, "It's okay, Charley. We're going to be okay." It is Beale, lying on his back next to him, nervously trying to get a clip in his M-14. "Here, can you get this sucker in?"

"The other way, dummy. Here, let me."

Charley is slamming the clip home when Jose Luis dropshis M-16 and clutches the top of his head. Blood runs between his fingers, and he

224

gives out one chilling wail, slumps to the ground and lies still.

The men from the 126TH settle down to firing short bursts into the trees. Machine-gun fire and the mortars join in from inside the compound. As the minutes drag on and dusk begins to settle, angry red tracers lace the dull gray sky overhead.

"Look!" Beale points to where two men are beginning to inch their way out from the compound. They had made their way past the barbed wire and now were crawling in a zigzag pattern across the bare ground.

"It's medics!" Beale sees the red crosses on their helmets.

"No, no, NO!" Jones screams, "The place has been re-mined!"

The two men pay no attention to his warnings, crawling slowly through the soft sand, their boots leaving trails behind them. Beale realizes they probably can't hear through the firefight. They get lucky and are only a few yards away from the Dimbos when they are enveloped in a jagged cloud of smoke and flame. When the low-hanging smoke clears, they both were still, lying twisted like broken dolls.

"Thirty yards to safety", Mad Denny moaned, "Thirty lousy, fucking yards!"

Charley is out of his mind. "We got to *do* something, Ong Be."

"Yeah, but *what*?"

Charley eyes the open mud field in front of him. "Look," he starts, not knowing what he is going to say, "everybody dies sometime anyway...." He senses something brittle snap in him, and physically feels the fear drain from him like an ugly brown-yellow liquid. He is amazed. He knows what to do. Charley has found his own monster.

"I just don't want to die alone! Follow me, Ong Be! He hunches over to Jose Luis, who is whimpering in Spanish ten feet away.

"Get down!", Jones roars, "What the fuck you doing, white boy?"

"Getting my ass out of here! Thought I'd take Jose Louis along, seeing as I'm going anyway!"

"You're crazy, man! I can't let you do that!"

"No choice, sarge. Ten more minutes it's so dark we won't be able to see the way the medics came."

"You'll never make it, here to there!"

"We'll talk about it on the other side." Charley strips the radio from Jose Luis's back. He pulls the man over his shoulders, and stands in a half-crouch, looking back at Beale. The fear, the nervous tension, the sick butterflies are gone. He is thinking the red, blooming shells and white-and-green tracer streaks overhead are beautiful. "What a way to die," he says, almost to himself, "Come on, Beale." Then he turns from them, grits his teeth, and trots straight for the medics.

The men in the compound see Charley coming, and send out a storm of fire over his head. Beale gives him a few yards head start and follows. After a moment's hesitation Larky goes after him, and then one by one the rest of the squad follows after. Finally Mad Denny brings up the rear, walking backwards through the mine field, snarling and spraying the hills with the M-16 Jose Luis had left behind, looking like an imitation G.I. Joe himself, but for all that, looking carefully around to make sure he steps as close as possible in their footprints.

In that way they made it across the unknown ground, and then retraced the boot-paths, dragging the dead medics after them, and finally a last dash between the heavy rolls of barbed wire and on into the compound itself.

Once they are back and the firing dies down, they crackle and pop with pent-up emotions, grateful to just be alive, slapping each other on the back and calling everybody *Lucky Sons'o Bitches*. Later, while they are drinking warm cans of Hamm's beer, Charley has a violent case of vomiting and diarrhea, both coming on suddenly at the same time. Beale helps him to the nearest shitter and stands by at a discrete distance. Long after Charley has emptied himself out his body is still racked with the dry heaves. Beale sits on a wooden crate, near enough if Charley calls for him. But he knows there is nothing anyone can do to help. Every warrior's monster extracts its price in its own way.

CHAPTER TWENTY SEVEN

That night a heavy fog laced with sudden gusts of rain moves over the sandy hump hills of Phu Bai. The enlisted G.I.'s who aren't on guard or night patrol stand around in their olive t-shirts and shorts under a canvas square lashed to four poles. They are a few yards away from the mortars, and they are intent on getting potted on warm beer and hash.

Beale and Charley are down to their last joint, but the Phu Bai crew produces a new stash, and everybody lights up.

"Where are the guys?" Charley still looks pale and weak.

Beale passes him the joint, "Larky's playing poker in the van. Mad Denny's sleeping it off."

Barf, who has been tinkering with the sights on one of the mortars, takes off his thick glasses and wipes the steam from them on his t-shirt. There is a flashlight at his feet, and he is reading co-ordinates from a frayed booklet. He looks a little like a white slug with the indirect lighting shining up in his face. "You guys know the captain's in town, getting his nuts cracked...."

"May he gather the clap unto himself."

"Amen."

Barf nods and takes a swig from a can of Schlitz he'd balanced on a nearby sandbag. "And....since he's not around, we wondered if you lingies might give us pore, mindless grunts a hand?"

"Sure - won't we, Beale?"

Beale takes a hit from the cigarette Charley hands him and stares off into the rainy night, "Sure. Anything."

The men gather around, and Barf begins to call on a field phone. Another G.I. is intently surveying something in the distance through an electronic night-scope. Someone brings Beale and Charley a couple of new beers.

Barf holds his hand over the mouthpiece. His eyes gleam in triumph, *"Got* 'em!" He holds the phone out to the two Dimbos. Charley takes it and handed it to Beale, who asks, "Got *who?*"

"Our Arvin buddies!"

"*Alloo*?", someone on the other end of the line says.

"*Un moment!*" Beale put his hand over the speaker, "What do you want me to say?"

Barf's eyes gleam in the strange light from his flashlight. "Tell them terrorists have planted a bomb in their parade grounds!"

"Whaaat?"

Charley, who sees the 81MM shell in Barf's hands, catches on immediately, "Just *tell* them, Ong Be!"

Beale uncertainly puts the phone to his lips and says in stumbling Vietnamese, "The hated *Cong San* baby-killers have put a bomb in your place of marching! Get away immediately!"

Barf twisted the nipple on the tip of the mortar with a sardonic little laugh, "No delay fuses - after all, we wouldn't want to *kill* nobody! Jones-y, you want to do the honors?"

The black sergeant shakes his head no. Barf looks around the group, "Well then, gentlemen...." He leaves the shelter of the overhanging ponchos

229

and drops the shell down the mortar tube he'd been adjusting, doing it casually as if he is throwing out the garbage.

There is a hollow POOMPH! sound. Silence for a few seconds. And then the shell explodes inside the barbed-wire perimeter of the ARVN camp on the next hill. The kid looking through the night scope chuckles and reaches between his knees for his beer can, "Hell, Barf - you just took out their johnny-tent! There must be shit all over the place! Half-a-notch left for sure!"

Barf adjusts the mortar and drops in another shell. Again a shell flies off in a neat parabolic arc through the night sky.

"Bullseye!", the man with the night scope cheers. They shout happily, like little boys with a pocket full of cherry bombs.

Beale watches in the darkness, "Now we're mortaring our own allies....Christ, Charley, what's this war all about?"

"I don't know, Be. It's too much for this old spy. Tonight I think I really want to go home." He nods over to where Jones sits unmoving, apart from the laughter and the cheers, "All I know for sure is the sergeant's buddy's dead, and Jose Luis got drilled with a bullet where his brain's supposed to be, and nothing's ever going to change that...."

Morning finds Phu Bai as damp and bleak as ever, and the Dimbos eager to leave for Saigon. Their deuce-and-a-half already has its motor warming. As Beale is throwing his gear on board, Barf shows up, chewing on an S.O.S. sandwich, "Just thought I'd say goodbye."

Charley takes a look at what he was eating,

"It's been fun, but I can't say much for your diet around here."

"Hear the news? The chicken-Arvins deserted last night."

"*Deserted?* You hear that, Beale?"

"Yep. Heard it at breakfast, such as it was. The ARVN unit's all gone, scattered like the wind."

"Probably went back to their village hamlets."

"Or over to Victor Charley."

Barf throws the end of his sandwich in the mud and steps on it, "Some war of independence we've got here, huh?"

Beale looks down at his own muddy boots, thinking about Dirty Mary and her nostalgic feelings for black and white heroes, villains and issues. "Lucky Strikes goes to war...", he says softly. "Lucky Strikes goes to war."

CHAPTER TWENTY EIGHT

After two more weeks of sitting out in the rain with headphones clamped to their ears listening to The Happy Jack Platter Shop on VTVN Radio Saigon the Dimbos are trucked back to the 3rd RRU. Mad Denny, sitting cross-legged and naked on his bunk, gingerly pulls at his balls until he comes away with a long strip of dead white skin. "Oh, no! Crotch-rotch!"

"Red ball." Larky grins, "You got to get to the medics, let em paint up your scrotus with red ball tinct-aid.or your balls will fall off."

"That's not true...and it's a *scrotum,* you nut-brain."

"Gospel truth, you gonna be deball-ated! Shore hell of a way to get a purple heart, huh?"

Mad Denny's eyes widen, "Charley?"

"Quiet, Denny." Charley waves the scrap of the San Francisco Chronicle in his hand, rescued from the wads of old newspapers he's been stuffing in his boots to dry out the rot before it eats holes in the leather, "Listen to this, Beale - some professor's organizing anti-war rallies in Berkeley!"

"Hey, I got a problem here," Mad Denny growls.

"They're calling us invaders, colonialists and baby-killers!"

Beale is sprawled across his own bunk, trying to write down his impressions of the past three weeks. He doesn't even bother to look up, "Old news, baby, old news. That's why I signed up."

"It's *right here in this paper,* Ong Be!"

Larky, who has his .45 lying in oily parts all over his footlocker, looks puzzled, "Didn't nobody back there ever hear of the draft? I mean, good old Beale here's the only one who *wants* to be here!"

"*What about my balls?!*"

"If they don't fall off tonight, get over to the medic station near the runway in the morning." Charley turns his attention back to Beale, "First this guy's family tree gave us Attila the Hun, then Hitler the Horrid, and now, Ladies and Germs - we present *Beale the Baby-Killer!*"

Beale snatches the crumpled newspaper from Charley's hand, "Give me that!"

It quickly absorbs his attention, and he reads in silence for a few moments before he hands the paper back to Charley. "It's the same thing every time.... these protestors use the same exact language, just like Victor Charley! *De Quoc Xam Luoc My* - 'invader-gangster Americans'. That's what the VC call us all the time. I heard those same exact words at UCLA, and it's right here on a poster in San Francisco."

"So what, Beale?"

"Don't you get it? *Invader-gangster?* It's an every-day, common expression. I say that all the time, 'That's my coffee, invader-gangster'....'Get out of my seat, invader-gangster'".

"You're saying we're being duped? Don't be so hyper, Ong Be."

"Yeah", Larky scoffs, "We got free press - they can't be that stupid!"

"I'm saying *America* is being duped!"

They are quiet for a while; Denny picking at his balls while the rest of them go back to their tasks. As if in harmony with their mood, there is a sudden irregular crackle of weapons fire in the distance.

"Hmmmm, fairly close."

"Probably the tree line across the runway."

Larky turns his radio up, "Hey, you guys heard this one yet?" It is Radio Saigon, throbbing with the Beatles' A HARD DAY'S NIGHT.

The wind shifts, rattling the rain harder against the gray, unpainted teakwood slats on one side of their barracks. Outside it is black as pitch. They hear the two night guards go by, miserably sloshing around their perimeter.

It makes Beale uneasy, realizing that the guards have their rifles slung upside down under their ponchos, and the clips are in their pockets, if they are even allowed to carry live ammo. Other guards are circling other units all over Tan Son Nhut, endlessly walking around marked perimeters.... while somewhere out there, moving almost at will like shaggy wolves in the night are roving bands armed with mortars and satchels of *ep plastique*, with captured M-1 and M-14 rifles, with borrowed AK-47 automatic assault rifles, RPG-7 rocket launchers and K50-M submachine guns.

"Hey, *Beale*," Charley shouts over the noise of the radio, "what are you going to do to further the fair Hoa's musical career?"

"Nothing. I'm still numb from Phu Bai...."

Charley waves a copy of The Saigon Observer, a weekly magazine printed in English that he'd picked up at the EMC. "No excuse, pal! I, the Italian Impresario, have found an idea for you! Some band leader named Leonard LeRoy's holding a singing contest!"

"Leonard LeRoy! What does he play, the sweet potato?"

"No. Accordion, I think. It doesn't matter. He's a bandleader, Ong Be. The U.S. Information Library sponsors him, and the winners get to compete nationwide for the top prize."

"Which is?"

"A Vespa motor scooter."

"Whoop-de-doo!"

"Prelims are next Sunday on the My Canh floating restaurant, by the river. If Hoa's more than just a roll in the hay, that is...."

"Thanks, Charley. You're always thinking of ways to better my life. Why don't you do it yourself?"

"What - bring Tuy? Tuy's blessed with the voice of a truck driver, Be. She ruined it screaming at men."

They are interrupted by Toady, who bangs his way in through the screen door, "Ohh! Good! You guys are back! It's a red alert - everybody grab your pots and get over to the armory room for your rifles!"

"What's up, Toady? Somebody steal the captain's little brass airplane?"

Toady is panting, and his eyes are wide saucers of fear in his pimply face, "VC snuck in past the tree line! Nobody knows how many! We got to defend the White Shack!"

"Who are *we*?"

"Uhh, *everybody* - a whole bunch of guys!"

Captain Nordoff has a truck waiting at the assembly area in front of his office, and in minutes the Dimbo Patrol is jouncing along the runway over to the White Shack where they are met by Taters Johnson, the night duty sergeant. The icy chill from the air conditioning hits them with the usual arctic blast as they rush into the workroom.

"Sure," Mad Denny mutters to anyone listening, "your balls fall off or they freeze off, and the uckin'-fay army doesn't care one way or the other..."

"Listen up here, fellers," Taters warns. He holds up a rusty incendiary grenade. It looks like a left over from World War II or a bright red can of hairspray with a pull-ring at the top where the sprayer should have been. The sergeant's face is pink in the glare of the overhead lights, "There's one of these in the top drawer of each file cabinet. If we're forced to fall back to this position and hold them off from here, the first thing we do is ignite everything...."

"But sarge, wouldn't we burn ourselves up?"

"We'll think about that when the time comes!"

Charley picks up the three-page set of instructions that Taters had been leafing through. They are stamped *Confidential* and look at least ten years old.

"That what it says in here?"

"Screw that, Jack! We might be dead by the time we wade through that!" He tears the manual in half and stuffs it in the nearest waste can.

Charley points to Beale, "He Jack -- me Charley."

But Taters isn't in a joking mood. He yells, "Follow me, men!" And then he leads them out the heavy steel back door. It was the first time any of them had seen it unbolted.

Mad Denny gives Charley a bemused look,

"John Wayne is alive and well."

"Green Berets forever."

The Dimbos spend the night in the rain, fifteen feet from the relative comfort of the White Shack, huddled in a two foot high bunker of sandbags that somebody had started on the cement slab near the rusty burn-bags incinerator. Two Puff-the-Magic-Dragon DC-3's circle endlessly overhead, just under the low clouds, dropping flares that etch the scene in stark yellow-and-black.

Beale huddles under his poncho, too numb and dazed to care that the rain is slowly working its way inside. His cigarettes are soaked and he can't get a Marlboro going, though he keeps on trying.

After a while Mad Denny begins to softly sing an old college song,

> Her mother never told her
> The things a young girl should know
> About the ways of college men
> And how they come and go.

Charley and Larky join in, and the mournful drinking song is sad rather than funny as it drifts through the rainy night

> Time has faded her beauty
> And sin has left its sad scar
> So remember your mothers and sisters, boys
> And let her sleep under the bar...

Beale clutches his damp M-14 and tries to conjure up some back-home images. *What was it like in America?* Hoa had asked. *What was it like in America?* as if the place was some fabulous,

237

unattainable legend of old, the G.I.'s wonderful and forbidden Camelot home. He remembers the snappy, red Schwinn two-wheeler he'd had in grade school, but there in his mind in the dark the image warped in a strange direction, and his bike was exploding in the schoolyard rack at St. Liborius because some greasy little peanut girl had been paid 200 P to stuff the handlebars with *ep plastique*! He shakes his head, chasing the crazy notion away. *Beautiful, ivy-covered Wrigley Field! The Cubs, and they're actually winning 4 to 3 in the seventh inning....* but his mind betrays him again, and a land mine planted by a gap-toothed cyclo-peddler out behind 3rd base blows Ron Santo to a million pieces in front of twenty eight thousand hot-dog munching fans. He grits his teeth angrily. *Disneyland! Disneyland, the beautiful and sacred, the family place of fun and laughter where you leave your cares behind!* But then sappers are crawling over the walls with satchels of explosives in their teeth, while a death-squad ambushes the little train, the tourists hanging out the windows with the blood running from their blank eyes. *Snowball fights!* Those were safe, they didn't *have* any snow in Vietnam, and he eagerly wraps his fraying mind around thoughts of himself tucked safe and secure behind the thick walls of a snow-fort back in the Illinois of his younger days. But the nasty, unwanted images sneak into his mind again like black spiders, and the shimmering snowballs melt and warp in mid-air, changing to olive-colored grenades, and the slick, glassy walls of ice turn to a bamboo walled prison.

"Nuts, Beale", he whispers to himself, "You're

going abso-fucking-lutely nuts!" Yet he can almost feel the fragments of steel and the slivers of shattered bamboo cutting and ripping into his chest as a make believe grenade goes off.

Finally he is too weary to be afraid any more. He knows the V.C. aren't coming anyway; Nordoff had panicked and called a full alert, and now he wouldn't have the guts or brains to call it off until morning. Beale slumps and stares blankly up at the sky, allowing the rain to hit his face and to run down his neck inside his poncho.

He runs a hand over his forehead, knowing the rain is mingled with his own sweat. *They tossed four living human beings out of a helicopter, like they were dogs or slabs of meat!* He still can't get over that one. Back home, the know-nothing protest bull-shitters are calling the troopers all baby-killers, and here in Vietnam the killing just goes on and on and on like they were pigs in a slaughter-house . . . *Is he learning the things he'd come here for? There was a time when he thought he was. But the Nam realities are so different from the incident-sparked features Newsweek and Time write about, so alien from the howl of anti-war protests, so unique to this place and time itself, so wrapped in the endless flow of arcane oriental belief and in the historical conflicts of the region, that he feels he has been time-warped to an existence he would never be able to explain to anybody.* One thing he thinks is sure; if he ever does get back, he won't be the same old Jack Beale, the young guy who signed up for three big ones just to prove to some girl he hardly knew that he could find out what was really going on!

Dawn comes and the sun lies like a great leaden egg trying to peer through the dull grey grill of the sky. Toady finally comes to pick them up at about 10 o'clock.

"What the hell's going on, Toady?", Mad Denny grumbles in a hoarse voice.

"Well, uhh- uhh, we've been *busy* too, you know!"

"What about the terrorists?"

"They were captured - sometime in the night."

"What time did the Red go off?"

"Uhh - about five or so, I think . . . "

"You went to sleep and forgot all about us, didn't you?" Mad Denny grabs the dumpy little clerk by the arm and pulls him out of the jeep. The Dimbos wearily throw in their gear and climb into their seats.

Toady stands up and rubs his back, "If you've broken anything - Wait! That's *my* jeep!"

Mad Denny drives in a big circle on the concrete apron around Maizy and Daizy and heads for the 3rd. They don't give Toady a second look, and that, too, is a mistake. For, as any Vietnamese will tell you, *When forced to share rice with a rabid rat, try not to ruffle his fur.*

CHAPTER TWENTY NINE

After procrastinating until it is almost too late, Beale talks to Hoa about entering *The Saigon Observer's* singing contest. At first, she gives him a dozen excuses: she isn't ready, it is too short notice, she is busy with her job, and so on, but he accuses her of not being serious about her singing career and so bullies her into agreeing. To make sure she won't back out, he takes her to the *Moulin Rouge*, an exclusive dress shop in the Edan Arcade just off of Tu Do Street, and buys her a dress to wear specially for the contest.

And then he doesn't see her for the rest of the week, because every moment she isn't at the Hong Kong bar, she is with her singing teacher. He can't get away from the White Shack to see her for even a few minutes, and so doesn't really know what she will be singing. Since he's never heard her sing in front of a crowd with a band backing her, he isn't sure what to expect. But that's the thing about Beale -- once he gets it in his head that the contest is good for her, he plows ahead full steam and damn the torpedoes.

At noon on the day of the contest they stand hand-in-hand looking out across the wide, muddy waters of the river. It's a Sunday and the moody clouds threaten more rain, but for the moment the showers have broken off and they can see to the far side of the turgid waters of the estuary where a few houses are crowded by mangrove swamps. There is enough sniping from those distant trees to discourage water-skiing, but there is still plenty to see; life on the river goes on, and the carefully-marked shipping lanes are packed with commercial boats from one-man pole dugouts with little loads of fruit or vegetables to huge ocean freighters. Heavily armored river gunboats cut trails of froth through the flat, brown water and the packed river ferry is making its hourly way across the wide expanse of open water to the other side.

Hoa is in high spirits. She breaks away from Beale and does a fanciful little spin to show off her new dress.

"*Dep lam, dep qua!*", he said. "Very, very pretty, too pretty for words!"

The dress she has picked is a touch more snug-fitting and colorful than he might have wanted, her practical mind reasoning she might wear it to work at the bar, and she still applies her make-up on the heavy side, but he is pleased anyway, *After all, it's who she is*

They join the Sunday crowd gathered on the sidewalk and watch a man carving vegetables in fanciful designs. Beale buys her a lavender balloon and they eat tiny scoops of French ice cream in hard little waffle cones.

Saigon has come out for this brief respite from the rain. Middle-class bureaucrats in their dull suits, wearing clip-on sunglasses over their plastic-rimmed bi-focals, point out matters of interest to their western-style dressed wives. ARVN soldiers in khakis and Rangers in camo and G.I.'s in civvies and a sprinkle of Frenchmen in short-sleeved white shirts stroll along the sidewalks of the carefully groomed little park. Matronly *bas*, their pear-shaped bodies covered with simple *ao gai* and their heads under conical hats, stroll by looking for a

Sunday morning deal on peanuts or bananas. Women sidewalk sellers wearing two-piece pajamas with brown tops and black bottoms wave slices of cold pineapple on sticks. White mice cops in their uniforms of snowy white strut about with an air of disregard. Bargirls move along like richly colored flowers in their tight-fitting silk dresses of heavily brocaded silk and Saigon cowboys in flashy polyester and fancy French sunglasses huddle in chatty groups and carefully examine the crowd.

There is no hurry and Beale and Hoa make their unhurried way to the My Canh floating restaurant where the contest is to be held. The restaurant is built on the main deck of an old river packet boat tied to permanent moorings between the ferry dock and the downtown small-boat docks. The black-suited waiters serve food that claimed French origins, but over the years had wandered into *pho* and egg rolls, as well as black market beefsteaks and chops from the American Bachelor Quarters and other mess halls. It is frequented by both officers and enlisted men who need a place to bring their girlfriends before they take them back to bed, and many an American has gotten his first real idea of what his night-time companion looks like in the light of day over a Bloody Mary or a Gin Fizz at the My Canh.

By the time Beale escorts Hoa along the ramps that lead over the water to the old decks of polished wood, the lunchtime crowd is gone, but it is still too early for dinner. At Beale's request, the waiter seats them near the bandstand at a table overlooking the river.

It isn't long before the band starts trickling in

and begins to set up their drums and loud speakers. Beale orders Hoa an iced tea and a whiskey-and-water for himself, and goes to talk to Leonard LeRoy.

There is a small crowd of people around the bandleader, who has a fleshy, red face and a spade beard. Beale sees money is changing hands.

LeRoy sizes up Beale with a glance. "One thousand piasters entrance fee", he says softly.

"For what? I thought this was a U.S. sponsored event!"

An older man behind Beale tries to push in, "Put up or get out of the way, soldier." The newcomer is a trim man with short hair and an erect posture. He looks like a captain or a major, and he has a girl half his age in tow.

The bandleader wearily eyes the crowd pressing around him and puts a restraining hand on the older man. "There's plenty of room for all." He speaks to Beale, "It's for expenses. Now I can't take all day, buddy. *Are you in or you out*?"

"In, I guess...." Beale fishes for his wallet and passes over five crisp, purple 200 P notes, accepting a mimeographed entrance form from LeRoy.

"Your girl is number six." He treats Beale to a wide grin, showing his large, yellow-stained teeth, "Which is better than if I said she's Number Ten, right?" Number Ten was an old joke, a bad number to the Vietnamese. Beale hurries back to his table without answering.

"What is this? What were you doing?" Hoa wants to know about everything.

"Entrance form. Here, just fill it out and I'll turn it in to grease-ball over there."

244

The band, with LeRoy on the accordion and two young Vietnamese musicians on drums and sax, lumbers through an opening barrage of old standards, doing fuzzy renditions of "Deep Purple" and "Louise" and an awful, sour version of "Autumn Leaves". After a brief intermission, the girls begin their numbers. They range from bad to terrible, and Beale feels better as he listens to an amateurish "Moon River", a pathetic "We Shall Overcome", and a "Mister Tambourine Man" that sounds like the poor girl was warbling through a mouthful of big grape-like *Trom Trom Trop* berries, "Hey, Meest-ah Tab-or-ee Ma, See a saw pho meeee. I lo-lee, an' tha' ai' no play I go-in'...."

Hoa twists her white handkerchief around her fingers and looks longingly at the ramp back from the My Canh to solid ground. "I don't feel so good, Ong Be. Maybe we still have time to go...."

"Okay, Hoa Night Bird. But you'll end up a bar-girl for the rest of your life."

Tears starts down her cheeks, "That is a mean thing to say!"

"It's just the truth, and you know it. This is a good opportunity, and you've got to go for it. Anyway, it's too late to leave now."

The fifth contestant is reaching perilously for the final notes of the smaltzy, old Debbie Reynolds hit, "Tammy", and Leonard LeRoy's bikini-clad young girl assistant is holding up a pink card on which is hand-lettered a large number 6.

Hoa stumbles out of her chair and nervously walks to the raised platform followed by a polite sprinkle of applause from the crowd. Beale watches as she gathers the three-man band around her and gives them a few instructions. They nod and go back to their instruments, beginning a slow, sad waltz time, while Leonard sets his accordion down and moves toward his whiskey glass.

She sings *"Em yeu Anh"*, a pop Vietnamese song that is on the Saigon music chart. Her sobbing voice breaks in over the backbeat like liquid gold, rising through the room easily, gliding from note to note. The crowd hushes, and Beale knows everything is going to be okay; there is no way she can lose in this field of turkeys.

Leonard LeRoy slips into the seat Hoa had vacated, "What's she singing, kid?"

"Vietnamese love song. It's very popular."

LeRoy sucks at his yellowed teeth and sips his rum and cola, "Couldn't you teach her something in the mother tongue?"

Beale frowns. "She's Vietnamese. She wanted to sing a Vietnamese song."

"You her agent?"

"No. Look, I don't get it - what's that got to do with anything? She's got a great talent."

"Look, kid, great voices is a dime a dozen. Take a tip from the king -- "On Top Of Old Smokey" is not too hard to learn. Great crowd-pleaser, too."

Beale feels himself getting angry, "You mean you're going to count her singing a Vietnamese song against her?"

Leonard thinks about it for a moment, studying Beale over the rim of his half-empty glass, "Naw, 'course not.... maybe it's actually good for a novelty item. Nothing wrong with a little variety."

"But - she's *great* ..."

The fleshy, little man runs his hand through

the black hairs on his chin, "Good, maybe, but great... I don't know."

Beale fumbles for his pack of cigarettes, "Yeah, what does it take to make *great*, anyway?"

"Well, in *this* case", Leonard answers with an expressionless stare, "I'll get her in the quarter-finals for fifty bucks *My Kim*."

Beale drops his Marlboro hard-pack and has to fish around under the table for it. His eyes came up over the edge of the table, "You're kidding?"

"I never kid, kid. Look around you - I got a colonel, a major, two lieutenants, five or six sergeants, that navy guy over there I don't know what-the-fuck rank he is, and about ten grunts like you. *All* you guys think your lay is the Songbird of the South China Seas. It's fifty for the quarter-finals, a hundred for the semi's and the winner goes to the highest bidder, a once-in-a-lifetime opportunity!"

Beale was stunned, "How much is that..."

"Who knows? Some of these officers got all the money in the world.... I mean, they *ain't* making it the army way, if you get my drift."

Beale reluctantly reaches for his wallet, "Fifty is going to make a big dent in my weekly...."

The band leader shrugs, sipping from Hoa's half-empty glass and spitting with a grimace when he realizes it is tea, "Hey - you're in love, you got to pay one way or the other...." He folds over Beale's five tens and stuffs them in a pocket of his wrinkled seersucker jacket, already standing to move on to the next table. "Another free tip, kid - she's drinking tea, so the king says, *if you think you're getting her loaded for the big score, think again*."

The waiter comes by with soup, and Beale says they will select the main course in a few moments.

The Vietnamese girls in the crowded room genuinely applaud Hoa's song, and the two musicians pat her on the back, clearly impressed by her performance. She is all smiles as she returns to Beale's table. Too full of nervous energy to sit, she places her hands on the back of her chair and gives him a shy, nervous smile.

"How did I do, Ong Be?"

He plucks a red rose from the small bouquet on the table, "A flower for my Hoa - the fairest song-bird in the land!"

She reaches to accept it, but her fingers never touch the stem, for in the split second before she could accept his gift there is a shock, and a huge wall of pressure from behind her - a sharp explosion and a great, whistling noise. As his chair is knocked backwards, Beale has a horrible flash-image of the top half of Hoa Night Bird, the love of his life's, head lifted off and tumbled into her soup bowl.

And then he himself is slammed back to crash to the floor, and his unbelieving, terrified cry mingles with a roomful of shrieks of pain and shock. Tables are overturned and glass shards fly through the air. Dead and dying bodies flop in their own blood like doomed fish.

Beale manages to crawl around their upended table and gather Hoa's still-shuddering body in his arms. He has to turn his eyes, he can't bear to look at her maimed head. He knows what has happened; he'd heard a sound like that twice before, in weapons training back at Fort Ord and then when the Dimbos were stranded outside the Phu Bai compound -- *A Claymore mine!*

Smoke hangs in heavy streamers through the room. The lucky ones who had been out of the direct line of the deadly spray of buckshot or who had been protected by the shattered bodies of others are now dragging themselves over the warm pulps that had so recently been human beings. They are panicking, crawling, clawing blindly, anything to get away across the catwalks to the safety of the shore.

Beale knows everything is hopeless, but he refuses to leave Hoa. He looks around in shock and horror. His ears are ringing. He can't hear anything, and he feels disconnected, like he is floating in another reality. Hoa had taken the full force of the explosion. She had died instantly, and her body had saved him.

Feeling a sense of dread, like he is doing something wrong because it is too intimate and personal even for a lover, he gently puts her head **back together as best he can. He sits on the floor, hugging her, unwilling to let her go; he is a numb, tragic figure drenched in her blood, and he has no idea of what to do next.**

From where he is, he can see the narrow ramp off the boat is jammed; everyone who can move desperate to get off the boat. He sees it isn't worth it – or even possible - there is no way he can carry his broken Hoa through that mob. And worse, he blames himself, he talked her into coming here with him. Now all he wants is to sink through the floor of the boat into the black, black estuary and float away into eternity with her. And that moment a second claymore detonates, overloading his already frayed and ringing eardrums, and sweeping the catwalks clean of the people scrambling to get away.

Again, Beale is spared. He lives on unscathed, breathing the acrid fumes and gazing on faces that mirrored his own agony until he can't bear to look any longer. He sits on the floor like a string-less puppet with what is left of Hoa limp in his arms. He sees the shattered dishes, the blood spattered bodies, the walls splintered and bent as if they will cave in. His lowered gaze spots the red rose he'd held out to her moments before the first blast, lying now in a pool of blood and broken glass. He clings to his own crushed and broken flower and little animal cries of pain and sorrow come unbidden from his mouth.

A team of Vietnamese in military uniforms finally takes her away from him. He is led to shore where he is poked and prodded and ordered into a long line that will be checked over after the seriously wounded and the critical are given their chance at survival. He stands there in a daze for nearly an hour while the rain starts to fall and night deepens and the See Bee with the gash over his nose in front of him still hasn't moved. He finally takes one step out of the line. No one says anything. So he takes another, and still another. Gurneys rush past and someone yells for more O negative blood. He turns for one last look at the still-smoking remains of the restaurant, and then walks away, disappearing into the night, heading back in the direction of the 3rd on foot until he gets lucky and hails down a cab.

CHAPTER THIRTY

A disgusted voice rings out from one of the barracks, "Somebody shut that Son-of-a-bitch up!"

"*He's* going to be dead if he doesn't put a lid on it!"

"Christ-sake, two in the morning!"

"I got duty coming up in less than four hours...."

Charley takes Beale by the arm, "Come on, old buddy - let me get you off to bed!"

Beale pulls out of his grasp and takes a sip from the almost-empty bottle of bourbon under his arm, "But she's deaaaaaaaaaaaad..." he starts all over again in a long, keening lament that carries through the 3rd like a coyote's howl.

On his way back to Tan Son Nhut, the taxi had let him out downtown, refusing to take him back to the airport. The White Mice had picked him up and taken him to Saigon General. They swabbed iodine on his cuts, gave him aspirins for his headache, and released him. He'd found another taxi and taken it back to the base, and started drinking whiskey-and-waters at the EMC. After the club closed, the Dimbos all stayed with him, even when he wandered around outside the barracks in the rain; but as it got later and he showed no signs of relenting, Larky went inside to get some sleep, and after another hour Mad Denny left. Charley stayed with him, trying to console him and assuring him over and over that it wasn't his fault.

Charley reaches for his arm again, but it is like grappling with wet spaghetti. Beale spins out of his grasp and staggers over to one of the cement culverts that ran between the barracks. They were only about three feet deep, but he doesn't see it and disappears over the edge with a heavy thud.

Toady shows up, wearing long underwear and rubber go-aheads. He holds a tattered black army issue umbrella and angrily points the beam of his flashlight at Beale, who is still thrashing around at the bottom of the culvert.

"*WILL* you stop this disgusting behavior *at once?*" the clerk hisses. He looks outrageous and foolish, like one of the befuddled German guards in "Hogan's Heroes".

"Toady, get out of here - Beale's lost his girl!"

"Look, mister - we've got a whole company of men here, not just one drunk pining for a lost hooker!"

"You're a real sweetheart!"

"Don't get on my bad side, mister!"

"You don't have any other side, you little prick!" Charley yells, "You're just a kiss-ass corporal!"

"You're going to get yours, Magnolia!" Toady backs away and vanishes around the corner of a nearby barracks.

Charley stands looking after the retreating corporal.

"Thanks, Charley", Beale says in a quiet voice, sounding sad and tired, but fairly sober. He is now sitting on the lip of the culvert. "Do you think you could take me to the medics?"

"Of course. But you can throw up anywhere you want, Be. Pick your spot."

253

"Naw, it isn't that. I think I broke my arm." He lifts his left arm above the edge of the culvert so Charley can see. It bends at a strange angle about halfway between his elbow and wrist. "In a way it feels good, you know? Pure, like fire." He tries to laugh, but the sound chokes out, more than half a sob, "I haven't felt so much pain since I put rubbing alcohol on my dick."

Charley helps him to his feet, and supports him as they walk out the front gate of the compound. The guard just waves them through, eager to be rid of Beale.

"Why'd you do that? I mean, with the rubbing alcohol."

"It seemed like a good idea at the time...." Beale gives out a mournful little laugh, "You know, cleanliness is next to Godliness."

"Yeah, and clap is the work of the devil. Rubbing alcohol really works, huh?"

"I recommend it every time."

It is a half-mile to the medic's station, where they put a cast around his arm and give him a sling. Charley supports him and keeps him babbling as they walk back to their unit down the dark road. Charley thinks talking it out may be the best way to get Beale going again.

The next morning Beale staggers into some civilian clothes and goes downtown to the white mice police headquarters, looking for her body so he can make the arrangements for burial. Hoa hadn't talked about any other family members, so he assumed she was alone in the world. He thinks she has to be Buddhist, though she'd never said. He plans to have her cremated and her ashes

254

placed in one of the lotus bud limestone urns that dot the countryside. He selected some lines from the tragic old Vietnamese classic "Kim Van Kieu" to place in the urn.

But there was no record of a Hoa or a Chim Oanh. Every Vietnamese casualty had been accounted for, and their families had claimed the several dozen bodies of the deceased. Beale went in a state of increasing desperation from department to department in the huge building, but everywhere he was met with shrugs, head shakes, and raised eyebrows. He feels resentment and unspoken insinuations, and the weight of middle class disapproval. *The Nguoi My who says he fell in love with the bargirl/whore. What kind of love could that be? Love, no; surely, it must be guilt.*

There is finally no one else left to turn to, and so he leaves. He knows he can't expect any help from the local authorities, and he also knows he can't go to the Americans who will worry whether and just how his emotional involvement makes him a security risk. He takes a cab to the little park by the river where he had spent some of his precious last day with Hoa. The place is deserted now, newspaper and peanut bags stuck in the hedges and puddles on the meandering gravel pathways; the fruit sellers and vegetable carvers gone, and the wind gusting through the tree branches, giving warning the rain will soon return. He slowly walks to the water's edge, where he reads the lines he'd selected from "Kim Van Kieu" in a low, sobbing voice, first in Vietnamese and then in English:-

What a harrowing destiny, that of this woman!

Speaking of cruel fate is speaking of us all!

Why are you so cruel, Creator?

Why did you make this green youth waste away and her rosy cheeks wither?

Alive, this girl was the wife of everybody.

Alas! She is now a phantom without a husband.

Where are her former lovers, phoenixes attentive to her?

Where are the wooers of her green youth, those who lusted after her rosy complexion?

Since no one has pity and mourns for her death, I want to burn a few sticks of incense.

Maybe you will see my gesture, you who are now in the Other World.

He lights the edges of the paper with a match, watching as orange flame bloom around the words, and then at the last minute he lets it fall into the swirling muddy water below. But there is no relief in the gesture; it isn't enough for him, and he only feels like he's failed her one last time.

In the next days, he sinks into a morose silence. He accepts the cast on his arm without thinking about it. He trudges back and forth to work, where he toys endlessly with the few scraps of intercept that come in. Every night he makes his way to the EMC, where he sits alone and drinks until closing time.

By Friday Charley decides he's had enough. He runs after Beale, who is walking along the tarmac from their barracks to the White Shack.

"Hey, Ong Be - wait up!"

Beale doesn't turn around, and so he was

forced to run an extra couple of steps.

"Hey, guy - we're all going to the Cherry Bar tonight! You got to come!"

"I don't *got* to do anything...." Beale says softly, almost to himself.

"Yeah, but we're gonna have a great time! Even Tuy misses you - she says you make her feel more wicked than she really is!"

"You guys go without me."

Charley takes him by his good arm and turns him around. "You can't go on like this, Ong Be. You don't eat. You don't sleep. You drink booze like water and smoke like a furnace - but you don't enjoy it! God gave man vices to be enjoyed on the way to hell!"

"That's my business...." Beale pulls away from him and continues down the runway.

Charley runs after him and turns him around again, "God damn it, it *isn't* your business! You've got responsibilities to your friends! Hoa died, but you got to stop acting like it's the end of your world!"

"It *was* the end of *my* world! You want me to pretend I didn't care?" Beale sounds hurt and angry.

Charley takes any emotion from Beale as a good sign. "Of *course* you have to care! But you can't walk around like a mummy for the rest of your life, soaking up whiskey in memory of the greatest love the world has ever known, which it was not-"

Beale turns on him then, furious at him, "We had a great relationship!"

"Yes! But you weren't going to marry her!"

"I might have....", Beale starts to protest.

257

"Never! Not in a million years! What would you have to talk about when you're a great and famous writer? The various grades of *nuoc mam*, Vietnam's famous fish sauce? Rice? *Babies?*"

"She had a great voice!"

"Right, but that's not the point either. The truth is, she was good for you. The guys and I all saw it. She gave you a lot. She taught you a lot. And she did love you, in her own way. And you, in your own weird and wonderful way, loved her. Did you ever stop to think, you owe it to her memory to go on?"

"Oh sure", Beale scoffs.

"Don't be so selfish! You *owe* her! Do you think she'd like to know you're wandering around in an alcoholic stupor?"

Beale turns away and starts down the runway again, but Charley keeps at him like a nagging little terrier, "Another thing - she didn't have any real family that we know of. They say the living have to go on, to keep the memory alive - and that's at least twice as true for you, a writer, who can give her life and memory a meaning!"

Beale stares at him, not wanting to accept that responsibility, but Charley sees he is making progress, and he plunges ahead, "Don't you see, Jack? You've got to write those stories, man - for her! You got to go on!"

Beale breaks then, and starts crying. He turns away so Charley won't see the tears coursing down his face as he walks on down the runway, still relentlessly heading for the White Shack. Charley catches up with him again, and they continue the rest of the way in silence.

That evening Beale eats a serving of

scrambled yellow re-do's and some army-burnt toast, the first meal he'd had in a week. And an hour later he scrawls his name in the sign-out log, blinking calmly into Toady's smoldering gaze.

The company clerk scratches an angry red zit on the end of his nose, "I don't think you should be going anywhere with that arm -"

"Who cares what you think?"

"-which, by the way, you deserved."

"Go bite a dink-dong, Toady." Beale fakes a punch with his good arm, and is rewarded to see the clerk flinch. Then he heads for the main gate before Toady has a chance to talk to the C.O..

Beale is pale and quiet as he makes his appearance at the Cherry Bar, and Charley notices his hands shake visibly when he lights his steady stream of Marlboros. But he eats a little cold crab that the girls bring, and holds his drinking down to a couple of Ba Muoi Ba's.

Charley nods quietly to the rest of the Dimbos, and they talk of other things. It is enough that Beale has decided to come back to the living.

CHAPTER THIRTY ONE

The days drag on and Beale does seem to slowly mend. Charley pens in the big black numbers 101, 102 and 103 on the calendar he is keeping. The Dimbos take turns with their Ong Be, not letting him out of their sight and trying to come up with things to keep him occupied. Charley even invents some intercepts that he has Larky type up on computer paper for him. Since they are total gibberish, they have no solution, and Beale works furiously on them for hours.

One rainy afternoon when the four of them are together in their bunk area, Charley finishes a barracks improvement he'd been crafting, "Look at this, Be!"

Charley pulls a little brass ring attached to some fishing wire. He is sitting on his bunk, and yet the bamboo rain screen outside his area lowers itself as if by magic. The split-bamboo screens are lowered down when the wind blows hard and the rain spatters through the louvered teak and wire-screen walls. They normally are rolled up on the side away from the rain, but when the wind shifted everyone had to run outside and get soaked as they lowered their shades.

"Terribly civilized, isn't it", Charley says proudly, running his screen up and down again. "A few bucks at the PX for nylon fishing line, and a few piasters in the Old Saigon Market for pulleys - what a fine thing is the mind of man!"

Beale nods, looking up from the scribbled pages on his bunk, "Now how about a dehumidifier?

They are interrupted by Toady, who pushes his pumpkin-shaped face up against their screen door, "Spec. 4 Magnolia! I should have known!" He comes inside and waves one hand at the brass ring while unconsciously reaching his hand inside his baggy fatigue pants and scratching at the rash of zits on his butt, "That's an unauthorized mechanism!"

"Come off it, Toady! It's an automatic rain shade! It's in the manuals."

"Get serious, Specialist! You're fooling around with army property!"

Beale tosses his pen down and rolls over on his bunk to look up at Mad Denny, who is grinning down at him from the upper bunk, "This cast itches so bad I want to smack it alongside the Toad-man's head."

Mad Denny waves a restraining hand, "No, let me. I'll handle it with diplomacy." He smirks at Toady, "Don't you have enough homo cock books and queer French postcards? You have to come jacking-off in here?"

Toady's face turns bright red, "This pulley-thing is unauthorized! That mechanism is causing damage to the bamboo shade!" As he speaks, he fishes angrily in his pocket, coming up with the small penknife he uses to clean his fingernails after popping his zits. "I'll cut it down myself!"

But as he moves forward, his momentum is frozen by the click of a monster switchblade that appears in Charley's hand. Toady gazes bug-eyed at the knife, hypnotized by the glitter of the huge blade.

Charley flicks his wrist. "Don't ever fuck with

a kid from Bayonne, Toad-shit." He stands and moves forward, flicking the blade back and forth until the clerk is backed up against the screen door. "You touch my automatic screen invention and I'll come for you some night - and you know what I'll cut off!"

Toady retreats through the rain to the scornful catcalls from the barracks, leaving his umbrella behind in his haste. He walks methodically, chin high, as if there are no Dimbos and the rain isn't really soaking him. He returns to his always-waiting desk in the C.O.'s office, where he sits like Job, picking his pimples. He tells himself they will pay. *They will pay! Oh yes, one by one, they will pay!*

CHAPTER THIRTY TWO

Three days after his run-in with Toady, Charley stops with Beale in front of the duty roster bulletin board. Charley stares in amazement, looking like he's seen a ghost, "Ong Be....I'm on intercept detail."

"What, the Otters?"

"No, in the bush!"

"That's got to be a mistake. You're not a radio man - and you're not allowed with your security clearance."

"It's *there*!" Charley jabs at the mimeographed list posted behind the damp glass.

"Let's go talk to the C.O.."

They walk over to the C.O.'s office, but he isn't there.

"What can I do for you gentlemen?", Toady asks.

"Where's the bird man? There's been a mistake on the roster."

"Your C.O. is on R&R, three days in Hong Kong."

"But we need him! There's been a mistake!"

Toady doesn't bother to look up from his religious crossword puzzle, "A well-deserved rest, after what you perverts put him through."

"Toady, this is serious! I'm not supposed to go on radio patrol!"

"A seven letter word, the only animal that lied . . . that would be "s-e-r-p-e-n-t" . . . What's the matter - don't like the bush, Specialist?"

"No", Beale says. "He's not trained for it.

Those guys are half way to Green Berets. We never even had Advanced Weapons Training."

Toady puts his feet on the C.O.'s desk, "Lot of bugs and spiders and *serpents* out there.... of course, you could take some of your inventions along to beat 'em off -"

"You *BASTARD*! I'm *NOT* going out there!!"

Beale has to hold Charley back to keep him from lunging across the desk, "I volunteer to go in his place."

Toady's eyes flicker= back and forth between the two of them. "Nope. You can't go with your arm in a cast like that."

"I *won't* go! You'll see!"

Beale pulls Charley to the door, "Come on - let's see what they say at the White Shack!"

Toady looks up from examining his nails, "Don't bother. Everybody who counts went along with the C.O.. Boo-Boo, Ball, everybody. I checked it."

I'll bet you did!" Beale yells at him.

Charley slams the screen door behind them so violently the damp wood gives and it comes loose on one hinge. That afternoon he had his first stomach pains. By six that evening he vomits up his greasy chicken supper. The next morning he hobbles over to Beale's bunk. "Ong Be - you've got to help me to the medic's."

Beale signs them out with a hurried scrawl, and they flag a cyclo-bus heading in the right direction. Beale sits quietly on one bench seat, blinking in the early light, while Charley retches over the back end of the bus. By now his stomach is empty, but he manages to come up with bits of sputum, and once he thinks he sees flecks of blood.

The medic station is the same place that had put a cast on Beale's arm. The doctors and nurses there spend most of their time fighting syphilis, gonorrhea and a variety of diseases like scalp fungus, red-ball and foot rot. It is a Thursday before payday, and Beale sees the white-painted waiting room is almost deserted. A thin captain looks up from an old Atlantic magazine, and then choses to ignore them. Beale quietly selects a thumb-stained Newsweek from the rack and sits in another corner. Charley paces back and forth while he hacks and clears his throat, convinced now that the disease that ravaged his intestines is moving into his lungs. After twenty minutes a nurse comes and the thin captain disappears around the corner into the inner room.

They are alone. Jets whoosh in for their landings on the adjacent runway, returning from raids on the north. Somewhere a cheap clock ticks. Beale looks up from his magazine, "Did you see these close-ups Ranger 7 sent back from the moon?"

"Jesus, Ong Be - here I am throwing my guts out with dysentery and you're talking about the man in the moon?"

"We don't know for sure it's dysentery", Beale responds mildly.

This seems to upset Charley. He goes into a coughing fit, and then shouts, "Well, for God's Sake, Beale - we know it's something *SERIOUS*!"

Beale shrugs and returns to his Newsweek. His concentration is broken as the outside glass doors slam open, and a team of medics rushes in with a bloody G.I. on a stretcher. They race past the two Dimbos and go directly into the inner rooms. Running footsteps approach from the outside and two more stretchers come in. Somebody yells, "Pound it - *Pound it*!"

Another medic yells, "No, bring him on through! We'll do it on the table! Leave the other one!"

The last stretcher is left in their wake as they rush past, left sitting on the floor in the middle of the waiting room, an intrusion from another, more violent world. Beale feels embarrassed that he is staring, but there is nowhere else to look. He peeps over his Newsweek and sees the guy's back is to them. There is a little blood on the back of his collar. Relieved that was all he could see, he looks over at Charley, who has stopped his coughing fit and now is looking pasty-white, like he is about to start another round of vomiting.

Charley picks up the Atlantic magazine and tries to read, but the wounded man is now moaning, making strange, muffled sounds, "Arrrrg....Arrrg..."

He gives out a louder cry and rolls their way on the stretcher. The two Dimbos stare in dismay - his jaw is hanging from his face, the right side of it torn away, most of his teeth gone and just a bloody red hole where his lips had been. He is doped up, but he sees them through glazed eyes. His gaze begs them, asking that it not be true,

Charley jumps to his feet, suddenly flooded with shame, "Come on, Ong Be - let's get out of here."

"But what about your dysentery?"

"I think I'll live. Come on." He practically
266

runs out of the room, leaving Beale to follow after him.

The cyclo-bus rattles and bumps over the road back to the 3rd. Beale still wants to protest Charley's assignment, "There's got to be something we can do. You're not supposed to be on radio patrol in the first place."

"Whatever will be, will be....", Charley says softly, looking at nothing in particular out of the back end of the bus.

CHAPTER THIRTY THREE

Beale has to work late at the White Shack, and Toady manages to get the other Dimbos on guard duty, so as night fell, Charley gets tired of waiting and catches a cab downtown by himself.

Charley doesn't like to watch Tuy work. It makes him jealous to see her play up to other guys for her Saigon whiskey. He turns away from the Cherry Bar, walking through the Edan Arcade, looking at the young kids hanging out at the milk-bars, and in the shop windows filled with silks, jewelry, fine tailored suits and expensive leathers.

He drops in on Kelley's Bar, but the place is deserted and gloomy. The Edan Theater signs say it is playing "Bonjour Tristesse", but after he's paid for his ticket and sits down inside he sees they are running something else, a Chinese historic epic with a cast of millions and a weepy heroine dressed in high-collared silk jump-suits. He tries to get interested, but the dialogue is harsh and intrusive and the subtitles printed on the bottom of the screen in Vietnamese and French make him dizzy. After twenty minutes his attention wanders, and since the movie looks like it will never end, he gets up and leaves.

Back out in the arcade, he hands the peanut kids a few piasters without his usual banter and heads across Le Loi Street to the U.S.O., which is two blocks toward the river on the Street of Flowers. He arrives just before they close the grill, and scores the last hamburger and a chocolate milk shake. He sets his paper plate on the glass top of a

Thunderbolt pinball machine, and eats while he runs up a string of free games.

He watches his time carefully, even while he expertly flips the balls and raps the edge of the machine, extending his string to 20 games. A half-hour before curfew, he hails a cab from the overhang of the sandbagged entrance to the club. The evening rain is still pelting down, and the windshield wipers make scratchy cat's feet noises as the driver takes him the few blocks to the Cherry Bar.

Tuy is happy to see him, and he buys her the mandatory drink. The bar closes at twenty minutes before midnight. His cabbie had promised to wait, but the driver has vanished. It takes a few minutes, but Charley manages to hail another. Tuy comes running out to join him, and the little blue-and-cream races to get them over to the Da Cau district before the curfew.

Tuy rents a little brick house at the end of a blind alley that is too narrow for auto traffic. Charley pays the cab, and they run for her front door with newspapers over their heads.

It is a humid night, and the house has no air conditioning. The fan Ranley had bought her slowly turns over their heads as they lay naked in bed without any covers. Tuy is on her stomach, paging through a Hollywood Star magazine that he'd brought her from the PX.

Charley lies on his back, looking at the ceiling and wondering if he should make love now or wait until it cools off. The fan blades make weird-monster shadows, and he feels uneasy. He sighs and takes a swig out of a warm bottle of Algerian red at his side. He is a long way from the comfort of the Italian ghetto in Bayonne, and from good old St. Pete's College. He finds himself wishing again that goddamn Beale hadn't gotten them into this bat-shit. Then he thinks about it again, admitting that it had been more than Beale. True, old Lemonlips' desire to see it all had been the catalyst, but the rest of the Dimbos had been bored out of their gourds at the Puzzle Palace, ready for the chemical change. *If he, Charley, himself, hadn't been so clever with Nelson and Captain James, would they still be back at the Puzzle Palace.... who could tell?* The war was heating up now, with thousands of combat G.I.'s streaming in every week. And they might have been stationed at Phu Bai or Nui Ba Den or some other hellhole anywhere from the central highland plateaus to the delta.

The fan swirls, and he imagines the shadows are Vietnam vampire bats, come to suck his blood - no, not bats, in this country they would be vampire dragons. What was it Beale was always saying? *The dragon rolls the dice.* He turns and rubs the back of his hand against Tuy's bare shoulder, "Hey love, what do you know about dragons?"

She puts a finger on the page to mark the place where she was reading, and pouts at him, "Aren't you going to make love to me?"

"Nah. Too hot. Later. Tell me about dragons."

"You don't know? Every schoolgirl and boy know about Mister Dragon. He the most famous guy in Vietnam."

"Yeah? How could a horrible-looking creature like that get famous? What does he do?"

"Never say that, Ong Charley!" She sits up, genuinely upset with him, "It is bad luck - very bad, Number 10 bad, to say any evil on Mister Dragon!"

"Yeah, well I'm sorry, I didn't know. Tell me more so I don't make any more mistakes."

"He is sign of Emperors in the old days - you know, ancient day? Even today, he our friend."

"The same dragon? How long does he live?"

"She eyes him with a solemn gaze; they are discussing religious things. "He never die!"

"Seems strange in a country where everybody else is popping off like flies...."

"You make fun again. Number 10 bad for you."

"Nah, not really making fun. I just don't understand." He smiles, "You see, I never saw a dragon, Tuy."

"They very hard to see," she admits. "They can live under ground, and in water, and in air with cloud! They can spit fire, too - burn you, very too badly! I don't think you like it if you see one for real!"

He smiles at her again, "I'm much more afraid of *Su Tu Ha Dong* than any old dragon."

She gives him a curious look, "I have that hot blood, yes? Not quiet and meek like the Japanese, or the China-woman who all the time say 'yes-yes' to their men. You make a Ha Dong mad, you run plenty fast!"

"Faster than if I trip over a dragon's tail?"

"You figure out for self; Mister Dragon has head of camel, horns on top, great big eyes bug out like devil-eye, ear of the buffalo, \body like snake, coat like fish, claw like eagle and foot of tiger!

271

How you kill something like that?"

"Why would I want to?"

"Many men try, for the precious jewel he hide under tongue!"

Charley props his chin on his hand and stares at her, "You're not making that up? You learned that in school?"

"I told you so just one minute ago."

She looks so young in the dim light from the bedside lamp that he feels a twinge of conscience. She is probably the youngest girl at the Cherry Bar. His curiosity gets the best of him, "Tuy, how old are you?"

She smirks mischievously, "Ohhh, what a very good question, my Charley. It is my birthday very soon, and you must celebrate with me – I think for my wish list you must buy for me a fine Sony radio from your PX store. After all, it is old American custom, yes?"

He swats her naked rump lightly, just enough to sting, "How *old* are you? Answer the question."

"Oh, you dare to strike a woman of Ha Dong!" She comes back fighting, and they wrestle on the bed. He manages an arm-lock, but she wiggles free and goes for his weakness, tickles to the stomach. Finally, he is laughing too hard and has to give up. He sinks back on the saggy old mattress with her on top of him. She holds his wrists and looks down into his eyes, "So you think you can get the best of a tiger-lady, is so, my Charley lover-boy?"

"Okay, okay", he says, trying to get his breath back, "a present from the PX. A *nice* present."

"She lowers herself until her hair covers his face, enclosing them in a dark tent, and her nipples

272

tease his bare chest. "Now you remember, Mister Charley, that my birth-date is two weeks from Friday....I will be sixteen years old!"

His blood pounds and his breath comes in little gasps. If he wasn't so involved....if, perhaps, she had been an American girl, or even if she had told him at some other time, it might have had more impact. But she has arched her back and is sitting on him, rubbing her hands gently up and down his thighs. He closes his eyes and lies back, shuddering with delight. She is old enough to do anything she wants to - and it wasn't going to be too muggy to make love after all.

CHAPTER THIRTY FOUR

"Just remember", Charley says as he waves from the back of a truck, "according to a recent Harris Poll, 85% of the folks back home approve of the war!"

Beale, dressed in civvies, has gotten out of bed to see him off. He scratches his arm, trying to get at the itch under his cast, and stares sleepily up at Charley, "What the hell are you talking about?"

"I read about it in Time! One hundred million Americans can't be wrong - therefore, I accept this sacred trust! It is the will of my people that I carry the Holy Grail north to victory!"

"Yeah.... well, just keep your head down and stay out of trouble."

The truck revs up, belching black smoke into the moisture-laden air. As they pull out, Charley has time for one last wisecrack, yelling back over the engine noise, "Don't forget your penicillin shots, Ong Be!"

The small caravan sloshes its way out of the 3rd's motor pool, two deuce-and-a-half's led by a jeep, and in a moment they are out of sight. Beale wanders back to the barracks, hoping Larky still had some Oreo cookies left from the care package his mom has sent him.

Fifteen minutes later, Charley's convoy rumbles out the Tan Son Nhut Main Gates, and after passing through the city check-points, heads inland and moves north along Route 20. After leaving Beale, Charley drops his mask of joviality. He doesn't have the foggiest idea of how to survive in the bush, and he knows it. He rides alone with the radio equipment and his gear so he won't have to get into any conversations with the regular radio operators, who are lifer-types, and passing he time playing pinochle in the back of the other truck.

Charley lights up a joint and glumly watches the green countryside string out behind him. After thirty miles they leave the lowlands and begin crawling up into the isolated hill country of the piedmont. There is a light rain, and fog drifts in and out of the scrub brush on the slopes.

They travel slowly, and by mid-day they are crawling up Bao Loc pass. The jeep goes on ahead, and radios back that the road looks clear. The further they go, the more Charley's tension increases. When they'd first left Saigon, he'd noticed spiders hanging from the few telephone wires along the road - spiders so big their feet hung from wire to wire. There were no telephone wires here, this far out in the bush; so all those creatures had to be running around loose in the grass somewhere. He chides himself for having such a vivid imagination. *After all, fucked-up Beale was the one who saw visions.*

The road finally branches off, and they take Route 21 northwest into the rain forests near Da Lat. Beale had done some research for him and had found that in another age, before World War II, and perhaps again for a brief time in the early '50's, Da Lat had been a famous resort town, a place where gentlemen hunters from Europe and America left their wives to dawdle at the spas while they disappeared into the deep jungle to stalk elephants and tigers.

Beale, doing his customary research into any

275

new subject, had found out some things Charley would rather not have known. He ran across a two year old Classified C.I.A. Area Briefing that claimed the forests were still supposed to hold native pygmies who used poison-tip blowgun darts. But when Charley worriedly asked Taters Johnson about it, he just scoffed, "I'm taking a tenderfoot cub scout into the wilds - you'll scare off any wildlife for miles around!"

"But what about the pygmies?"

Taters shrugs, "Map says the area is uninhabited." He hands the map across, "See for yourself!"

Charley sits alone in the truck and worries his ass off. He listens to the rumble of the engine carrying him north to the jungles. *Pygmies or no pygmies, he could hardly wait until the C.O. got back so he could fry Toady!*

Late in the day the trucks halt by the roadside in a small, saddleback valley. The forest is a dense green wall on both sides of the road. Charley sees it lean over the asphalt, and knows it is full of creepy, bad things. Taters walks by and hits the fender with his fist, "Alright, pop up, Little Scout, time to take a hike!"

Charley crawls out of the truck and stretches his legs. He looks around doubtfully, "Where *are* we?"

"A couple clicks out of Da Lat. You're the first drop, Scout. Get your gear and follow me."

The sergeant hoists the heavy intercept unit on his back and disappears into the jungle, hacking with a machete as he hikes along. Charley grabs his heavy backpack and his M-14 and runs after him. Moving through the heavy vegetation, they

276

go in about a hundred yards. It is impossible to see the road from where they are, and difficult to move because Taters insists they go the last fifty yards without clearing a path.

At last he leans the radio against a clump of thick bamboo in a small clearing between several trees. "This is far enough. You set up here."

"Alone?"

"Sure, alone. What do you think this is, a convention?"

"I'm not staying out here by myself."

"This is a secure area. And I'll be back to check up on you myself. Late tonight, or tomorrow for sure."

Charley takes hold of his arm, "I thought we worked in teams."

The sergeant shrugs him off, "Well, we're a little short-handed right now. You can handle it."

Charley looks around with a sense of growing panic. Everywhere he looks there are leaves that probably are poisonous, and thorn branches, and weird and colorful caterpillars and ugly-looking insects.

Taters tosses a little wave of farewell over his shoulder as he disappears into the green jungle, walking back the way he came.

"You're coming back, right?"

"Sure. Tonight or tomorrow morning, maybe. Keep in touch with the other units. Use the radio, nug. You'll be okay."

The sergeant was gone. Charley finds a stick and quickly lays it on the ground, pointing in the direction he has disappeared, so he might at least know which direction the road is. He glances around nervously, his eyes moving from point to point in the forest of green that surrounds him. Moving quickly, he picks up his machete, which he has leaned against a tree, but in doing so, he kicks the directional stick. He *thinks* he's put it back the way it was, he is almost certain he has it right. He sits down on his helmet and breathes deeply to control his panic.

When he feels a little calmer, he hacks furiously around where he's standing until he has a clear space about two meters in every direction. The humid heat quickly saps his energy, and his fatigues are sweat-soaked under his poncho. He is exhausted, and has to sit down to rest. His eyes wander to the direction-stick, and he realizes he doesn't remember which end points the way back! Neither end looks right! And worse, the stick doesn't seem to be pointing where he remembered it - he must have kicked it again in his wild hurry to clear the area!

His breath is coming in gasps. Is it his imagination, or is the jungle all around him getting darker? His original plan had been to clear a wider area, but swinging the big hatchet-knife in the fetid closeness has been tough work, and he is not in very good shape.

He looks at the fresh blisters on his hands and decides to leave the clearing go and erect his makeshift tent as fast as he can. He throws some lines around the trunks of trees in roughly the four corners of his clearing, and manages to get his spare rubber poncho up overhead, and then to string his hammock under that.

A few days before, he'd bought still another poncho from a peddler on Le Loi Street. He spreads this one under the hammock, hoping it will keep away the hated bugs and spiders. Finally, he adds four mosquito nets - his own, and three spares, also acquired from the Le Loi black market.

He is trying to figure out how to keep the rain from coming in through the head-hole in the poncho that was serving as his roof when Taters unexpectedly returns with the batteries and the rest of the radio gear. He takes one look at Charley's tent and lets out a loud guffaw, "Where do you want this stuff - in your living room or the den?"

Charley immediately sets his direction-stick right.

"Sarge! I never thought I'd be so happy to see a lifer! Can't I come back with you now?"

Taters grin isn't a pleasant sight. "I accepted your friend Beale. He works hard, and he used to hang out with Ranley. But I don't got much patience for the rest of you lingies. Now you kin' put this inside your little shack, or work outside with the bugs chewing on you all night. Your choice."

"But, sarge, I *know* we're *supposed to work in pairs* -"

Taters gets serious about what is what, "Listen up close - You ain't alone, you're part of a triangle team. Your second unit's five miles south, an' the third's seven miles west. The others went on north to build their own triangles. That's *it*, nug. See you Tuesday."

"B-but - it's only Sunday!"

The receding voice comes at Charley for somewhere in the green beyond, "You got rations and water. This is a *secure* area....secure as anywhere else in this god dam shit-coolie land!"

279

And then he was gone again.

Charley looks around, swallowing in fear and frustration. He finally drags the heavy receiver/recorder inside his makeshift tent, dropped it next to his hammock, and goes back outside for the solid battery packs.

He eyes his watch, which he can now read by the green radium dial. It is past four-thirty in the afternoon. Very little light filters through the trees. It will soon be too dark to see. He takes a quick look around for bigger animals, dreading that he might see a huge, man-crushing snake in the trees overhead, or a black panther, it's shining red eyes looking at him through the bamboo thicket. Seeing nothing, he goes quickly back inside his netting.

Inside there it is already almost dark as night. He again feels the panic begin to swell up in his consciousness. The heavy jungle air smells of decaying vegetation, and several very large bugs already hang on the outer netting, looking in at him. Every once in a while a small lizard chases up or down the nylon mesh, making a weird *eeeeeeeeekkkkk* noise. He hurriedly tucks the bottoms of the nets under his ground-poncho, anchoring the corners with the batteries.

He shivers with fear and flicks at the bugs on the netting from inside with his rations spoon, thinking over and over again, *Fuck, oh fuck, oh fuck, how did I ever get into this? Sure, the times in Saigon had been great; a little light crypto-work and then the wild taxi rides downtown to beat the curfew. A few Ba Muoi Bas and some knocking around the nightspots with the Dimbos, and then to bed with lovely, fresh-limbed Tuy.*

280

He grits his teeth and tries not to think of Tuy. *Sure, she said she was his, but now he would be gone for almost a week. The guys would move in like vultures, and when that happened, what would she do?* He shakes his head and drags his thinking back to his present situation. He can't find his M-14! He crawls around his poncho, digging frantically through the mounds of clothing and equipment, but it was nowhere to be found. He finally spots his rifle outside, leaning against a nearby tree, and quickly crawls out and retrieves it.

Then he scurries quickly back inside his bug-fortress. Once he feels he is safely inside with no insects hanging on him, he takes off his undershirt and wipes the beads of water from his M-14. *This baby wouldn't let him down!* He snaps a clip in, makes sure it is ready to fire, and places it on his hammock along with his big switchblade.

Setting up the radio takes over an hour. He isn't familiar with the procedure, and finally discovers some wires he'd forgotten to connect. When he gets it cranked up, it is so dark he is working by the light of a big-beam flashlight. Taters had told him to work in the dark, but he knew he'd never get it fixed without a little light. He puts on the headset and turns the radio on, but only was rewarded with a flat, static hiss. He decides the others must not have set their gear up yet.

He sits on the edge of his saggy hammock, exhausted from the humid heat and the unfamiliar work. He takes off his boots and the rest of his clothes. They are soaked both from perspiration and the rain that drips steadily from branch to branch through the thick canopy of forest overhead. He hangs his fatigues on a rope he'd strung under the roof-poncho, knowing that if he neglects his clothes they'd be mildewed by morning. Then he sprays his naked body with a can of Yard Guard his mother had sent him from the States, and finally climbs in and tries to rest on the hammock. He jerks to attention almost immediately as some animal makes a rustling sound nearby, and the bugs are silent for a moment before they begin again to click and creak around him like a strange insect orchestra..

He simply cannot get comfortable, and after a few minutes of squirming around and trying to keep his rifle handy without it poking him in the side, he rolls out of his hammock. Lighting the big flashlight again, he digs in his pack for a big nose-spray bottle. Nervously unscrewing the cap, he holds the plastic bottle in one hand and works at the spray plug in the top with his nail-clippers file. After some manipulation, the plug pops out. He fishes around in his pack some more until he comes up with a small packet of Zig Zag papers.

He is getting to be expert at roll-your-own; he deftly touches his tongue to the top paper in the pack, and pours out a small pile of gray-green Laotian Gold on the paper. In a moment it is licked and rolled, and he is able to light up. Snapping off the flashlight again, he feels his way back into the hammock with the smoking joint hanging from his lips. He leans over and grabs the headphones; he'd pre-set the band knob to the USIA station in Saigon.

It is raining harder now, and the drops work their way down through the leafy canopy overhead to fall on his poncho with heavy plopping sounds before they slide off onto the ground. *I guess I'll manage,* he tells himself. *I always make out somehow.* He knows it doesn't really matter if he picks up any code or not. The other guys aren't working yet. And he can always tell Taters the radio broke down. *Hell, the guy should have been out here anyway, HE was the goddamn expert!*

Charley builds another smoke and lies back on the hammock, aware of the light film of sweat on his skin. He drags the sweet, blue smoke into his lungs and holds it there. He can hear his heart beat, and the raindrops are in sync with the Beatles as they wail

I wanna hold your ha-a-and
I wanna hold your hand!

After a while he drifts off into sleep. He dreams he is back in Saigon, riding deep in Tuy while a dragon hovers somewhere overhead. He doesn't notice when he rolls over on his side, the short earphones cord pulls away from his radio. Unplugged like that, the Beatles begin to play soft and clear from a small speaker in back of the intercept unit, the friendly rock an' roll spreading out into the listening night air of the jungle.

CHAPTER THIRTY FIVE

Beale has come back from the White Shack and is chewing his way through some fried chicken in the 3RD's mess hall when Toady comes running to get him. "Phone call, Beale. From somebody back stateside."

For some reason Beale flashes on Mavis. Maybe she has found his address somehow, is tracking him through the army. Maybe she is pregnant. Maybe she wants to kill him. He gulps the last of his coffee, grabs his Marlboros hard pack, and runs after Toady.

"They say who it was?"

"Said her name was Tweedildee-dee."

Beale's heart sinks. Charley had given Tuy the company number for emergencies, and that was her code word. He hurries into the C.O.'s office and picks up the phone. Toady sits on the C.O.'s desk, well within earshot, until Beale waves him away. Even then he only retreats to his own desk, still obviously hoping he can overhear something.

Beale speaks into the phone, "This is Ong Be. What's happening?"

"Ong Be?! You must rescue my Charley. He is in great danger!"

"What do you mean, Tuy? Did you have a nightmare or something?"

"Tuy!" Toady says angrily, leaping up from his chair and grabbing for the receiver, "that's a dink girl's name!"

Beale pushes Toady away, speaking into the

phone, "Hold on a minute, Tuy." If Beale had to pick an exact moment when he changed, when he stopped being, for a time, the meticulously careful person who thought everything through before acting, it would be then. Of course, war changes people, and this time his monster came practically unbidden. There was no real sign of the transition.

Beale sets the phone on the desk. He waits for Toady to reach for it, and then smashes the corporal across the back with his interlocked fists. His arm under his cast feels a sharp jolt of pain, but Toady goes down like he's been felled by an ax. Beale picks up the phone again.

"Tuy? What is all this? Did you have a nightmare?"

The voice on the other end of the line sounds half-crazy with worry, "No, no - Charley - he - he *talked* around the Cherry Bar. Many people knew he was going in the bush."

"But surely not *where* he was going."

She is clearly frightened, her almost-perfect speech breaking down under the strain into typical bargirl English, "He say one time 'near Da Lat'. People at Cherry Bar *hear* him. And he laugh at Mister Dragon, Number 10 bad luck!"

Toady shakes off his dizziness and comes up snarling and grabbing at the phone. Beale hits him on the side of the head with the captain's ashtray and he groans once and rolls off the desk onto the floor.

"Anything else, Tuy?"

"Is plenty enough, already! Mister Dragon loose tonight, Ong Be! He fly over Vietnam!"

The line clicks off and Beale is left with the disconnect humming in his ear. He sets the phone
285

back on the hook and pulls Toady to his feet. There is a big lump on the clerk's head and a little blood where the heavy brass tray has gashed him. His head lolls to one side as Beale gives him a violent shove into the C.O.s seat.

"You personally fudged papers to send Specialist Magnolia out into the bush, on a mission he had no right to be on. Now he's in danger, and you're responsible!"

"Danger's everywhere. What kind of crap are you - ?"

Toady felt the lump on the side of his head, and fell silent for a moment, gauging what Beale might do to him next, "-you're going to get a court martial for this."

"Toad-shit, I *out-rank* you!"

"I was acting on the captain's orders."

"I don't think so. Anyway, we'll find out when he gets back. Right now, you're going to issue me a jeep."

"Why should I do that?"

Beale picks up the ashtray and speaks quietly, "Because I'll kill you if you don't."

Toady's eyes widen. "Okay - okay! Put that thing down." He tosses over the vehicle requisition slips. "But you can't drive with your arm in a sling. And you don't have any idea where Magnolia is. He could be anywhere."

"I'll find him. I'd better - for your sake!"

"You're going by yourself?"

"You want to go?"

"N-n-*no!*"

Beale locks him in the C.O.'s steel wall locker. He was going to sign Toady's name to the rec slip for the jeep, but then he changes his mind

286

and scrawls his own. The motor pool orderly doesn't even give it a second glance.

Beale finds he can shift by holding the wheel briefly with his right knee while working the stick with his left hand. No one stops him as he jerkily makes his way out the main gate and in a moment he is lost in the downtown traffic flow.

He stops by the NCO's villa and throws Ranley's Beretta and a bigger pistol, a shiny silver Colt Python, into a small gym-bag. He thinks for a moment, and then dumps the packs from a carton of Marlboros and a carton of Kools on top. He's hoping, with any luck at all, he can be well out of the city by curfew.

He knows the way to Da Lat because, once Charley committed to going, Beale had gone over the map with Taters at the White Shack and then committed it to memory. He even knew within a mile or so where Charley was supposed to be located; he'd seen the neat pins on a wall map at the White Shack and transcribed the positions to his own smaller topo map.

And he knew something more. All the hours sipping whiskey over at the EMC were about to pay off; he'd soaked up endless lifer talk about what they did and how they did it. That included bragging about the easy-outs, counting the bennies and the scores, and chuckling over what they got away with in the name of duty. Taters Johnson liked Da Lat because he had things comfortable up there. And Beale knew the name of the hotel/bar where in all likelihood he would be shacked up for the next couple days, and even the name of the girl he'd be with.

CHAPTER THIRTY SIX

Van Thiep has personally never given an American more than a passing glance. He is not even thinking of the hated *Nguoi My* as he and his friends hurry along the roadside, moving through the rainy night with a swift certainty. One of them carries a flashlight muffled in a dirty piece of cotton. It is pitch dark in the highland jungle, and they have much to do yet that night. Their mission is to intimidate the local populace, to convince parents to keep their children home, not to attend the local schools that are run by the South Vietnamese government. To do this, they target certain hamlets, slashing the throats of cows and sheep and sometimes dogs, anything they can run across.

The evening birds have long since silenced their chatter, and the monkeys no longer call out to one another. The rain shows no signs of letting up. Van Thiep's group, a band of six rural Vietnamese teenagers, are used to such weather, and to walking swiftly over long distances.

He gives a short sound, *Zut!* from his lips, and they all pause. Hoang is lagging behind again. "Here," he says to Hoang, "Give me the damn thing. The spot is almost directly ahead."

He carefully accepts the cloth sling containing the mine. It is a Russian land mine, and makes a very heavy dead weight when you have to carry it for a while. In spite of what he had said to Hoang, by the time they get to the low cement bridge he himself is tired enough to want to pass it on to someone else.

It is an excellent site; several days before he had noticed a pothole just before the bridge where the road asphalt had spalled away from the harder concrete surface of the bridge itself. He was their expert; he'd been to *Bac Viet* and all the way north to mighty *Chung Hoa* itself to study such things. But at the time they had been carrying tribute-rice and couldn't detour to pick up a mine and bury it in this spot..

Now the others step aside and hand him the flashlight. He is disappointed to see the government workers had filled the hole in. He is about to get his team to move on to another site when he more carefully inspects the hole. The new asphalt, laid in the rain, is already crumbling like stale bread. Hoang fashions a short, sharp stake, and the asphalt gives way easily, it is rotten throughout and only held there by its own inertia. It is an easy matter to remove it and lay in the flat, disk-like land mine. The hardest part is covering it back up; Van Thiep waits until the last moment to arm it. Then he sprinkles a last few handfuls of the crumbly, wet asphalt over the site, spreading it carefully so the detonator doesn't project above the level of the road.

The spot is perfect. The hole had been worn in the road because the vehicles always lined up there to traverse the narrow bridge. There is intelligence from Saigon that the Americans are to run some exercises in this area. American trucks had been sighted the day before, and Van Thiep hopes to blow up such a prize.

He stands and stretches his muscles, aching from the strain of activating and positioning the

289

bomb. He is about to motion his men to retreat with him back down the road the way they had come when he notices something. At first, he isn't sure what.

He pauses, his lean body tensed in the slight chill of the breeze, his every sense straining. He motions to the others with the flashlight, and they stand around him in a silent body. *Madness! Someone was playing a radio in the jungle nearby! He is sure of it - there it is again, snatches of music!*

290

CHAPTER THIRTY SEVEN

Two ARVN corporals stand on the road waving government flags, looking surreal and unnatural in the foggy mist, like dancers in a ballet about automation. The gears on his jeep grind down and Beale pulls over to the side of the road. He is still in the flat paddies area of the delta, and the sides drop quickly away from both sides of the elevated road. There is no way he could squeeze past.

He sits there, rubbing the cast inside its sling. The jeep rides hard, like all jeeps; his left shoulder is already aching, and he has been slipping his right arm out of the sling and using it for short periods to help hang on to the steering wheel.

He is only about ten miles out of Bien Hoa. He figures it has to be a roving checkpoint as there is no guard-shack, just a small military pickup truck that is parked to block the road. He sees the tip end of a cigarette brighten in the passenger seat of the truck blocking his way.

"Khong phai di." One of the men says. *You can't go.*

Nobody moves, and after sitting impatiently for a few minutes Beale says in Vietnamese "I'm in a hurry. Why can't I get through?"

"Very dangerous up ahead. You must wait."

"Well, I *can't* wait! One of my men is in danger."

"Ahh....", a voice at his side says in heavily accented English, "You speak Vietnam!" It is an ARVN captain. The man puts his revolver away

291

as he slides into the passenger seat next to Beale. "We very sorry for inconvenience, but you must wait here. There is no alternative. V.C. ahead. *Beaucoup* V.C. We are the saving of your life."

"How soon can I go on?"

"Oh, very soon. I find it a bore out here. We can talk to pass the time away."

The minutes drag by. The captain says his name is Tan.

"Tell me about Beach Boys. The singers."

Beale has no choice. "Yes," he says. "I saw them once. In concert at UCLA.

"Ahh. You are very lucky for that. Is surfing hard to do?"

"Not too hard. You have to watch out for sharks."

"Do the blond girl have bigger breast than the brown hair or red head?"

Beale answers his endless questions, regretting he mentioned he came from California. He is thinking of reaching for one of the pistols in the handbag on the floor under his seat when a set of headlights approached from the direction of Saigon.

"Ahh," Captain Tan comments, "soon enough all is settled. You stay here. I go see who is it." He leaves Beale's jeep, shrugging his way into his yellow rain slicker as he goes.

The set of headlights resolves themselves into a deuce-and-a-half with a white star on the side.

"Who the fuck is that?" Someone thunders from inside the cab of the newly arrived truck. The ARVN captain hurries over to the truck. He shrugs, he talks smoothly, pointing to Beale. The two men argue for a short time. Tan seems to be

292

assuring the newcomer he would handle everything. Beale hears Tan say, "...I handle it." In the dim light from the headlights of both trucks, Beale sees the newcomer is a U.S. Army buck sergeant.

The two ARVN corporals, directed by Captain Tan, are swiftly unloading boxes from the army truck and putting them on their own pick-up. They are mostly cartons of American hard liquor - whiskey and scotch - and one crate that says SONY on the side in big, black letters.

Beale reaches down and pulls his flight bag from under the seat. He has no illusions about what happens to strays who witness black market deals. He fumbles around until he comes up with the Beretta. It has a solid, reassuring feel, and he puts it on his lap. He takes the Python, and, for lack of a better idea, puts it there too.

While the last of the merchandise is being transferred, Tan takes a small white parcel from his pickup truck and hands it up to the sergeant. There is a brief pause while the American inspects his goods. Then he says something abrupt that sounded suspiciously like *Handle it!* and turns the big truck around. In a few moments, his taillights are disappearing, heading back toward Saigon.

Beale sees Captain Tan speaking briefly to his two soldiers. The two pick up their M-1's and head his way. Tan himself also comes over, but on the passenger side. This time he doesn't get in the jeep. The light from the pickup shines on his calm features as he asks Beale to step out of the jeep.

Beale has crossed his arms, with a pistol in each armpit. He holds the Python in his good left hand, hidden by the sling. He grits his teeth and

293

squeezes both triggers. But nothing happens. *He has forgotten the safeties!*

Fighting down his panic, he sets the pistols on his lap. He reaches in the bag at his side and tosses a handful of cigarette packs out each window. "Hey, you guys like some *thuoc la My?*"

"Very interesting", Captain Tan says. "What else have you got in there?"

Beale quickly slides the safeties off and crosses his arms, again with one gun uncomfortable under each armpit. At that moment he doesn't even remember which is pointing in which direction. oor open. "Okay," he says in a much less friendly tone, "Fun and game is over for you."

The captain jerks the passenger door open. Beale sees a pistol come up in the officer's hand and he fires at him with his left hand gun, which proves to be the python. The bullet catches the captain over his right eye, jerking his head back out of Beale's line of sight. Beale feels a burn mark on his cheek, realizing Tan had fired, at least once.

Agonizing squeals come from his left; he sees one of the Arvins has a bullet in the throat. Blood spilling over the man's ches t in the moment as he slumps to the ground. *Two at the same time!* The thought flashes through Beale's mind. *But he hadn't fired his second pistol, had he?* It was a moment before he realized Tan had killed his own man in the crossfire.

The last ARVN soldier stands rooted to the ground, clutching his cigarettes and his M-1, staring at Beale. He is a little guy, barely a teenager, and he has bad teeth. Beale hears him

294

breathing through his mouth, a frightened, gasping sound.

"*Di, di - mao len!*" Beale yells at him.

The soldier drops his M-1 and disappears into the night, still carrying his few precious packs of *thuoc la My.*

Beale hurries out of the truck. Blood is running down his face from the cut on his cheek, and his right armpit is burning from the flash of the Python. Both the ARVN soldier and Captain Tan are dead.

His first instinct is to panic, to turn around and head back to Saigon. But then he sees the M-1's; the soldier would not be coming back, and the other two won't be bothering him. The road is deserted. No one had passed in the long time while he'd beenforced to wait. *What were the chances any of this would be reported? The American sergeant was long-gone, and wasn't going to say anything. If the V.C. happened along, they would enjoy a once-in-a-lifetime prize of G.I. booze and booty. If the Arvins got there, they would, like as not, take the prize and blame the deaths on the V.C.!*

And then it strikes him that he has killed a human being, and been responsible for the death of a second person. His lip quiver, and he sinks to the ground, stunned at what he has done. Yes, they had tried to kill him a moment before; but they had been living, breathing human beings. *Who has the bigger breasts, blonds or brunettes? the captain had asked, his eyes glittering with amusement.* And now they are cold, dead things that can't breathe any more. The simplicity and completeness of their deaths overwhelms him, and he stares out into the night, wondering how all this has come about in the first place.

The minutes tick by, and he finally is able to still his shaking hands and concentrate on what has to be done. *There would be time to pay the monster later, whatever price he asked. For now, Charley's in trouble, and Charley is depending on him.*

Beale stands up, staring around at the still-unbelievable scene. He goest over the way it has happened, and his shock is replaced by a hard, cold anger. *After all, they were going to kill him! Captain Tan wasn't going to let him go on. Rather than kill him right away, he'd chatted for a few moments. He just wanted somebody to pass the time while he waited for his American black-market contact. What kind of person would insist on a brief anatomy lesson on the girls of sunny California, knowing all the time he was going to kill the person he was talking to? Troi, dut, nuoc, oi! The lousy, rotten dink bastard!*

Beale takes a deep breath and blows the air in his lungs out slowly. *Okay, go forward. It isn't your fault. Just go forward!*

He uncertainly eyes the scene, trying to think what to do first, then starts up the pickup truck and moves it out of his way. He remembers to wipe his fingerprints from the steering wheel and from the keys. After another moment's thought, he takes the nearest case of whiskey from the bed of the pickup truck, struggling to one-arm the carton of Jim Beam to his jeep and put it on the floor in the front seat.

Back in his own jeep, he clicks the safety on the Beretta and pockets it. He keeps the safety off the Python, placing it carefully in his travel bag so he can retrieve it at a moment's notice. The engine on his jeep grinds and grinds, but won't start. Near panic, he pushes the gas pedal to the floor and tries again. This time it catches, sputtering at first as it wakes to the cold, damp journey that lies ahead.

Beale awkwardly puts it in gear, and, jerking a bit, starts on up the road. It is approaching midnight and he is barely out of Saigon.

297

CHAPTER THIRTY EIGHT

Moving without artificial light through the nearly absolute dark of night a few miles south of the war-tattered and neglected resort town of Da Lat, Van Thiep separates his forces into two groups. The plan is to move in from all directions. If there are too many of the enemy, they will slit a throat if possible and run away. They have heard that sometimes the Americans sleep when they are supposed to be on guard duty. In any event, there should be little danger; if the Americans are heavily armed and alerted, they will simply vanish into the night and move on.

Van Thiep and the others had been born and raised in this area, and had evaded the draft and the conscripting government soldiers for years -- as their fathers had hidden from the French and their ancestors from the Chinese, the hated *nguoi Trung Hoa,* ever since time began. And they knew this forest like a childhood playground.

They leave the road and creep carefully through the thick foliage, feeling their way with their hands and bare feet. They only have two pistols, and of these, one was almost out of ammunition. Van Thiep hopes almost desperately they might be able to lift something of value from the Americans. *What a way to run a war, on stolen bullets!*

Twenty yards away, lost in the jungles of his own mind, Charley snores peacefully, with his blanket pulled up around his ears. Some time during the night it had cooled off, but rather than get dressed in his damp uniform, he had simply rolled up in his army blanket. He feels okay now, still slightly ripped with the afterglow from the good grass. It is a mellow melody hour from USIA, and he half-listens to last year's pop-hit

When the Deep Purple falls
Over sleepy garden walls
And the stars begin to twinkle
In the sky....

He thinks he maybe ears a slight rustling noise. He pushes back the dim urges of panic. *He is okay. Everything is Aaaaaa-O-kayyyyy.*

At that moment, someone rudely dumps him from his hammock. He lands hard on the ground, already cursing Taters, who he is sure has gotten drunk and come back to get him working, "Sarge, that isn't funny, goddamn it!!"

There is no reply. Someone cuts the strings on his makeshift tent, and the poncho and all his mosquito nets drop over him.

"Son-of-a-bitch, who -?"

Two or three people jump on top of him. He thrashes about in the netting, feeling for his rifle. *He didn't give a goddamn if it was Taters, he'd blow his brains out!*

But he is too close to his M-14, actually pinned to it by whoever is on top of him. *It feels like several people! Taters must have gotten his guys to pull this cheap shot on him!* Charley is furious, and he flails around, almost throwing them off in his anger.

But they were hitting him, punching him hard! He feels something solid, like a bat or a gun butt

299

smack him in the chest! *They are going to kill him!* He can't believe it!

"Wait! It's a mistake! I'm Charley! Charley Magnolia from Bayonne, New Jersey!"

He manages to get his pig-sticker open and feels a brief satisfaction as someone grunts in pain and rolls off him. But there are too many of them, and he can't untangle himself.

He screams again and again as the sharp blows crash in on him through the netting and the rubber poncho. The brutal punches go on forever. Finally a stunning smash catches him full in the face and he goes limp, falling down a long, dark tunnel to nowhere.

CHAPTER THIRTY NINE

Though there is a dim, golden lamplight coming from the window, the guard post looks deserted to Beale as he slows his jeep to a crawl. He has been through half a dozen check-points by this time, and he doesn't want his head blown off by some raw recruit with a couple of weeks in uniform and a nervous trigger finger. *If the place really was abandoned, why the light?* He feels chill fingers running up and down his spine.

Leaving his jeep on the road with the motor running, he takes the Python in his good hand and cautiously enters the guard-shack, wary of booby traps. Three guards are sitting around a table, playing cards. Teacups are on the table, and the light comes from a kerosene lantern burning dimly over their heads.

No one looks up or greets him as he enters. No one moves at all. The floor is heavy with their mingled blood, each having had his throat neatly slit. One wall is crudely finger-painted in blood. The slogan reads in Vietnamese, "Death to the puppets of the American Invader-gangsters."

Beale runs for his jeep and drives on in a numb, cold sweat. As he pulls over for the last checkpoint before Da Lat, gray dawn is already blooming like an evil flower in the east, lighting up a dull sky that promises more of the endless rain.

With the light he sees that he is in hilly country, heavy with vegetation. The checkpoint is a little, six-sided stone building with slits where rifles could be stuck out at waist height.

A lone ARVN lieutenant comes out to greet him, holding a shoe in one hand and a polishing rag in the other. "Good spit-and-polish, yes?" he says with a bright smile.

Beale is at his wit's end, "Very good," he says. "I see you use Kiwi."

"It is good polish?"

"It has always - been my favorite... Would you like some *thuoc la My?* I have some Marlboros or some Kools."

"I should prefer the Marlboros. The other is for women."

"Uhh, yes - the betel nut urge. Have you had a bad night?"

"No trouble. But you cannot pass here for another two hours." The Lieutenant pockets the cigarettes and picks up his shoe again, carefully rubbing the tip in an endless little circle with a blackened piece of cotton.

"Why is that?"

"Captain's orders. He has gone to breakfast. He will return to clear you. You will have to wait."

"You like Whiskey *My?*"

"Yes. Very much. Jack Daniels, yes?"

"Jim Beam. Jack's uncle." Beale hands a bottle across for the lieutenant's inspection. The man sets down his shoe and accepts it with both hands. As he does so, Beale calmly takes the big Python out of his travel bag and points it in his face.

"I am a *ma,* a ghost. I don't exist, and therefore you never saw me."

The ARVN lieutenant starts back a moment, the pleasure lines around his eyes freeze into

302

something else. He takes in a startled half-breath before he catches himself. "Of course. A *ma My*...."

Beale lets out the clutch and drives off, weaving around the sandbags that had been placed across half the road. He hunches down and leans toward the door, half expecting a bullet to scar the windshield. But this time there is no bullet, and in a half hour he is driving down the main street in Da Lat.

The carpets in the hotel lobby once had been splendid Persians, but now they are tattered and worn. Beale marches through the hotel lobby carrying his travel bag. No one is behind the desk, so he finds the sergeant's name in the sign-in book by himself. There is a spare key in the message slot for 219. He takes it and walks up the arched marble stairway that leads to the second floor.

Taters is right where he thought he'd be - in bed with Lan-Ly, the dark-eyed half-Chinese beauty with the big jugs that he'd described to his envious friends back at the EMC as *Hot to trot in Da Lat*.

CHAPTER FORTY

The pale light of early dawn has given way to the heavy grays of mid-morning when Magnolia slowly swims up out of unconsciousness into his new world, which is one of agonizing pain. His hands are tightly bound behind his back. There is a tight cord running up from his tied wrists in a loop with a slipknot around his neck. This makes the slightest movement of his arms enough to start choking him. There is a stick in his mouth, holding his jaws apart and tied tightly behind his head. His mouth is also stuffed with rotten leaves and dirt; someone has scooped a handful of rot off the jungle floor and crammed it in.

He cranes his neck to look around. He is alone, tied not four yards from where his tent had been. But now everything he brought with him is gone – ponchos, rifle, the radio receiver, his clothes, and the food he'd brought, his precious mosquito nets. It was all taken by whoever jumped him. *Why hadn't they just killed him?*

To the limited extent that his neck rope allows, he looks down at his naked body. One of his eyes is puffed shut, but with the other he sees he is bruised and cut, all evidence of the beating he has taken. He coughs, almost gagging on the jungle dirt in his mouth, and tries to spit some of the junk out, but it is hopeless.

As feeling flows back into his body, he tries to raise himself to his feet; only then does he realize that he is tied in a sitting position, with his legs spread-eagled and his hips pinned tightly to the ground with stake-tied ropes. He notices angrily that the rope is his own nylon cord that he had earlier used to string up his poncho! His back is against a clump of thick bamboo, and he is also tied tightly to that. He cannot move an inch in any direction.

As he comes more and more out of his dizzy mental fog, waves of pain roll through him. Now that he was tied and helpless, he is doubly aware of the little things of the jungle, the things he hated, that now could do as they would with him. It feels like bugs and ants are crawling all over his body. He shudders and struggles fiercely for a moment, but all that he accomplishes is to tighten the cord around his neck until he nearly strangles himself.

His situation, the way he sees it, is serious but not impossible. *It is Monday, and he has no water. Taters said he would pick him up on Tuesday morning. He might still be in pretty good shape - if the creepy bugs, the big spiders, the poison snakes or the jungle animals didn't get him!* He shudders, and tries to shake off a large red-and-black beetle that has landed on his chest. It falls down into the hair between his legs, and then crawls back up across his lower stomach. Magnolia tries to shake it off, but it is impossible, he has been tied so he can't move. *Why did the stupid dinks - for by this time he realizes it had to be the V.C. - tie him up like this? It is a weird way to pin a person down - why had they gone through all the trouble?*

Charley figures he has one other chance. *If they try to raise him on the radio and he doesn't answer, then they might come sooner to see what the problem was!* But even as he thinks of this possibility, he knows chances are slim that might happen. He'd never done radio work before and he knows in his heart they weren't counting on him for anything.

The rain starts, and after fifteen minutes, begins pelting down. He wants to direct the trickles of moisture into his mouth, but the wad of rotten stuff blocks him from doing anything. He concentrates on trying to work it out, and in a few hours has cleared most of it by pushing it around the end of the stick with his tongue, and swallowing the rest of it.

It has to be about ten in the morning. He can't move, no matter how hard he tries. *Why had they tied him so oddly to the ground?* His vision blurs and he passes out again.

At the same time, back in a hotel room in Da Lat, Taters Johnson couldn't remember when he had been so furious. *To have a lowly specialist barge in on him like that!*

But he had to admit, he had been fairly caught, and Beale did ignore the girl, ranting on about his friend Magnolia being in terrible danger.

Taters has no choice but to be professional about it. He sits naked on the edge of the bed and reaches for his pack of Pall Malls, "Beale, don't get your balls in an uproar here - Spec.4 Magnolia's just one person. What about the rest of my guys?"

"Charley's the only one who's had no jungle training! He never even was a boy scout! He has no idea what to do out there!"

Taters pulls his olive t-shirt over his head and steps into his boots, "I'd have never let him come with us if I'd known that." He doesn't believe
306

Charley is in trouble for a minute, but now he needs Beale. He was supposed to be out swatting mosquitoes with his men. He gets his Pall Mall going and reaches for his fatigues, makes his apologies to his girl and heads for the crapper down the hall. Fifteen minutes later he grabs a loaf of fresh French bread from the kitchen on their way out, breaking the still-hot bread and tossing Beale a steaming chunk, "You say you got intelligence that a bar-girl compromised our operation?"

"*Charley* mentioned where he was going, and it got out! A bar-girl called to warn me!"

You sure she didn't *do* him?"

"*No*, I'm *not* sure! We'll sort it out later. We've just got to get out there!"

"Okay, okay, we're doing our fastest!"

Taters throws the gear slung across his back into his truck. "He's back the way you came. Three clicks out of town. Just past the first stone bridge and in the green soup on the right. *Hey -* wait for me!"

Beale is already gunning his jeep out of the gravel parking lot. He shifts jerkily and drives at the jeep's top speed, which was nearly sixty miles per hour by the speedometer, with Taters' truck right behind him.

The bridge Taters has mentioned comes up faster than Beale expected. He is fighting a curve, driving the jeep one-handed, and he looks up from shifting and there it is, spanning a fairly steep ravine. His jeep is at an odd angle, and slides on the gravel to barely miss the low wall on the far side of the bridge. Taters, who knew the road, has a better angle and approaches more normally, and that was his undoing. He has just made the near end of the bridge when the front wheel of his truck hits the mine and his deuce-and-a-half goes up in a huge ball of angry black smoke and flame. Van Thiep and the V.C. terrorists are batting two-out-of-two.

308

CHAPTER FORTY ONE

Charley wakes, groggily swinging his head back and forth, wondering if he has dreamed the sound of an explosion. It couldn't have been over a half-mile away. He is half-conscious, and begins to drift off again.

He comes back to reality as a sharp pain jabs up into his bowels from the ground. *Something is stabbing him!* He panics, his breath coming in raw gasps. *An animal! Something is eating him alive, burrowing up his ass, eating into his insides!* He struggles violently, shaking his body to try and clear whatever is piercing him. *What the hell is happening?*

He stops struggling as the cold realization sweeps over him that his movement has only resulted in several puncture wounds deep inside him. He strains to look down as much as the rope around his neck will allow, and sees a widening patch of his own red blood spreading on the leaves between his legs. The pain mounts up and up beyond anything he can bear and he passes back into blessed unconsciousness\.

Beale sits in his jeep on one side of the bridge. *Shelled!* He thinks wildly, grabbing the travel bag and diving into the ditch at the side of the road, *We're being shelled.... or mortared, maybe!* After a few minutes, the smoke hanging in the heavy air begins to dissipate, but Tatters' truck is nowhere to be seen. The jungle returns to its normal brooding, watchful way, and Beale starts to think there had to be some other explanation. *If it were mortars, they would have taken out the jeep by this time. Unless maybe they only had one mortar shell.* But he'd heard somewhere it took several rounds to zero in on targets with a mortar. *But maybe they had locked in on that exact spot near the bridge.* His tired mind is a jumbled mass of contradictory notions, but he knows he has to do something. He makes his way along the roadside ditch back to the bridge, and then quickly runs across it, crouching for protection behind the waist-high concrete walls.

He is nearly on top of it before he sees it -- a four-foot deep hole in the road where the explosion had gone off. Wisps of smoke curl up from the hole. He looks around; sees the shattered remains of the truck have tumbled down into the ravine. Beale scrambles down after it, slipping and sliding on the steep slope, and slowing his descent by hanging on to vines and roots..

What is left of Taters is hanging halfway out of the truck, lying face down in the swollen stream that rushes through the ravine. Beale pulls him out of the water, but there is nothing else he could do. Taters is dead, dead, dead. *What had Taters said? Magnolia was off in the green soup somewhere.*

CHAPTER FORTY TWO

Charley swims up into a haze of red pain, delirious and too weak to move. He finds himself thinking of girls he'd known, all the nice ones, and all the hookers and whores. He thinks of Tuy, trying to use her image to push away any thought of his wife Beth, the girl he'd met at Carmel Beach when life was a game and playing spy was good for a roll in the sack almost every time. He'd tried not to think of her at all, but now her memory flooded his mind until he could think of nothing else.

"Beth....", he mumbles softly around the stick in his mouth, "Beth, I'm so sorry...."

While Beale searches in vain, methodically combing the woods on the far side of the bridge, the pool of his own blood that Charley sits in widens and he slowly begins to slip away.

What Charley doesn't know is that he is just a joke, a propaganda victory for the cause. Van Thiep had noticed this stand of bamboo right next to where they had overcome the American gangster They all had chuckled as they tied the unconscious man firmly to the bamboo, and made sure a fresh new shoot was properly positioned up his ass. As they had observed countless times during their childhood spent in these woods, this particular type of bamboo shoot was hard and sharp as a metal spike, and grew upward with a force that was impossible to deny. And in the wet it grew fifteen to twenty inches in a single day.

Beale pulled his way out of the ravine, his one good arm clutching vines and weeds to help him out. Then he runs in a low crouch back across the bridge. *Somewhere nearby in the green goop. Charley is nearby. Taters had said so.*

Beale runs a hand over his face, realizing he is exhausted. He can't be thinking well now. But Charley is somewhere close. *The dragon is rolling the dice.*

The land slopes gently but persistently uphill to the right from the road, on the side Taters said he'd left Charley. Beale begins sweeping the jungle, walking a quarter mile in, and then moving over fifty feet, turning around and making his way back to the road. It is slow, hot work, and he is soon exhausted. The steadily falling rain slows his progress, and he is covered with muck. After his fifth trip, even the python is too heavy to carry, and he slips it under the driver's seat in the jeep. The Beretta will have to do.

The long morning drags on into afternoon, and still he continues, not daring to widen his tracking pattern for fear of passing Charley unseen in the thick vegetation. *Does he dare call out?* He hasn't seen another sign of anybody, except for a big, old French Renault and a Saigon blue-and-cream that had made their way to the bridge and then turned back. *The lifers all said the V.C. came out at night like spiders, and hid during the day. He would have to rely on that.* He begins calling, at first softly, then louder, "Charley! Where are you? The Dimbos are here!"

In spite of all his care, he nearly passed him by, only pausing when he heard a muffled moan. And in another few seconds he finds his friend, head lolling to one side, tied and staked to the ground in a strange sitting position.

He carefully unties the stick from Charley's mouth.

"Ong Beeeee," Charley whispers, "What took you.... so long...."

Beale's fear mounts as he looks at Charley's battered body, and sees the pool of blood surrounding him. He quickly unties the rest of the bonds and manages to lift him off the cruel stake that by this time has driven itself deep into Charley's body.

Awkward and frustrated by the cast on his arm, Beale manages to lift Charley over his shoulder in the carry they'd learned in basic training. He staggers back to the jeep, falling twice on the way. He cracks his cast, and his arm aches like it had when he'd first broken it, but he keeps going

He doesn't know how to support the limp and unconscious Charley in the jeep. The back seat is too small to lie him down, and he will fall out of the front. Beale runs back to the woods and gets the rope to tie him in the seat. Rain is battering the canvas top of the jeep. It's raining so hard he can barely see the road in front of him.

Da Lat is the closest town of any consequence, but Beale can't get past the hole in the road. He jerkily turns the jeep around, honking and weaving his way through a short line of civilian cars and trucks, blocking his path. His plan is to stop the first G.I. or ARVN unit he comes in contact with.

Charley's hand weakly flutters to him.

Beale slows to a stop, "What?"

313

"You got.... the letter. Beth's letter"

"*Yes,* but we won't be needing it."

Charley smiles through the pain of his smashed lips, "Means everything.... to me."

"What?"

"Couldn't stand to.... die alone."

"You're *not going to die!*"

Charley shakes his head, "No....*you're* not going to die. Remember.... *you* don't roll the dice.... *Scribe*...." Charley drifts back into unconsciousness.

The rain clears to intermittent light showers. Beale drives like the cruel claws of the dragon that had become his Vietnam are closing in behind him, which, in the truest sense, they are.

He gets lucky about ten miles down the road, running into an armed convoy that is able to radio for help. He stayed with the unconscious Charley until the helicopter came, and then stood watching as the plump Jolly Green flapped away toward the hospital at Bien Hoa, flying low above the hills and just under the solid lid of gray clouds. And the last time he felt for his weak and fluttering pulse, Charley was still alive.

314

CHAPTER FORTY THREE

"You fucked the duck", Toady says. "Now you pay."

Beale doesn't have time to reply as the C.O. enters the room. The colonel ignores them both in his official way, pawing through the mound of paperwork on his desk for five minutes. Finally, without looking up, he says, "Toady has reported enough infractions here to lock you up and throw away the key."

A grin lights the clerk's pimply face under the big, loose bandage he is wearing for effect, "That's right Mister Better-Than-Thou Specialist Fifth Class."

"However," the C.O. continues, "I have read your report and fully concur Specialist Magnolia should not have been sent on that mission. *How* you found out he was in danger will not be the subject of this conversation. It is a matter of grave security concern, and will be handled by your superiors at the White Shack."

The smug expression drops from Toady's face, "Sir - you can't just let him go!"

"I'll handle this, Toady!"

Beale knows what this means. The C.O. isn't letting the matter drop because he wants to; this *the army way,* this is just a sham, back holing to cover what has happened. And Toady is too dumb to realize that with Taters Johnson out of the picture it is his tail that is on the line.

The C.O. riffles through his paperwork, "Specialist Beale, I have an ARVN report indicating a great deal of activity on Route 21 the night you went to Da Lat. Do you want to illuminate me on that?"

"It's a long, dark stretch of two-lane blacktop, sir."

"Come off it, Specialist. There were at least five ARVN soldiers - one of them an officer - killed in two separate incidents along that road. And you know *nothing?* You had to drive right past both of them."

"Nothing at all, sir." Beale is busily unscrewing the captain's brass airplane from its heavy ashtray base.

Nordoff sees what he is doing and thunders, "Leave it alone! Do you have *any idea* of the artistry and craftsmanship that went into making that plane?"

"A World War II P-38, isn't it, sir?"

"Get out of here!"

The C.O. buries his nose back in his paperwork; Beale gives Toady the finger and flips off his head bandage with the same finger on his way out the screen door.

The Dimbos take turns staying with Charley, taking the Grey Snail up to Bien Hoa and bunking down in spare hospital beds, or falling asleep in the chair at his side.

Two nights after his talk with the C.O., Beale is working at the White Shack when he gets a call from Larky. He sets aside the hopelessly jumbled message he is trying to crack and runs down the long hallway to the front office to pick up the phone, "Larky - what's up *nguoi my*?"

"I'm over here in the C.O.'s office, Be."

"But - it's your night. You're supposed to be in Bien Hoa with Charley."

"He's dead, Be. Charley's dead."

"No. That can't be. Not our Charley...." The phone hangs limp in Beale's hand. He raises it slowly back to his ear, "That - that's impossible - I only just the other day -"

Lieutenant Boudreaux, who has been sitting across the workroom doing a crossword puzzle in an old issue of Stars & Stripes, catches the edge on Beale's voice and comes over, "What's going on, kid?"

Larky continues over the line, sounding thin and frustrated, "I *know* you did just the other day, Beale. We all did. But that was *then* and now it's *now*, and Charley had this fever and they told me it was okay and then he was god-awful still and I called them and they came and it was too late and they say it's peritonitis and I don't even know what that is just some infection and he was too weak to fight it off."

"I don't understand -"

"Me, either. I don't understand *anything* about this stupid, rotten pig's ass country!"

Beale hangs up the phone. The room around him seems wrong-spaced and remote. From a great distance away he hears Boo-Boo asking what he can do.

"Nothing, Lieutenant", he says, "It's just that now I got this friend gone...."

He doesn't say anything more, and Boudreaux has to call up the C.O. to get the story.

They ask Beale the usual things; can they take over his shift for him, and does he want some

317

coffee? Beale doesn't say anything. He does no work decoding the jumbled message. He just sits at his desk for the rest of the shift, refusing to leave until the day is finished.

Boudreaux wishes he would break down and cry. But he doesn't.

CHAPTER FORTY FOUR

Beale, Larky and Mad Denny sit up all night in the empty mess hall, crushed and silent. When morning comes, Beale pours a last cup of bitter army coffee for each of them.

"I've got to go up there. You guys want to come with me?"

Mad Denny shakes his head, "It won't do any good. It doesn't make any difference."

Beale hears his voice rising, even though he doesn't want to argue, "I've got to go anyway! You want to come with, Larky?"

His pudgy friend just stares down at his boots, "No - I can't, Ong Be. We got to each say goodbye in our own way."

Beale thinks about that. "Okay. I get that.. But I have to go."

Dawn is turning the eastern sky a pearly gray as he slowly walks along the runway to the tarmac where the Otters are parked. Lieutenant Boudreaux gives him a ride up to Bien Hoa, and later the same day he rides back in a truck with the silent box. It is a long, bone-jolting ride, but he feels out of it anyway, and he is too weary and numb to pay much attention. He sits on the bench in the flatbed back of the truck and steadies the coffin, which tends to slide around on the curves.

Beale finds himself thinking about Meade and the last burn bag detail, remembering Rafaelson being chewed up by the pulper. *Was this what his vision meant? Had the curse come full circle,*

319

leaving his girlfriend Night Lark and his best friend Charley dead? He has brought along one of the bottles of Jim Beam from the carton he'd taken on the night of his wild ride to Da Lat. He unscrews the cap and takes a drink. The alcohol burns its way down his throat and he can't stop thinking. *Maybe the lesson was the pulper itself, brass gauged, aluminum-nippled, impersonal, symbol of the Agency, waiting for victims. He had wanted to see the face and form of war, and now he knew it for what it was. War itself was the great pulper, its blades howling under them all, whistling death and waiting for men to fall into its teeth!*

He drinks some more, and the torturing thoughts of what might have been swarm through his mind.... *If only he hadn't wanted Nam so badly, if Charley only hadn't listened to him, if Charley hadn't pulled his trick to get him out of the Puzzle Palace, if only he hadn't talked Hoa into that damn singing contest, if he hadn't fallen in the ditch and broken his arm, if Charley hadn't ragged so bad on Toady.... if, if, IF!!*

Beale stays with Magnolia as they check him through the Tan Son Nhut gates. They fill out the paperwork in a warehouse near the runway. Charley now is nothing more than a coffin draped with an American flag. They place him in a row with six others. Beale overhears someone say it had to be a big day for Victor Charley, seven grunts with one swat; and someone else mentions the plane will be here in a few hours to take them back to the States.

Beale gets a cup of coffee from a machine in the warehouse and sits on top of a crate. His hands

320

shake so violently he has trouble keeping the chain of cigarettes burning in his mouth.

He can't think of anything to say to Magnolia. And worse, he knows his monster will soon be returning, going for the big time. He feels he is starting to crack; he keeps hearing Charley's voice in his mind, clear as if he is right there next to him in the hanger. They are at Chez Anna, back in Tay Ninh. Charley is grinning at him, the grin that he could never completely relax with. "You're my best friend, Be....I must be really hard up, huh?" And then that little laugh that brought it all back together and made it all right. Charley could say anything he wanted to him. He was the *best friend*.

They had done all their things together, and now he can't think of what to say.... he remembers Charley going for his sex-endurance record. Now he can almost feel the arm around his shoulder, almost hear that energetic East Coast twang, "It isn't so bad, Ong Be. Come on, buck up, *stugatz*....you see, now that I'm a *real* spook, I can lay any broad I want, and she won't even know it!"

Beale shakes his head like a dog shaking off water. It's only his overworked imagination. Charley is never going to say anything again, and nothing he can do will change that. He knows it is dumb, it won't help at all, but he starts sobbing anyway. He can't stop, and he doesn't know how long he carries on like that, bent over into a fetal ball on the crate.

He finally sits up, feeling hollow and spent. He sees a scatter of snubbed-out cigarettes on the concrete floor surrounding him. The bottle of Jim Beam is half-empty, but suddenly it was right and very important that enough of it remains for one last round. He takes it and walks over to his best friend. He pours Charley a drink, letting the golden-brown liquid tumble to the floor in front of the coffin.

"Hey!" A corporal with a clipboard angrily tries to take his arm, "What are you doing?"

"For the spirits", Beale says, pulling away from him.

"Buddy, I have to *mop* this floor!" The corporal is going to get into it big time, but a lifer sergeant who'd seen Korea and the mess up on the highlands near Ban My Thuat comes over and takes him away. Beale walks the line of coffins, pouring each in turn their drink. The whiskey splatters and pools on the smooth concrete floor.

"I'm sorry," he says out loud, talking to Charley, talking to them all. "I honestly don't roll the dice. I'm just . . . . just . . . the scribe."

Beale looks out from the wide hanger doors across the sweep of the runway. The grays of late afternoon are thickening. A wind is stirring, and he sees the clouds of Vietnam bunching together to dump on his friend once more before he can get away.

A detail comes across the apron driving an electric mini-truck with empty freight wagons strung behind. There is no honor guard, no witnesses except himself, no crowds of pretty Saigon girls in gaily-colored *ao gai* to throw flower pedals and wave the brave dead away.

The work-detail of G.I.'s talks about Johnny Unitas' arm and the Colts' chances as they lift the silent, star-spangled boxes onto the little wagons.

322

It doesn't take more than five minutes. Then they climb back on the mini-truck and drive away.

Beale stands looking after them, wanting desperately for there to be more to it. He looks around frantically at the hanger, the wide, wet runway, the dark tree line in the distance, the low clouds overhead. *A sign! Give me a sign! -- Something to prove this was necessary!* But there is no sign and no answer for what he wants. There is just the gloomy bowl of the sky, the first drops of the next rain shower spattering the concrete apron, and the electric whine of the mini-truck procession getting smaller and smaller in the distance.

THE END

OTHER BOOKS BY JOHN KLAWITTER

NOVELS
Crazyhead
Codes & Decodes
Hollywood Havoc: The Trouble With Fat Boy
Hollywood Havoc: The Llama Goes Up
Devils
Foul
The Save Your Planet Show
Orange Glory
AAARG! (short stories)

NON-FICTION
Tinsel Wilderness
That Ain't No Shit (Stories of the Old Spooks & Spies – Vol I-IV)
Headslap: The Life & Times of Deacon Jones
The Book of Deacon (Afro American Oral Wisdom)

More about John Klawitter, his life, books and films at
www.amazon.com/author/johnklawitter